OLIVIA'S AWAKENING

What Reviewers Say
About Ronica Black's Work

Freedom to Love

"This is a great book. The police drama keeps you enthralled throughout but what I found captivating was the growing affection between the two main characters. Although they are both very different women, you find yourself holding your breath, hoping that they will find a way to be together."—*Lesbian Reading Room*

Snow Angel

"A beautifully written, passionate and romantic novella."—*Sunset XCocktail*

The Seeker

"Ronica Black's books just keep getting stronger and stronger… This is such a tightly written plot-driven novel that readers will find themselves glued to the pages and ignoring phone calls. *The Seeker* is a great read, with an exciting plot, great characters, and great sex." —*Just About Write*

Flesh and Bone—*Lammy Finalist*

"Ronica Black handles a traditional range of lesbian fantasies with gusto and sincerity. The reader wants to know these women as well as they come to know each other. When Black's characters ignore their realistic fears to follow their passion, this reader admires their chutzpah and cheers them on… These stories make good bedtime reading, and could lead to sweet dreams. Read them and see." —*Erotica Revealed*

Chasing Love

"Ronica Black's writing is fluid, and lots of dialogue makes this a fast read. If you like steamy erotica with intense sexual situations, you'll like *Chasing Love*."—*Queer Magazine Online*

Hearts Aflame

"Sleek storytelling and terrific characters are the backbone of Ronica Black's third and best novel, *Hearts Aflame*. Prepare to hop on for an emotional ride with this thrilling story of love in the outback… Along with the romance of Krista and Rae, the secondary storylines such as Krista's fear of horses and an uncle suffering from Alzheimer's are told with depth and warmth. Black also draws in the reader by utilizing the weather as a metaphor for the sexual and emotional tension in all the storylines. Wonderful storytelling and rich characterization make this a high recommendation."—*Lambda Literary Review*

"*Hearts Aflame* takes the reader on the rough and tumble ride of the cattle drive. Heat, flood, and a sexual pervert are all part of the adventure. Heat also appears between Krista and Rae. The twists and turns of the plot engage the reader all the way to the satisfying conclusion."—*Just About Write*

Wild Abandon—*Lammy Finalist*

"Black is a master at teasing the reader with her use of domination and desire. Black's first novel, *In Too Deep*, was a finalist for a 2005 Lammy. …With *Wild Abandon*, the author continues her winning ways, writing like a seasoned pro. This is one romance I will not soon forget."—*Books to Watch Out For*

"Sleek storytelling and terrific characters are the backbone of Ronica Black's third and best novel, *Hearts Aflame*. Prepare to hop on for an emotional ride with this thrilling story of love in the outback… Wonderful storytelling and rich characterization make this a high recommendation."—*Lambda Book Review*

"This sequel to Ronica Black's debut novel, *In Too Deep*, is an electrifying thriller. The author's development as a fine storyteller shines with this tightly written story. …[The mystery] keeps the story charged—never unraveling or leading us to a predictable conclusion. More than once I gasped in surprise at the dark and twisted paths this book took."—*Curve*

"Ronica Black, author of *In Too Deep*, has given her fans another fast paced novel of romance and danger. As previously, Black develops her characters fully, complete with their quirks and flaws. She is also skilled at allowing her characters to grow, and to find their way out of psychic holes. If you enjoy complex characters and passionate sex scenes, you'll love *Wild Abandon*."—*MegaScene*

"Black has managed to create two very sensual and compelling women. The backstory is intriguing, original, and quite well-developed. Yet, it doesn't detract from the primary premise of the novel—it is a sexually-charged romance about two very different and guarded women. Black carries the reader along at such a rapid pace that the rise and fall of each climactic moment successfully creates that suspension of disbelief which the reader seeks."—*Midwest Book Review*

In Too Deep—*Lammy Finalist*

"Ronica Black's debut novel *In Too Deep* has everything from nonstop action and intriguing well developed characters to steamy erotic love scenes. From the opening scenes where Black plunges the reader headfirst into the story to the explosive unexpected ending, *In Too Deep* has what it takes to rise to the top. Black has a winner with *In Too Deep*, one that will keep the reader turning the pages until the very last one."—*Independent Gay Writer*

"…an exciting, page turning read, full of mystery, sex, and suspense."
—*MegaScene*

"…a challenging murder mystery—sections of this mixed-genre novel are hot, hot, hot. Black juggles the assorted elements of her first book with assured pacing and estimable panache."—*Q Syndicate*

Visit us at www.boldstrokesbooks.com

By the Author

In Too Deep

Deeper

Wild Abandon

Hearts Aflame

Flesh and Bone

The Seeker

Chasing Love

Conquest

Wholehearted

The Midnight Room

Snow Angel

The Practitioner

Freedom to Love

Under Her Wing

Private Passion

Dark Euphoria

The Last Seduction

Olivia's Awakening

OLIVIA'S AWAKENING

by

Ronica Black

2020

Acknowledgments

Thank you to the entire Bold Strokes crew, you are all amazing and you continue to bless my life by taking my work and turning it into something incredible.

CHAPTER ONE

Olivia Savage sat in her Prius, staring endlessly at the mountain in front of her. She'd been doing so for a half an hour, and she still couldn't bring herself to budge. She closed her eyes and hoped that some inner focus might do the trick. She breathed deeply and concentrated.

The air seeping through her lowered window was cool, indicative of an Arizona dawn in early spring. She loved the way an awakening desert smelled as new life bloomed, growing and thriving, eager for the rays of the sun. She, too, was eager, wanting to grow and thrive herself. She'd already made some big changes. Like leaving her marriage and her mind-numbing job as a medical assistant and going back to school. But she also had a secret longing for something that she thought of often.

Love.

Real love. True love.

She wanted to know what it felt like to really love and be loved. She'd been married, but she knew that wasn't love. She still didn't quite know what that was. But it definitely wasn't love. Would she ever find it? Would she recognize it if she did? She didn't know. The whole thing seemed more like a pipe dream so she kept her line of sight on her other, more realistic wish.

She wanted to get into shape.

But so far, she just hadn't been able to get herself started. And today, it seemed, was going to be a repeat of other previous attempts. Because instead of just climbing from the car and walking straight toward that mountain trail, she was sitting there overthinking, unable to move. Too stuck in her head to get herself going. The negative thoughts just kept coming, replaying in her mind like warped film on an old projector. The voice in her twisted movie sounded like a drone, and the images contorted and skipped on the screen. The message, however, was still the same.

You're fat.

You're useless.

I'm not going to tell you you look good when you don't.

She'd left her husband, Kenny, a little over a year ago, yet she couldn't shake him from her thoughts. He was always there, an ever-evolving demon slinging insult after insult. She was so familiar with his evil song his words had become a mantra.

And that mantra was killing her.

Things hadn't started so bad with Kenny. They were compatible and she really did care about him. He had been kind and even a little reserved when they'd first met. His gentle manner had put her at ease, and she never would've guessed he had a mean or angry bone in his body. But his behavior changed. Slowly at first, with subtle jabs at her abilities as a wife or her cooking or the way she organized things in the house. She blamed stress and his job, and when they'd discussed having children and agreed to try, she thought for sure a child would change everything and he'd be happy. That they'd be happy.

But children were not in the cards for her. She couldn't get pregnant, and when they went to the doctor and found out why, Kenny's behavior grew worse.

She couldn't conceive and she would never be able to.

She had been devastated.

Kenny blamed her, like she had somehow caused her condition. He barely spoke to her for weeks, and when he did, he wasn't kind. He was angry, and his once few and far between insults of her became an everyday thing. His disdain for her dripped off of him, and there had been many times when she'd worried for her safety. Thankfully, he'd never physically harmed her, but that fear alone had been traumatizing. No one should ever have to be afraid in their own home.

It had been that realization that had helped her find the strength and courage to end things. He hadn't been happy about it. Not in the least. But she had been determined. She'd told him she was leaving whether he tried to physically stop her or not. There was no way he was going to be able to prevent her from leaving forever. He'd finally come to realize that and he'd backed off.

The day she walked out of that house for good had been the best day of her life so far.

But now there were other hills to climb.

She squeezed the steering wheel and opened her eyes. The mountain loomed in front of her, waiting. Though it was just a huge mound of rock and dirt, it seemed to hold her entire future. All she had to do was get out of the car and claim it. But she still couldn't bring herself to move.

She pushed out a long breath and considered her options. She could remain in the car, restart the engine, and drive back home. Doing so would definitely save her the pain of having to conquer the mountain. There would be no struggling for breath, no certain but irrational feelings of dying, no horrible, awful stabbings or aching. She wouldn't be sore tomorrow, and she wouldn't risk injury or have to worry about waking up extra early to return day after day.

Staying in the car would be easy. Safe. She would know exactly what to expect.

While being pain free and continuing with her predictable, easy physical life sounded great, she knew in her heart it wouldn't work.

Because that's what she'd been doing. And she was beyond miserable.

The only way to the top of that mountain was to climb it, plain and simple. She knew it. Now all she had to do was do it.

"Damn it." She slammed her hands down and then quickly grabbed her phone and earbuds and climbed from the car before she could change her mind. She closed the door and stood looking at the desert trail ahead. The gentle coo of stirring doves tried to soothe her, but she couldn't relax. She was too worried about failing. No, what she needed was music. She needed it loud and she needed it now.

With her earbuds in place, she strapped her phone to her forearm and turned on her playlist. She began to walk, leaving her car and any temptation to escape behind. Instead, she allowed the music to move her, to ready her for her ascent.

Excitement and motivation began to grow. Soon, she was walking briskly, happily breathing in the crisp morning air. When she reached the base of the trail, she began to jog.

This isn't so bad.

Sure, it had been a while since she'd run, but so far it wasn't hurting. Why hadn't she done this more often? She'd ran off and on throughout the years strictly for exercise, to lose a few pounds here and there, but it had never become a habit and she hadn't beat herself up over it. Athletics in general had never interested her. She didn't consider chasing a ball for over an hour fun. She didn't like watching others do it either, so why would she ever want to play?

She continued and tried to remain focused on her music. The trail began to incline, and she slowed as she pushed her body forward. She became aware of her breathing, feeling as if her airway had tightened and oxygen was struggling to get through. Her mouth was drying out, and she realized she was counting her steps. She tried to ignore it all and just run, but soon an onslaught of other things came at her. Her legs began to burn, something stabbed at her ribs, and her heart thudded hard and heavy like it was lead.

She recalled why she'd never made running a habit.

It felt awful.

She made it up an incline only to turn at a small bend in the trail and find another. She tried to curse, something she very rarely did, but instead she choked, too starved for air to speak. She stumbled to a stop and bent with her hands on her knees, trying desperately to breathe. But it only caused her chest to ache. Wincing with pain, she straightened, only to feel another pierce to her ribs. She glanced back at her car. It sat next to another in the dirt lot, looking like a pod of failure with wheels, waiting for her to return and crawl inside like a defeated, dying animal.

No.

She couldn't.

Wouldn't.

Oh, but the seat would feel so good. And the drive home would be so nice with the windows down. And she could stop at Circle K and get a Thirst Buster full of icy Diet Coke. Yes, that would be so nice.

But Kenny's words came at her again, slapping her in the face, just as they did each and every day. Tears brimmed in her eyes. Not just because of the insults, but from the pain of the run and the struggle to change. Why was it so difficult? Why couldn't she do this? Why was it so many other people could? Maybe he was right. Maybe she was useless. But that thought only made her angry. Because she'd believed him for a long time. But toward the end, she'd stopped. She'd stopped and fought. He wasn't right. He'd never been right.

And she'd be damned if she'd admit that he was now.

"No," she said. "Not today."

She walked on, despite the pain. With her fists clenched, she pushed herself to run. She climbed step after step until she was forced to stop to regain her bearings and strength. Once she recovered, however, she started again, urging herself up the mountain, until eventually, she reached the top where she staggered, like she was no longer used to level ground. Her head pounded, her body shook and screamed with pain, and she couldn't catch her breath. She fought passing out and stumbled again, this time off the trail where she bent to vomit. Though there was very little in her stomach, the retching was relentless, punishing her body even more. When it finally ended, she hobbled to a large rock and sat, hoping to put her suffering at ease.

She removed her earbuds, the music now loud and intrusive. She closed her eyes, way too physically overwhelmed to enjoy her success. Yes, she'd made it to the top but she'd paid the price. Her entire body trembled and hurt so badly she wondered how she was going to make it back down. And how in the world was she going to be able to do this every day?

Tears formed again, and this time she let them. They were warm, like she imagined her blood to be. Maybe that's what they were. Maybe she was bleeding out the pain with her hot tears. She stared down at her hands, unable to enjoy the view of the valley below. She looked up at the sky and prayed for the shaking and aches to stop. She prayed for the ability to walk back down the mountain. But most of all, she prayed for the calm that only inner peace could bring.

CHAPTER TWO

"Are you okay?"

Olivia startled from her position on the rock. She stood and turned, hurriedly wiping the tears from her face.

"Ye-yes."

A woman, very fit and well-muscled with streaked blond hair, slid her sporty sunglasses to the top of her head, rested her hands on her hips, and stared at Olivia as if she were some kind of rare, delicate creature.

Olivia's heart fluttered and her breath caught in her throat, the vision before her seeming surreal.

"You don't look so hot," the woman said, taking a step toward her. "You look like you could use some help." She was wearing tight black yoga shorts and a matching sports bra. A light sweat coated her chest and face, causing her tanned skin to sparkle in the dawning sunlight. Her heart-shaped face had a tinge of pink to it near her cheekbones. As if a painter had lightly brushed on some color with a single, deliberate stroke.

Olivia blinked. This woman, this incredibly beautiful woman... she was *real*.

Oh, God.

This wasn't going to be like the past. She wasn't going to be able to look away and forget her.

Not this woman.

She was going to impact her life somehow.

She already had and Olivia didn't even know her name.

The woman's brow crinkled as she studied Olivia. Her hazel green eyes were seeking and penetrating, even from a few feet away.

"I'm okay," Olivia said, needing to break the building intensity.

But the woman kept her gaze transfixed, and after another silent moment passed between them, the corner of her full, mauve lips lifted.

Olivia's heart quit fluttering and stopped altogether. Quickly, she forced a relaxed smile and tried to look casual by placing a hand on her hip.

"Really, I am." But as she shifted her hip into her hand, she felt awkward and ridiculous.

Her legs shook worse with the passing of every second. The standing wasn't helping. Her left knee buckled as a sudden weakness overcame her. The woman stepped toward her, but Olivia managed to recover.

"Whoops." She smiled again. "Lost my balance there."

The woman's face clouded, and Olivia's knee buckled again, and she went down in an instant. But to her shock and amazement, she didn't feel the impact of the ground. The woman, who must've moved with ninja like speed, had caught her. She was gripping Olivia's arm and helping her stand.

"You are far from fine, I'm afraid."

Olivia flushed, not only at the feel of her hands, but at the sheer strength she felt in her as the woman walked her back to the rock. She encouraged Olivia to sit and then knelt in front of her. She placed her hands on Olivia's legs, and the heat of her palms penetrated just as powerfully as her gaze.

Olivia had been stirred by beautiful women all her life, but she'd always managed to push the feelings down, to keep them tucked safely away. She'd been taught by her very religious parents that such feelings were wrong and immoral. So, any time she had a reaction to a woman, she distanced herself and prayed the feelings would stop.

That was what she had to do now. It wasn't going to be easy.

"You're still shaking," the woman said. "And you got sick. Didn't you?" She rested her hand on Olivia's. The gesture was so moving and so unexpected, Olivia felt something deep within her unlock and ease open. She fought against it, trying to distance herself. Even if she couldn't get away physically, she had to try mentally. But a strange urge overpowered her attempt and she suddenly wanted to confess everything, to relay her entire life, her secret feelings, her failed marriage, and her current struggles. She was ready to share it all, lay it all out there for this woman to see. She didn't understand any of it. She just knew she was feeling something she'd never truly felt before.

Safe.

"Yes," Olivia finally said. "I—" She stopped herself. The reason and resolve that had failed her moments before began to take root. She couldn't blurt out her entire life to this woman. She didn't even know her. She was probably only being kind for God's sake. Was she really so starved for a little attention and human kindness that she was ready to completely spill her guts to a stranger? Simply from the mere touch of a hand?

Get a grip, Olivia.

"I'm okay. Just had a little trouble."

The corner of the woman's beautiful mouth lifted again.

"First time running up a mountain?"

"First time running. Well, at least in a few years anyway."

She grinned and patted her hand. "Yep, that'll do it."

Olivia laughed.

The woman stood and extended her hand. "I'm Eve."

"Olivia." Olivia shook her hand, and when she felt her body begin to react again, she tried to release her grip. Eve, however, held fast.

"And what, my dear Olivia, are you doing trying to run up a mountain with no preparation and no water to boot?"

Olivia shrugged and prayed Eve couldn't feel her racing pulse through her hand.

"I want to get into shape."

"Ah." She pulled a water bottle from her belt and allowed Olivia to take a few squirts before returning it to her waist. Then she gently tugged on Olivia, helping her stand. Eve lightly squeezed her arms. "I think maybe you got a little ahead of yourself here. Bit off more than you can chew."

"I see people running up this mountain all the time," Olivia said. Her legs weakened again, and Eve steadied her.

"Keep breathing nice and slow. It helps if you raise your arms." She demonstrated by interlacing her fingers behind her head. Olivia did so as well and took deep breaths.

"Good. Now walk around slowly for a little bit. We want that blood to keep circulating." She rested her hand on the small of her back and walked with her. "Those people you see, the ones running up this mountain? I guarantee you they didn't start out that way."

Olivia knew what she was trying to say. "I thought about walking. Knew I probably should. But walking won't get me into shape."

"Actually, walking, especially up inclines, does a lot for your health and fitness."

Olivia shook her head. "But I want to run. Like those people I see. And I want to look like them. Look like you."

"You look pretty good to me."

Olivia flushed again.

Did she really just say that?

Could she really think that?

No way.

"I'm too big, too flabby. I need to lose weight." She hated her thighs and she had gained some in her middle. The mirror didn't lie, and her ex-husband had definitely made sure she knew she was out of shape.

"I understand that you want to tighten up and maybe lose a few pounds. Most people do."

"Yeah, that's an understatement." She'd never been happy with her body. She'd always felt bigger than the other girls, and her mother hadn't helped any by constantly telling her she was too muscular for a woman. "I just wish I could be skinny. I'd be so happy."

She felt Eve look at her.

"Olivia."

"Yeah?"

"You realize that skinny is not realistic, right? Nor is it healthy. Especially for someone like you."

"Someone like me? What does that mean? I'm hopeless?"

"Of course not. I just mean that you have a lot of muscle. And curves."

"I know. I hate it."

"Well, then, you're crazy. Because you're beautiful."

Olivia heated again, not only at her words, but at the soft way in which they'd been spoken. This incredibly gorgeous woman, who had vigorously moved her within the past ten minutes of knowing her, was now telling her she was beautiful. A tiny spark of excitement came to life in Olivia, and it grew quickly, awakening every single part of her.

But even though she felt elated and somewhat giddy, she wondered if Eve was truly being sincere or if she was just being nice. She decided, however, for the moment anyway, not to question her or her compliment.

"I," Eve said, "like those people you see running, am in the shape I'm in, because I put in a lot of time and hard work. It didn't just happen overnight. And you forcing yourself up this mountain when you're not ready won't make it happen quickly for you either. I know this because I've lived it and also because I've made it my job to know. I help people like you every day. And I'd like to help you, too."

Olivia wasn't sure what to say. Eve was not only helping her, but also willing to continue to do so in the future. The suggestion made her mind spin with thoughts of seeing more of her. But despite wanting to stare at and be near her, she knew seeing more of her could possibly send her long reined attraction to women free. Was she ready for that kind of madness? She was already feeling crazy and struggling to control her heart rate, and they'd only just met. What would more time with her bring?

Eve led her back onto the trail and encouraged her to lower her arms.

"Feel any better?"

Olivia exhaled long and slow. "Much."

"Great." She tucked her arm inside Olivia's and pulled her close, as if they'd known each other for years. "Let's get you back down this mountain."

Olivia caught her scent and felt the heat of her body pressing against hers. That growing excitement inside burst into a white-hot flame. Soon she was heady with it, almost like what she imagined being drunk would feel like.

The light-headedness caused her to get lost in her thoughts. At some point, she realized Eve was speaking. She didn't know what had been said, but she knew Eve could have said anything and she would remain in step next to her, captivated. Like a magnet, she was pulled to her and quite literally stuck to her. Yet it wasn't enough. She wanted to get closer. She was suddenly desperate to do so. She didn't know how she could possibly get any closer than she was, but she wanted to. Needed to.

She kept her want and need quiet. Walking with her as she was, was almost more than she could handle. How did she think getting any closer would make her feel?

By the time they reached their vehicles, Olivia was nearly limp in her arms. Not just exhausted from physical exertion, but from being completely overwhelmed with new, powerfully potent stirrings for Eve. She almost collapsed with a smile on her face when Eve stood before her and once again slid her sunglasses to the top of her head. She unzipped the small pack on her belt and held out a business card.

"I would like it very much if you called me."

Olivia felt her heart jump to her throat.

She wants me to call her?

She took the card and read the name.

Eve Monroe. Fitness trainer.

A phone number followed.

"Oh."

"Something wrong?"

Eve looked concerned as she searched her face.

Olivia shook her head. "Nothing. I'll think about it." She opened her door, still upset at herself for her disappointment. Of course, Eve wanted her to call. She wanted her business. To think she wanted anything more was ridiculous and most likely brought on by the foolishness of her feelings. Which were something Eve knew nothing of and never would.

I would die of embarrassment if she knew.

And then there was the added reminder that being around Eve might illicit more of what she was currently experiencing.

So, her disappointment was absurd.

"I can help you. Truly."

"I don't know."

Eve held up a palm. "Hey, I get it. This process, it's hard and it's grueling, and it can be very personal. But you need some help. I don't want you to hurt yourself."

Olivia sighed, knowing she was right. She didn't have a clue what she was doing.

"At least meet with me. There's no charge and we'll go over your goals and fitness history. We'll feel each other out. See if we're a good fit."

Olivia lost her breath as thoughts of them literally feeling each other swirled in her head.

But Eve didn't seem to notice.

"What do you say?"

"I—" But Olivia could only stare at the tempting beauty of her mouth and imagine how it would feel upon hers.

"You okay?" Eve pinned her once again with her gaze. Just like she had up on that rock.

And she was doing the same thing here, drawing Olivia in, like a moth to a flame.

I want her.

The declaration rocked her and started a throbbing between her legs. For a split second, that throbbing confused her, having never experienced anything like it before. But then she knew. She understood what she was feeling.

It was desire.

And it was fierce and more formidable than anything she'd ever felt or ever could've imagined feeling before.

It scared the hell out of her.

"I have to go." She scrambled into her car and yanked the door closed, just as Eve stepped away.

"Olivia."

But Olivia couldn't look at her. She tossed the business card onto the passenger seat and started the engine. She backed out quickly, put the Prius in drive, and sped away, kicking up dust, leaving Eve Monroe and all the feelings that came with her, far behind.

CHAPTER THREE

Eve stared after the gray Toyota Prius as it sped out of the dirt parking lot. When she lost sight of it, she finally lowered her hand, knowing her brief wave good-bye had been futile. Olivia had literally just run from her as quickly as she could, leaving Eve completely perplexed. No one had ever actually *run* from her before.

Mind still reeling, she got in her late model Tahoe and followed Olivia out onto the paved road. Normally, on a Monday she'd run the mountain trail twice before meeting her first client of the day. But the morning had been unusual. She'd seen Olivia at the bottom of the trail beginning her ascent when she'd first parked. She'd noticed right away that she was having trouble. Her form was sloppy and she was staggering as she ran, her legs seeking a strength to climb that they obviously didn't yet have. Eve had seen the signs of a novice before. People starting the process of getting fit at step nine rather than step one. Many of them she'd seen on this very mountain. Some failed and she'd never seen them again, and some got injured. One woman even had to be rescued by the fire department because she'd broken her ankle and couldn't descend. It was that particular memory that had driven her to hurry after Olivia and keep an eye on her.

She could've caught up to her and tried to talk some sense into her. But Eve had done that before, and more than once she'd been yelled at and told to mind her own business. So, she'd stayed back, watching her closely, hoping like hell she didn't trip or collapse or somehow hurt herself. To her relief, none of those things had happened. Olivia had, however, stopped several times, leading Eve to believe she might give up and come back down. But she hadn't. She'd kept climbing despite her obvious agony.

"She's a fighter," Eve said as she drove south down Fifty-ninth Avenue, leaving the mountains of Thunderbird Park behind. She took a few squirts of water and shook her head in disbelief as she recalled Olivia not bringing any of her own. She was definitely out of her league, and Eve could only hope that she would call. But the way Olivia had looked at her just before she'd taken off, Eve knew she most likely wouldn't. The soft look of what appeared to be interest and curiosity had morphed into fear and panic. Eve had been dating a long time, and she was pretty sure she knew what was going on.

Olivia had felt the palpable energy between them.

Eve had been just as surprised as Olivia apparently had been at their immediate attraction. She'd been so awestruck when Olivia first turned to look at her, she'd taken a small step back. Thankfully, Olivia didn't seem to notice, but that was only because she was just as awestruck at seeing Eve. It had been written all over her face and the way she'd struggled to speak. And her eyes, God, her eyes. Like storm clouds heavy with rain. They'd told her all she needed to know. Olivia's heart might as well have been beating just behind her irises, her gaze was so candid and seeking. And when her gaze had settled, obviously finding what it sought, Eve felt a heat and heaviness, like a flame was being held next to her skin everywhere Olivia's eyes traveled.

Eve hadn't ever felt like that under someone's stare before. She'd seen desire and interest, but nothing like what had happened up on that mountain. That had looked and felt like hunger, which wasn't very unusual. But what was unusual was the sense that Olivia was trying to hide those feelings.

Eve wasn't certain of that, of course. And even if she had been certain, she would have no idea as to why Olivia would feel like she needed to hide her feelings. She glanced at the clock and increased her speed. She needed to arrive extra early so she could burn off the energy she still felt from Olivia. She needed to get a head start on taming that brewing attraction. She didn't have the time to try to figure out the mystery of Olivia. And she didn't need any unnecessary distractions. Olivia probably wouldn't even call or ever return to the mountain. Eve needed to let it go.

She thumbed up the volume to the stereo. She liked her life the way it was. Home free and drama free. That was how she preferred to live and she was very happy in doing so. She had no interest in a serious, long-term relationship. Relationships like that required settling down and focusing a lot of your attention on another person. You became a family, whether there were only two people or not. And if the other person wanted more, like children, well, then you really had yourself a family. None of that was for her. She'd experienced all the family she could handle growing up. Being the youngest of five children with apathetic parents had taught her a lot. The most important lesson, of course, was to stay unattached. So she kept her relationships with women casual and her career front and center. Olivia and her inner turmoil…whatever that might be, could go ahead and stay far, far away.

She increased the volume even more and sang as she drove, leaving Olivia in the dust of her mind just as Olivia had left her in the dust in the parking lot.

It was time to focus now.

It was time to get to work.

She parked and slipped on a loose tank top, then grabbed her gym bag from the back of the Tahoe and headed for the door. U-Fit was a small and privately owned gym, tucked away in an old shopping plaza in Glendale. She loved U-Fit because even though it was small, it was often full of people like her, people committed to their fitness. She loved the familiar sounds of clinking weights and deep grunts and shouts of exasperation. Those were the sounds of growth and progress.

The air hung warm and heavy as she walked in through the open front door. It was March, so she wasn't surprised. Early spring in Phoenix brought cool nights and increasingly warmer, but still balmy, daytime temperatures, leading many people to put off turning on the air conditioning, hoping the last hoorah of mild temperatures would be enough to keep them cool before the heat arrived.

She wound her way through people and machines, giving a few nods hello to those she knew. She was a familiar face, having been a member for years. And Bobby, the owner, had become a good friend. He smiled at her as she approached the counter where he sat and kept watch over his kingdom.

"A little early for a Monday, Monroe." He was leaning on the elbows of his massive arms, his bald head shiny with sweat. He smiled, causing his blue eyes to dance. "To what do we owe the pleasure?"

She wasn't about to tell him about Olivia. He'd only tease her, just as he often did when it came to her dating life.

"I want to get in a quick workout before Karen gets here. Is that a crime?"

He straightened and handed her a towel. His scissor-cut sleeveless shirt was two sizes too small, making his thick pecs look as though they might tear through the thin material at any moment. With moisture beading on his skin and the full, ropelike look to his veins, she guessed he'd already put in a good workout. He'd no doubt have another before the day was through. Bodybuilding competitions left him training year-round. He was still trying like hell to get her to compete. But she'd never been interested in showing off her own body. What floated her boat was helping others so they could feel good about showing off theirs.

"Not usually," he said. "But for you, and the way you obsess over absolutely nothing *but* your career and daily routines…I'd say something was up. You don't drive in other lanes when it comes to your schedule."

She rolled her eyes. "Only you would read into my showing up early as some kind of sign that strange things were amiss. I think you sitting there behind that counter day after day has atrophied your sense of reason. The shit you've come up with recently concerns me a little."

"What?" He chuckled.

"Uh, last week you said something about alien abduction and how you believe it's real."

His eyes widened. "It is. I read this book called *Communion*. Scared the total shit out of me. You gotta read it."

"Okay. Sure. I'll get right on that."

"I'm not joking."

"Hey, whatever does it for you, buddy. To each his own."

"Having belief in something does not mean I'm losing it. I'm just opening up my mind a little. You should try it."

"Well, what about last month? You were convinced that someone was breaking in here at night and working out."

"I swear. That happened. Things were not how I left them."

"Right. Yeah. I know getting ripped would be on the top of my list if I were a criminal and an expert at breaking into places. In fact, a gym is the first place I'd go. I'd totally risk getting arrested to work out. So worth it."

"Shut up."

She laughed.

"You aren't funny."

She couldn't stop laughing. "Why the hell would someone break into a gym to work out? Night after night. Without taking anything. Honestly, I don't know how Trish puts up with your crazy ass."

"Hey, what can I say? When you got it you got it." He wiggled his eyebrows and kissed his biceps.

"Oh, how she must swoon." She flicked him with her towel. "I'm off. I'll see you later." She left him laughing and walked to the row of elliptical machines. She chose one on the end, dropped her bag nearby, and climbed on. She started slowly at first, allowing her muscles to warm up once again. Then she went hard and fast for thirty minutes straight. Until sweat ran down her body and her heart thrummed at a rapid but steady pace. The endorphins she craved rushed through her as she slowed to cool down. And for the first time since she'd laid eyes on her that morning, Olivia was completely gone from her thoughts.

CHAPTER FOUR

Eve was continuing her cool down on the elliptical when her long-time client and best friend, Karen, walked in. She, too, was a little early for a Monday. But nonetheless she appeared bright-eyed and bushy-tailed as always with her perfectly highlighted brown hair in a tight ponytail and eyeliner and lip gloss accenting her face. Eve watched as she spoke to Bobby, waving off the offered towel. Whatever was said, it left Bobby cracking up. Karen had a wicked sense of humor, and Eve was often in stitches even in the middle of an intense workout. It was one of the things Eve loved about her. Her giant heart was another.

"Hiya, hot stuff," Karen said as she tossed her bag next to Eve's. She knelt and unzipped it to retrieve a bright pink towel that she slung over her shoulder. The pink matched her snug athletic top as well as the wide stripe running down the side of her black yoga pants. She climbed on the machine beside Eve and started her warm-up. "Did you run today?"

"A little." Eve gripped the upper part of the handle to get a read on her pulse. Her heart rate had slowed considerably so she picked up the pace, wanting to stay in a higher performance zone as Karen warmed up.

"A little? What in the world does that mean? Did the mountain shrink in size or something?"

Damn it.

Olivia was right back in her mind again. Front and center.

"No, nothing like that."

"Then what?"

"Really? Can't you just accept my answer and move on?"

"Oh, wow, Evie-Eve is hiding something. I wonder what it could be? Hm."

"I just ended up stopping to help someone. Okay?"

Karen grinned. "Would this someone happen to be an attractive woman?"

"It wasn't like that, Karen."

It wasn't. She'd hadn't intended on anything happening.

"So, she *was* attractive."

She wanted to argue, but she knew Karen would see right through her. She might as well admit that she'd liked what she'd seen. Olivia was thick with muscle and her body curved deliciously in dangerous places, making Eve think about her full breasts and ass all over again.

"That's not why I helped her."

"Uh-huh."

Eve could feel Karen's stare boring a hole into the side of her face.

"And she just happened to be brunette, right?"

Eve shook her head, knowing there was no safe answer. She did like brunettes and her track record proved it. Damn Karen for knowing her so well.

"That's what I thought," Karen said.

"I would've helped her regardless. And I can't help what color her hair is. Or how she looks."

"I know, honey. No need to get all frazzled on me." She finally turned to look straight ahead, and Eve almost breathed a sigh of relief, hoping the inquisition was over.

"She has light eyes, doesn't she? What, green, hazel green? You're a sucker for the dark hair and green eyes. Yes, sir, that's it. That's your mashed potatoes and gravy. Gets you every time."

Eve heated.

"Mashed potatoes and gravy? That's a new one. And no, her hair isn't that dark and her eyes aren't green. They're more of a gray."

"Forgive me, I was *way* off." She moved on.

"So, did you offer her your services?"

Olivia laughed with frustration. "I don't want to talk about it."

"Oh, okay. Now you're going to pout because I've got you pegged. Poor Eve. Her best friend knows her too well. How awful."

Eve turned to tell her to shut up, but Karen was giving her an exaggerated look of sadness and Eve couldn't keep a straight face.

"I hate you."

"Oh, you do not."

"Do so."

"You love me. You adore me. You want to marry me."

Eve scoffed.

"Admit it, sunshine. I've got your number. I know you better than anyone else and it infuriates you that I can read you so well."

"Are you warmed up yet?"

"Nope."

"How much longer?" The urge to bust her ass with a killer circuit was growing.

"Long enough for you to tell me what she said."

Eve clamped her mouth shut.

"I'm waaaiting."

"She said she'd think about it, okay?" Eve halted and stepped off the machine. She grabbed her bag. "Come on, you're warm enough."

"All right, all right." Karen followed her back to the large mat area near the free weights. They tossed their bags aside and went carefully into stretches in front of the mirrored wall. "You like her. You like her and something happened. Otherwise you wouldn't be so cranky."

"I told you what she said."

"You're leaving something out."

"No."

"Yes."

"Christ, will you let it go? Nothing happened. I helped her and I gave her my card and she said she'd think about it. End of story."

"Then what's with the attitude?"

"It's Monday."

Karen laughed. "Since when does a Monday bother you? You don't take days off, so I'm not buying it."

Eve assisted her with a stretch and continued to fight the battle inside. She'd already gone over what had happened with Olivia and she'd decided to let it go. She needed to let it go. Thinking about their overwhelming chemistry again would only get her going and she wouldn't be able to do anything about it. She'd end up going nuts. And self-torture…well, that wasn't exactly her thing. Besides, she knew what Karen would say. She'd reiterate the couple of times she'd attempted to date women who had been hesitant or shy about their attraction and how they'd ended in disaster for numerous reasons. She'd lay into her for even considering it. Eve would tell her that while she couldn't control who she was drawn to in life, she did ultimately agree with her. But that wouldn't be good enough. Karen would still go on and on about it, and it would probably lead to her trying to set her up with someone again.

Something she preferred to avoid at all costs.

"I know you don't practice this, but it is okay not to share every single thing that pops into your head. Some things can be kept to yourself. In fact, some things should be kept to yourself."

Karen straightened, placed her hands on her hips, and cocked her head. Then she shook all over as if trying to rid the idea from her body.

"Yeah, no, not for me."

They finished stretching and both picked up a pair of free weights. Then they widened their stance, slightly bent their knees, and with their backs straight, they began doing bicep curls, alternating arms.

"Since you won't fess up," Karen said, pushing out a breath through pursed lips. "I'm going to assume that whatever happened shook your world a little bit. I'll leave you alone about it if you promise me something."

"What's that?"

"That you'll tell me if anything else happens with her. This mysterious woman of yours."

"Her name is Olivia, and I promise." Eve was pretty sure she wouldn't call so she wasn't worried about making that commitment.

"Oh, Olivia, eh?" She made a ticking noise. "I can't wait to get the goods on this one."

"Yeah, well, I seriously doubt there will be anything to share."

"Okay, whatever you say."

Eve pumped the weights while watching their form in the mirror. Karen was fit from years of working out with lean muscles and a strong core. But she wasn't as built as Eve and not nearly as cut. That wasn't the look she was going for. So Eve had her using lighter weights and doing more reps to ensure she didn't get the bulk of muscle.

"We're going hard with cardio tomorrow," Eve said, hoping to change the subject. Karen had been a long-time client, but she'd often take breaks, swearing she could maintain on her own. But eventually, she'd start complaining about her appearance or health again. Just as she'd done three weeks ago. This time around she said she'd gained a little weight and no longer felt as tight as she used to. Eve thought she still looked good regardless, but Karen wanted perfection.

Eve had told her repeatedly that she was too hard on herself and that perfection didn't exist. And while the talks had helped some, Karen still had trouble with self-image. And honestly, so did the majority of the women Eve worked with.

"Whatever you say, Evie-Eve. I am at your command."

"That'll be the day," Eve said as she finished and lowered her weights. She adjusted Karen's stance as she continued with her reps. "Come on, keep it up. You've got to push until burnout. Good. Five more." Her arms were trembling as she struggled to lift.

"That's it. Four. Come on, Karen, fight through."

Her face contorted and the veins in her neck popped as she pushed through.

"Last one," Eve said, lightly cupping the bottom of the weights for support. Karen cried out on the last curl and knelt to drop her weights.

"I swear to God if you weren't so good at sculpting my body, I would've killed you a long time ago."

Eve laughed. Threats on her life were something to be expected from clients being pushed to the brink. Karen was no exception, and as she watched her shake out her arms to do another set, Eve thanked the universe for the hundredth time that she had a job she loved and that it made a difference in people's lives. She thoroughly enjoyed helping her clients, and there was nothing quite like being there alongside them as they evolved into healthier, happier beings. The days when she hugged successful clients to say good-bye were initially bittersweet. But receiving the emails and texts that often followed, reporting their continued well-being and ability to thrive, made every tough moment completely worthwhile.

She smiled to herself, feeling extremely fortunate. But as she did so, her gaze fell upon a brunette on a treadmill in the distance. Her face was red and her body soaked with sweat. She was struggling, not only to breathe, but to keep her pace. Olivia's face flashed before her, and Eve felt the smile fall from her face. Her insides tightened as she thought about Olivia over-exerting herself, just like the woman across the gym. Would she try to run up that mountain again in her current condition? Would she get hurt?

Eve palmed her forehead. Why did she care so much?

She lowered her hand and refocused on Karen as she started in on another set. But Olivia's face remained despite her best efforts to push it away. And she wondered, for the first time in her life, how a woman she'd only spent minutes with had claimed so much space in her mind. She wondered how on earth she was going to get her out. And better yet, if she even really wanted her out.

CHAPTER FIVE

What does organic mean? Can anyone tell me?" Olivia's professor, Dr. Rosenberg, raised her eyebrows, searching her quiet class for a voice or, what Olivia imagined, a bright beacon in the dark. "If I say something is organic in a chemical sense, what does that mean?" She stood behind her desk, waiting.

Though she wasn't fond of doing so, Olivia spoke up, unable to take the anguish any longer. "It means it contains carbon."

Dr. Rosenberg pointed directly at her. "Exactly." She turned quickly to scribble something on the whiteboard. "It contains carbon."

Olivia underlined those words in her notes to remind herself of their importance. She did so to a few other phrases and definitions as well. She knew the material inside and out, but marking her notes was something to do. And she needed something to do in order to stay awake.

Dr. Rosenberg continued, and Olivia couldn't help it when her mind wandered to other things. She'd paid attention almost the entire fifty minutes of class, which was something of a feat for her. Now, however, she was just too tired to care. Fortunately, she was one of those people who could read something once and have almost complete recall afterward, which enabled her to drift off from time to time during the lecture. Sitting in class had become more of a formality, in case the professor took attendance, or on the off chance she mentioned something that wasn't in the text. Dr. Rosenberg did require attendance, but she rarely ventured from the required reading, leaving Olivia bored to tears and fighting off fatigue.

But truthfully, anything was better than where she'd been a little over a year ago. Ambling zombie-like through a small doctor's office as a medical assistant, calling patients back to be seen, and taking vitals. It had become mind-numbing and tedious, and she'd longed to break out, to be free, to go off and learn something new. After years of unhappiness, she'd finally gained the courage to make those changes and some days she still had a hard time believing she was actually in school and working toward her degree in nutrition. She was more content now than she'd ever been. So feigning boredom during long lectures was something she was more than happy to put up with.

Dr. Rosenberg closed her lecture for the day, and the class stirred slowly to life, as if rising from the dead. Olivia put her notes in her satchel and had an urge to groan as she stood. It had been a week since she'd run up the mountain, but her body still ached like it had just happened yesterday. The continued pain and stiffness of strained muscles frustrated her and tested her patience. She wanted to pick things back up again. Get moving. Continue on her journey to change. But her body wasn't having it.

"Tomorrow," she mumbled as she stepped out into the bright sunshine. She recoiled, shading her eyes with her hand, like a vampire terrified of evaporating. But soon her eyes adjusted, and she walked toward the student union. "Tomorrow I'll go and try again." Even if she was too sore to run, she'd still try. And if she couldn't, she'd hike. She'd do anything to get and keep a momentum. If she didn't, if she waited much longer, she feared she'd lose her ambition. And God only knew if it would ever return.

She tried to relax a little at having made up her mind about returning to the mountain. But thoughts of Eve came. There was a chance she'd run into her again on the trail. If not tomorrow, then another day. But what could she do about it? She wasn't about to stay away or change her plans. Eve was just a woman. A nice woman. And Olivia had the ability to tell her no. It would just be a little difficult is all. Maybe more so than usual. Okay, a lot more. Because unlike the other people she had to tell no, Eve was someone she actually wanted to say yes to. And good God, was it tempting.

She fought off a curse, still well trained from her childhood not to do so, and forced herself to focus on her surroundings, hoping against hope it would keep the thoughts of Eve at bay. Dozens of students bustled about the campus of the community college, with their minds no doubt on their own problems. Most had eyes trained on their phones, only glancing upward every so often to make sure they were still on the right path. Others whizzed by on their longboards with music loud enough for her to hear blaring from their earbuds. Some days being surrounded by all those young adults made her, at thirty-two, feel ancient. But today, she just felt grateful to be there with them, building her brain, ensuring herself a better life. It also helped that she'd met several other students around her age or older also seeking an education.

She crossed the busy sidewalk to the union. It was early afternoon, so the heavy lunch crowd had mostly dispersed, leaving a few tables open under the ramada. She slid onto a bench seat and placed her bag on the table. And just as she was about to check her phone for any messages, her friend and fellow student, Jake, eased in across from her.

"Ugh, can this day get any worse?" He handed over her Monday afternoon coffee and then slurped his own.

"Thanks." She took a sip and wanted to melt. It was still piping hot, and the smell and flavor of the caramel seemed to saturate her senses immediately. She couldn't have needed this more. "Thank you so much."

Jake was always good for their Monday afternoon coffee. He never forgot and he never got her order wrong. Her schedule was full on Monday mornings, so by the time afternoon rolled around, she almost always needed some sort of caffeine. She took another sip and winced as she readjusted herself on the seat. She just couldn't get comfortable anywhere, not even at home on her couch. She was really paying the price for that run.

"You okay?" Jake ran his hand through his striking blond locks and then rested his elbow on the table. "You're not still sore, are you?"

"Mm, a bit." That was the understatement of the century.

"You know I so badly want to say it, but I won't."

She swore she could see the playfulness in his eyes through the lenses of his Prada shades.

"Please, don't. Believe me I got the message."

Jake had flipped out when she'd shown up last Monday barely able to move. And after he'd heard what she'd done to cause such misery, he flipped out again, furious that she'd done something like that without telling him first. Because, according to him, he would've stopped her. He would've told her she was crazy. She'd told him she was going running, yes. But she'd never said anything about running up a mountain.

"I hope so. Because I hate having to tell you you're a moron." He shook his head as if he still was going to do so, as if he couldn't stop himself.

She braced herself for the onslaught.

"I swear, Olivia, you are like the most clueless smart person I've ever known. You are super intelligent with this incredible photographic memory, which, as you know, I seriously hate you for, and yet you have absolutely no common sense whatsoever."

"That's so not true." But as the words fell from her mouth, she recalled her sheltered life. She'd been raised in a very strict religious household. One where, next to God, her parents were the center of her universe. They made the rules, they made the calls. She was never to question them, even when she knew they were flat-out wrong. And friends? Sure, she had them. But most were from the church and brought up just as she was. Her world was very carefully controlled, and there were many, many things, she now knew, that she hadn't been exposed to. And very little of that changed when she got married. Control had shifted from her parents to her husband and the church had still been a big influence. Outside of work at the doctor's office, she knew very little of the world around her. But that didn't mean she was clueless did it?

"It's not," she said again, this time more for herself.

He gave her a look. "Please, honey. Don't even."

"Okay. Maybe I'm not up to speed on everything around me, but I can figure out how to exercise."

"Obviously not."

"I can. I just…" Eve's words came to mind. "Bit off more than I can chew."

"I'll say."

"I just want it so much. You don't understand."

"What, you think I don't understand what it feels like to want something right away? Sweetie, my least favorite word is *wait*. My middle name is *now*. I hate waiting more than anything. But I've learned that some things take time, whether I like it or not. Getting into shape is one of those things. You're going to have to accept that."

She lowered her gaze to stare at the grated table. She didn't want to wait. She wanted her new life now. All of it. She'd waited long enough. Stood stagnant for years in a smothering marriage. Wasn't that enough? Hadn't she put in her time?

"Olivia, look at me." He held her hand. "Think about all the changes you've experienced in just a little over a year. You left your husband, moved into your own place, quit your job, started school. It's mind-boggling what all you've done and had to adjust to. So, cut yourself some slack. Take some time to breathe. Getting fit is going to take time whether you slow things down or not. That's just a fact. So why not just relax and go about it the right way? You know, the way that won't get you killed?"

He squeezed her hand. She had been through a lot. More than she ever had before. Maybe she should think about slowing down.

She nodded. "I'll consider it."

"That's a girl."

She smiled and squeezed his hand in return. She might decide to slow things down, yes. But stop altogether to rest? Even for a short while? No way. A week had been long enough. Possibly too long.

She was going to return to that mountain. And she was going to do it tomorrow.

CHAPTER SIX

Eve inhaled the beautiful morning air as she walked along the top of the mountain after a second successful yet rigorous run up the trail. She kicked out her legs and kept moving, hands on hips, chest and chin up. She checked her pulse and took a few small sips of water. The view of northern Glendale was spectacular in the sunrise, and she usually enjoyed taking it in. But every trip to the mountain brought with it the secret hope that she'd see Olivia. And every time she'd left, after having to accept Olivia's absence, she felt both relief and disappointment. She'd never been so confused by her feelings for a woman.

She jogged a little in place, the orange and pink bursting sky doing little to ease her mind. She knew she should head back down to go start her day, but a part of her wanted to stay for a while. She could kid herself into believing she was doing so simply for the beauty of the view. But truthfully, she knew the longer she hung around, the better chance she had of running into Olivia.

She checked her pulse again and stared out at the dozens of Spanish-tiled rooftops. She imagined people tucked away in their quiet homes, some probably slightly stirring from sleep by the sound of the mourning doves. Sunrise was her favorite time of day and had been since she was a child. She could still remember waking early and sitting in the backyard, enjoying the calm, the stillness, watching as the gray world around her began to tint with color as light crept in. Those quiet moments alone had been her safe haven, her only peace in a house full of chaos. It had been difficult to find any moment alone, much less a peaceful one. But then there came a day when she'd awakened early from a dream. The calm of her house had felt strange, and she'd ventured into the kitchen for a glass of water. She'd been standing at the sink when she'd seen it in the first light of the day. A hot air balloon. Big, beautiful, and bursting with color, it was moving slowly above the homes, gliding across the sky. She'd rushed outside and stood in the middle of the yard staring. She could see the people in the basket and they'd waved at her. More than excited, she'd waved back and watched as flames torched upward into the hollow part of the balloon. She could hear the distant, deep hiss of the heat, and she'd felt so special, knowing she'd witnessed something her siblings hadn't. Seeing that balloon by herself in her backyard, it had felt like that experience was solely hers. Something no one else could take away, something she didn't have to ever share. And she hadn't. She'd kept it to herself and she'd set her sports watch alarm to wake her the next morning and the one after that. She'd eagerly bolted from bed and dashed into the wet grass in her bare feet and waved at the subsequent balloons as they floated by. None had ever come as close as that very first one had, but there they'd been, gliding across her sky, day after day, for weeks at a time and every early spring thereafter. She'd never told a soul.

Sometime shortly after that first spring, she'd learned that the vacant desert just beyond her subdivision, where all the kids liked to explore, was a popular place for crews to unpack and stretch out their balloons for launch. When she'd grown older, she'd taken her bike there and watched as a dozen or so balloons were raised into the awaiting dawn.

She'd stared up in amazement at all those bubbles of color dotting the sky.

It had been a sight to behold.

She blinked back into the present as she caught sight of a balloon in the distance. It was that time of year again, and soon there'd be more. She pulled her leg up behind her for a hamstring stretch. Then she lowered it and did the same to the other. She caught sight of something out of the corner of her eye. She turned and saw someone emerging, having reached the top. The woman was wearing a white ball cap, matching tank top, and dark blue athletic shorts. She bent over with her hands on her knees. Eve pushed her sunglasses up on her head for a better view. She moved closer and noted similarities. Her heart fluttered a bit at the possibility. Then the woman straightened, and Eve got a clear view of the beautiful, classical features of her face and those delectable, head-turning curves.

Olivia.

Absently, Eve put her hand to her chest. She felt the hard pounding of her heart and wondered if she'd subconsciously put her hand there to keep it from leaping from her body.

"Olivia." She hurried toward her, and concern grew as she drew closer. Olivia had a plume of red on her cheeks and neck. Her legs were shaking, and she couldn't seem to get enough oxygen. Eve was almost to her when Olivia spotted her, and within a split second, her face seemed to brighten with surprise and then fall with what looked like guilt. Eve skidded to a stop feeling like she'd been slapped.

She stood still, unsure what to do. An awful gut-wrenching feeling set in. It had been a long time since she'd last felt rejection, but she'd know that soul crushing feeling anywhere. And as if to solidify the reality of the rejection, Olivia raised her hand to keep Eve from coming any closer.

"I'm fine," she said. She bent once again and rested her free hand on her knee. Her breathing was sporadic, and she was covered in sweat. She didn't look good at all.

Eve worried she might even pass out. The strong pull to help her doubled, despite the rejection. Her concern for her was very real, and she didn't understand how she could continue to care so much about someone's well-being when they obviously didn't want her to. But at the moment, it didn't matter, her need to make sure she was okay won out, regardless.

"Let me help. I can—"

"It's not as bad as last time," Olivia blurted, before Eve could finish. "I didn't run the whole way up."

Then why do you look like you're going to die?

"I don't think I quite believe that, based on your current state." She spoke softly, careful not to be too hard on her. "But it ultimately makes no difference because the bottom line is you shouldn't be running *any* of it. Not yet, anyway." She rubbed her brow. "You're going to seriously hurt yourself."

Olivia glanced away from her, and Eve studied her closely, more curious than ever. What all was she hiding? Was she afraid to tell her the truth about how much she ran because she feared criticism and judgment? Or was it the attraction between them that was bothering her?

"I'm good. Really." She straightened and smiled. It looked forced. Like she was trying to convince Eve that she was fine.

She failed. Miserably.

Eve searched her mind for the right words. Words that would break through Olivia's stubbornness.

"Please, at least let me help you back down the trail."

That look of panic, the one she'd seen just before Olivia had climbed in her car and sped away, was back.

"Oh, no, no, no. That's not necessary."

Am I really that scary? And what exactly is it that she's afraid of? At the moment, with the current look on her face, Eve honestly couldn't tell. Eve felt herself soften.

Maybe Olivia didn't dislike her.

Maybe she was just uncomfortable. For whatever reason.

Eve spoke again, and she did so gently, as she had before.

"Olivia, you can hardly stand. And you know it would be a lot safer if you had some support walking back down."

Olivia continued to avoid her gaze, choosing instead to look out at the vast array of houses below.

"I'm fine. Really."

Eve didn't believe her. Not even for a second. There was no conviction. And the words had been said so softly she'd barely heard them.

Olivia's stubborn barrier was crumbling.

Eve struck again, hoping to knock the cement blocks down once and for all.

"Look, no strings attached, okay? I won't pressure you to call me and I won't tell you what you should or shouldn't do. I'll just be a beam of support, holding you tight, making sure you don't stumble and fall."

Eve smiled, convinced Olivia would see that things were okay, that she was safe, that she could trust her. But to her shock, the promise only seemed to reignite Olivia's panic.

She shook her head vehemently. "No. No, thanks. I got this."
What the hell?

Eve exhaled and gripped the back of her neck. That was it. That was all she had. There was nothing more she could do. Absolutely nothing.

Olivia was on her own.

"Okay, then. I'll leave you to it." She kicked absently at a pebble. "Just…" She looked up at her and was a little taken aback when she saw Olivia's eyes already trained on her. "Just be careful, okay? I truly only want for your happiness and your health."

Eve lowered her shades and turned to head out.

"Thank you." The words came on a breeze. Eve straightened her shoulders and accepted that those would be the last words she'd probably ever hear from this mysterious woman named Olivia. It was a finality that left her with a surprisingly deep and nearly overwhelming sadness. It was so heavy and so powerful, she hoped she'd never feel anything like it again.

Chapter Seven

Olivia watched helplessly as Eve walked away from her. She wanted to call out to her, to stop her, to apologize to her for being such a jerk. But she didn't. She couldn't.

She winced in pain from the pressure she'd had to put on her foot. She lifted it slightly but remained where she was. Eve couldn't know she was hurt. She'd absolutely insist on helping her, fighting her harder than she'd just done. But the mere thought of Eve next to her, pulling her in close and tight, close enough to feel her body and strength again, to smell her enticing scent, really worried her. And she didn't even want to acknowledge what having her so close would do to her loins. After their first encounter, it had taken hours before she'd regained some control over her thoughts and body, despite the rigors she'd felt from the run. The heat and the throbbing Eve had caused, they'd been new to her and overpowering, and the long, cold shower she'd taken hadn't doused either. She feared if those feelings came on again, she might do something crazy. Like act on them.

She swayed and for a second thought she might pass out. Was it because of Eve or because of her injury? She wasn't sure. The light-headedness and the race of her pulse were probably more intensified by both. Both had to be dealt with, whether she wanted to or not. The injury, she'd have to handle herself. And Eve, well, she'd done what she'd had to do and told her to go. It had to be done.

But watching her walk away was awful. She knew she had hurt her. The pain from that alone was seriously surpassing the pain from her ankle. But she couldn't afford for these feelings to continue. Her future depended on what she did right now. She needed to concentrate on school and continue to rebuild her life, her way this time. Besides, she wouldn't know what to do with her desire even if she allowed it to overtake her. She could never tell Eve. What if she freaked out? Where would that leave her? Even if Eve somehow felt the same, what would happen next? Touching? Kissing?

What would touching her feel like? What would kissing her feel like? Just how soft was her skin? Just how warm and supple were her lips? She shuddered as her imagination went into overdrive. This was the very thing she was trying so hard to avoid. Eve would soon disappear back down the mountain, and hopefully, so would her lust for her. She took one last look at her and tried to memorize her body. She started with her toned, tanned legs and moved up to her high, tight behind. Then she went on to the muscled contours of her back, which led up to her perfectly etched shoulder blades. The alternating shift of them as she walked was mesmerizing.

Olivia stared after her in awe. Why were things like this in life so cruel? Why did she still have to find Eve so beautiful and so desirable even as she walked out of her life forever? Why couldn't her feelings go with Eve instead of remaining inside to torture her for what? Eternity? Would it ever cease?

The way Olivia felt right now, she doubted anything having to do with Eve Monroe would ever dissipate.

I'm going to miss her so much and I don't even know her.

She tore her gaze away from her, needing desperately to regain some semblance of control before she was completely consumed by her grief. The large rock she'd sat on before was nearby. Only a few steps and she'd be there. She quickly hobbled toward it, but the pain was so bad she cried out, unable to hold it in. But she carried on regardless and let out a few more cries until she finally reached her destination and braced herself, dying for some relief. The rock's rough surface was an instant comfort, and she carefully sat, grimacing as a few more sharp stabs resonated from her ankle. When they lessened, she sighed, but heard the sound of hurried footsteps. She searched the path and saw Eve running. She slid to a stop right next to her. Olivia didn't speak, the agony of crossing to the rock leaving her too exhausted to even try to downplay her situation.

Eve wrenched off her sunglasses and shoved them into the center of her tight athletic top. The look of worry and determination on her face was so strong Olivia knew she wouldn't be able to fend her off at this point even if she tried.

"What's wrong?" she breathed.

"I turned my ankle on the way up."

"While you were running?"

Olivia nodded. "I stepped on a rock."

"And you were trying to hide this from me, because?"

"I wanted to handle it myself."

She chuckled and shook her head as she knelt in front of her. "You are something else, Olivia. You are something else."

"What's that supposed to mean?"

"Nothing, I—"

"I was in pain. So, trying to manage that was quite enough. I didn't need to be yelled at on top of it."

"I would've never yelled at you." She tried to touch her leg, but Olivia wasn't having it.

"You know what? Just stop." She shifted, trying to move away from her. "Your laughter is far worse than yelling." The movement, even though she'd done her best not to use her foot, hurt tremendously. "Ow, God dammit!" She clenched her fist and hit her thigh. She was so angry and upset and she couldn't seem to budge an inch without it triggering some sort of god-awful torture. She just wanted to be left alone.

Eve stared at her for a long moment.

"I wasn't laughing at you; I was trying to figure you out. I wanted to know why you tried to hide this from me instead of just accepting some help. And when you gave me your answer, I got it. I thought you were being a little irrational and I wasn't sure what, if anything, I was going to do about it, but I still got it."

"Got what?"

"That you're a very proud, self-reliant person who fears judgment and admonishment."

"What? Oh, my God, whatever." Eve had hit the nail on the head, and it made her feel all the more vulnerable. And that pissed her off.

But Eve continued.

"Now, is that fear the sole reason why you try to keep me away, or is there some kind of additional trepidation I haven't totally figured out yet? Probably."

She reached out again, and Olivia was too overwhelmed with feelings of exposure to swat her away. She was having enough trouble trying to maintain basic human functions, like breathing and swallowing.

Both became even more difficult as Eve touched her knee and kept talking.

"But there is one thing I am now very certain of."

Olivia scoffed.

"You don't want me to get close."

Olivia let out a short laugh. "Oh, please."

"I'm not trying to upset you. I'm just being honest."

"You're being ridiculous. Why would I care if you got close?"

Eve merely looked at her, and Olivia once again had trouble swallowing.

Does she somehow…know?

"This isn't a good time or place for speculation. So, let's just focus on your ankle."

Her fingertips grazed a path down her leg to just above her ankle. Olivia shivered, and if Eve noticed, she didn't act like it.

"How bad?" she asked.

"I don't think anything is broken. But it hurts pretty bad."

"From the look on your face when you tried to move, I'd say pretty bad stands for downright unbearable. Can you put any pressure on it at all?"

Olivia tried to rest her foot on the ground and yelped.

Eve gently cupped her heel and examined her as best she could without touching her further.

"We'll leave your shoe on. I know you don't know me or trust me or anything, but I'm really not into torturing people. So, you can rest assured there. Do you think you can make it back with my help? Or do you want me to call someone?"

"Call someone? Like who?"

"The fire department. They can—"

"Oh, God no." She was hurt, but not *that* badly. Just thinking about all those people having to come to rescue her because she'd been stupid made her stomach churn with dread. But still, she had to get off that mountain. And she now knew she couldn't do it alone.

She breathed deeply as she realized what she really hadn't wanted to have happen was about to, indeed, actually happen.

She'd already cursed once, and if she were someone who did that often, she'd definitely be doing so now.

She steeled herself and once again did what she had to do.

This time she didn't have to tell Eve to go.

No, this time she had to allow Eve to stay.

She had no choice.

CHAPTER EIGHT

So, no on the fire department means you're going to allow me to help you, right?" Eve asked.

Olivia nodded, knowing without a doubt that her previous rejection had affected her. She felt really bad, but she'd thought she was doing the right thing.

Eve brought her to a stand. She wrapped her arm around her waist and pulled her close. Olivia tried her best not to notice the merging of their bodies or the way the cherry blossom smell of her seemed to come alive in the moisture of her skin, causing Olivia to wonder if she used scented lotion rather than perfume.

"Drape your arm over my shoulders."

Olivia did and her moist skin once again caught her attention. It was warm and silky along her shoulders beneath Olivia's arm.

"Okay, just like before." Eve took hold of Olivia's hand dangling from her shoulder. "Lean into me and use me for support. Use me as your leg."

"Okay."

"You ready?"

"Yes."

They began to move.

"Good. Nice and slow."

They left the rock for the trail. The pain was sharp when it came, but soon, she was grateful because it seemed to come just as her body began to thrum in response to Eve's proximity. So back and forth, the feelings went, one on top of another. One second, a sudden rush of rising desire and then another, a sudden dousing of sharp pain.

"Lucky for us the walk down isn't as steep on the back side," Eve said when they finally began to descend. "We should still be good even though you're hurt worse this time." She smiled at her. "You got this, Olivia. You can do it."

She spoke like that off and on, upbeat and positive, praising and encouraging her. She never allowed fear or doubt to take root in her mind. She consistently cut both down with the mighty sword of her optimism, and Olivia was just as captivated as ever. She began to realize just how special the woman next to her was.

Eve was nice.

Really, truly nice.

Eve had been kind and caring before. But this went beyond a stranger doing a single good deed to help another.

This was deeper.

This was Eve's core.

"Thank you," Olivia said.

Eve kept her eyes focused on their footing. "You don't need to thank me, Olivia. I'm only doing what anyone else would do."

"No, not for this. I mean, not just for this."

"For what, then?"

"For not yelling at me and calling me an idiot even though I deserve it."

"No one deserves to get hurt, Olivia. And I did lecture you a little about the running as you may recall."

"Yes, but you weren't mean about it. I didn't expect that."

"What good would yelling at you do? Other than make you feel shitty? You're very much aware that you made a mistake, and a mistake is all it is. God knows I've made plenty so what would give me the right to lay into you for doing the same?"

Olivia had never heard someone speak from such an understanding viewpoint. It was empathetic, thoughtful, considerate. Not in any way angry or blaming or judgmental. It sounded nothing like what she'd heard growing up or what she'd heard from her ex-husband. She found it sad considering how religious her family and community were. Everyone should think this way and forgive this way. That was what love and acceptance were all about. Right?

They continued to descend, slow and steady, both concentrating on the trail while seemingly lost in their own thoughts. Olivia enjoyed being near her, despite the crazy chaos of pain and attraction both fighting it out inside her. But eventually, she knew their time together would have to end. They were almost to the base of the mountain. Sadness loomed, and Olivia spoke, wanting to stop it in its tracks.

"I don't think I've ever met anyone like you, Eve."

She laughed. "Is that a good thing or a bad thing?"

Olivia thought about all the uncontrollable feelings Eve evoked and how, even though they scared her, they seemed to be drawing her in, no matter how hard she tried to avoid it.

"Mm, a good thing."

"You hesitated," she teased her.

"Oh, I did not."

"Did so. You aren't truly convinced your meeting me is a good thing, are you?" She grinned.

Oh, my good God, she is so beautiful.

"Well, I don't know everything about you, do I? So how can I be totally sure?" She was teasing her right back, and it felt good to be light-hearted.

"Well, maybe you'll just have to get to know me then."

Olivia started to respond with more playful banter, but she quickly closed her mouth as the meaning of the comment settled in.

Eve's grin faded at her silence.

It hurt Olivia to see that. She wished she could tell her that she wanted, more than anything, to get to know her. Now more so than ever. But she couldn't tell her that. Because if she did, then she'd have to explain why doing so wouldn't be a good idea.

Eve, however, didn't seem to sense her plight. She was too caught up in her own.

"I'm sorry," she said. "I didn't mean anything by that."

Olivia was a little speechless. "You don't have to apologize."

"I feel like I do. I think I may have offended you somehow."

"I'm not offended."

"Then, what are you?"

They reached the bottom of the mountain and headed toward their vehicles.

"I don't know."

How could she put words to such turmoil?

"A little bewildered, I guess. Like I said, I've never met anyone like you."

"If you really think meeting me was a good thing, then why do I sometimes get the sense that you don't like me?"

"I do like you," Olivia blurted. "Very much."

"But?"

I keep thinking about kissing you. And it's scaring me so badly it's killing me.

Kissing. Killing.

Can I really be equating the two?

Oh, my God, I am.

The fear of what kissing Eve would do to her was what was truly terrifying her. Because if she did kiss her and faced the attraction she felt, and she…liked it, her entire life would be upended. Her life, as she knew it, would change or end.

"I don't know. It's all so confusing." She had no way of explaining herself without exposing her feelings. And Eve was wonderful, with an inner beauty that somehow rivaled her outer beauty. She was oh-so-tempting, and Olivia wanted so badly to confess everything to her. To just let it out and hope for the compassion and acceptance Eve had shown her thus far.

"What is?"

Olivia laughed, trying to hide her nervousness. "Me. I mean, my feelings—no, I mean—"

"Your feelings?"

They stopped at the Prius. Eve gently removed Olivia's arm from her shoulders and faced her. Olivia immediately fell into her eyes as they completely enveloped her. She was looking at her with such sincerity and acceptance, it made Olivia feel like she could float away.

"My feelings…I don't—I can't—I don't know how to explain them."

"Oh," she said softly. "I think I know what you mean." She reached up and, with a touch so delicate Olivia wasn't sure she'd actually felt it, stroked her cheek.

Olivia burned fiercely beneath her fingers.

She knows. She has to. She's touching me like…oh my God, like a lover would.

"You do?"

"You're scared. And uncertain. I absolutely understand that."

I am beyond terrified. You're right about that. But you don't know how much I want you. So, you couldn't possibly understand everything.

"Then can you help me?" She wasn't really serious with her request, more overcome with nerves and a need to break the tension than anything. She kept rambling, feeling a need to explain her foolishness. "Because I can't totally comprehend what's happening. I have no idea what to do."

"I can empathize with you in more ways than you know. Trust me on that. And as far as not knowing what to do, you don't *have* to do anything." She smiled. "But if you choose to, just look inside yourself."

She hadn't expected Eve to respond to her silly, half-hearted plea for help so thoughtfully. She wasn't sure what to say and her nerves continued to grind on her. "Great. I have no clue how to go about that." It was true, even if it did sound absurd. She'd always been taught to rely on her faith. That that alone would see her through and show her the way.

"Just try to relax and allow yourself to really feel these feelings you're having. Learn how they are a part of what make you you. You'd be amazed at what all you can discover when you look inward. I'm not saying you'll find all the answers you're looking for right away, but I know you'll find some. The rest, if you keep your mind and heart open, will come eventually."

"You sound so wise and insightful. I wish I could put you in my pocket and take you with me."

Eve made her feel like who she was was okay, even with all the madness running amok inside her. Even though she didn't know what Olivia felt for her.

Olivia didn't want to let her go. She was like a life-saving buoy in a wild, turbulent sea.

"I'll help you any way I can, Olivia. All you have to do is ask."

I want to. Oh, dear God, how I want to.

Olivia wished she could somehow solidify that moment into something tangible. That way she could pick it up and hold it and re-experience it whenever she wanted. She never wanted to forget the warmth of Eve's fingers on her face, the thoughtfulness of her words, and most of all, the way she was looking into her eyes and caressing her soul.

"Thank you," she said yet again. There simply weren't any other words.

Eve lowered her hand. "You're welcome."

Another car pulled in, breaking the intensity.

"Will you be okay?" Eve asked. "I know it's your left ankle, but still it might be difficult to drive."

"I think I'll be all right."

My ankle, maybe. Me? No way. Not anytime soon.

"Will you go to the doctor?" She raised an eyebrow, letting her know that she thought she probably should.

"Yes."

They both waved as the two people from the newly parked car walked by and greeted them.

"You have my number, yes?"

"I do."

"Glad to hear it wasn't immediately tossed into a bin." She grinned.

"Yeah, well, I thought about tossing it, but it seems you're not that easy to get rid of."

"Oh, really?" She clutched her chest. "I'm not sure if I was just insulted or complimented. I think I better go before you say anything more."

She backed away with a smile. "Elevate and ice that ankle."

"I will."

"And for God's sake, no more mountains for a while, okay?"

Olivia laughed and waved good-bye. She watched as Eve climbed into her dark red SUV and drove away. Then Olivia hobbled in behind the wheel of her Toyota, closed the door, started the engine, and stared straight ahead.

Had all of that really just happened?

She couldn't believe it.

A little over a year ago, she'd wanted, more than anything, to change her life. And boy, was she getting what she wanted. As she drove from the parking lot she thought about that old familiar saying.

Be careful what you wish for.

Because it just might happen in ways you never dared dream.

CHAPTER NINE

I don't think I've ever seen you this down," Karen said from across the table.

Eve could still see her sipping her margarita even as she stared beyond her into oblivion. Her ability to focus had disappeared, taking along with it sleep and motivation. Crankiness and frustration, however, had moved in, attempting to set up permanent residence.

"Um, hello? Anyone home?" Karen was leaning forward, trying to get her attention.

Eve forced her gaze back to her friend. Normally, she'd come back at her with something clever, funny even. But she just didn't have the will.

"My God. You're really jonesing for this woman, aren't you? Why don't you just call her and put an end to all this suffering?"

Somehow, Eve managed a sigh. She'd been pining over Olivia since she'd last seen her, wondering why she hadn't called, complaining that she hadn't called, moping around because she hadn't called.

"Well, for one, I don't have any way to contact her. And for another, this needs to be her decision. I'm almost certain she feels the same attraction I do, but the way she behaved the last time I saw her and the things she said…I think she may be struggling with it."

Which is why I'm so confused over my reaction to her silence. I shouldn't be surprised or upset over her avoidance if she's struggling with those feelings. Not only that, but dating confused women in the past has never ended well for me. So what the hell is going on here?

"Oh, now that's news. You've failed to mention that little nugget of information." She seemed to think for a moment. "What about your rule? About dating women who aren't secure in their sexuality? Or have you forgotten?"

"I remember my rule."

"Then that must be why you conveniently left out the bit about your suspicions. You knew I'd kick your ass for even considering dating her."

"Yes. That's exactly why I didn't tell you." She spread her hands and gave her an incredulous look. "What do you want me to say? You want me to deny it? I can't. I knew you'd kick my ass, and honestly, Karen, I've been kicking my own ass over it plenty. I've gone over and over my rule and the fiascos in the past and I'm still thinking about her. I can't seem to stop."

"So if she calls are you going to throw your rule out the window?"

"Yes."

"Wow. You didn't even hesitate."

"I don't need to. I've done nothing but think about this. About her. She moves me, Karen. She is on a whole different level."

"How so?"

"Well, she's honest. Even when she tries to hide something, I can tell it's not who she really is and that she feels discontent in not divulging everything. It's an innocence I think, and her being that real, that authentic, to me, a virtual stranger, is very unusual and it shows me who she is inside."

"And who is she?"

"She's…good."

"Good? Since when does Goody Two-shoes do it for you?"

Eve gave her a look. "There's depth to this woman, Karen. Real depth. The way she seems to feel and process the world, it's profound."

"Okay. She's deep, sensitive."

"Yes. But there's more." She couldn't help but smile. "She's got some fire in her."

"Really?" She eased back and crossed her arms.

"She's headstrong and stubborn and she can be temperamental. She's a fighter and she's ambitious and extremely determined. There's a definite passion there. I don't think she even realizes it, because she's been so repressed, but it's there. Especially with me. She reacts so strongly when I touch her, I almost expect her to spontaneously combust." She wiped at the sweat on her glass and got lost in the marks from her fingertip. "And the way she dives into my eyes." She shook her head. "It's like I'm the rarest most beautiful thing she's ever seen and she's trying with all her might to commit me to memory."

She returned her gaze to Karen, who also seemed to be caught up in her description of Olivia.

"But the thing that gets me the most. I mean really tunnels down deep and stirs me, is how everything she says and does and feels, it all seems to be one hundred and ten percent…" she paused, searching for the right word.

"Heartfelt."

Karen was quiet for a few long seconds. "I'm at a loss for words. I've never heard you talk like this before."

"I'm a little surprised as well."

"You know who you sound like, don't you?"

"No, who?"

"You sound like a romantic."

Eve spun her glass slowly around and around.

"Yeah," Karen said. "Try that one on for size."

"I guess, I do, don't I?"

"You're admitting it? You make fun of romantics, Eve."

"I have before, yes."

"So, what's happening here?"

"I don't know. And don't think that doesn't scare the shit out of me, because it does. But, Karen. Jesus, God, Karen. I want her. And not just physically, either. I want all of her. I want to know this woman inside and out."

"I know you don't want to hear it, but you've got it bad, my friend. You're well past Go with two hundred dollars in hand and you're headed straight for Love Boulevard."

"No," Eve said, resting her elbows on the table. "Saying I sound like a romantic is one thing, but no, I don't do love."

"Eve, you're love bound, babe. You are riding that wild train of helpless devotion like a demon, pulling on that whistle something fierce."

"Okay, I get your point." She massaged her brow while focusing on the table.

"You know I'm all for you meeting someone special and settling down. I want that for you more than I can express."

"But?"

"It's not what you want. You just said so."

"Right."

"Then you need to let this go. Let her go. Because, I'm telling you, you're going to fall for her. Hard. It's already happening, and I know you think you can control how you feel and delve into this woman with sex and passion and an exploration of who she is and somehow keep it casual. But you can't. Not when it comes to love. There is no way to control that. You wouldn't know because you've never felt like this before. I have. So, please, listen to me and save yourself and this woman a lot of trouble and forget about her."

Eve almost gulped her margarita, too worked up to sip.

"I must've said something that reached you, because you're stressing."

Eve took a break from her consumption of her drink even though there was very little left.

"She's not going to call, so this whole conversation is moot."

"She could still call."

"It's been weeks."

"Just be ready if she does. Know what you're going to say."

Eve downed the remainder of her drink in a single shot and placed her empty glass on the table. "Let's just talk about something else, please."

Karen patted her hand.

"Look outside. It's a beautiful day. A glorious day. And look at us. We're alive, we're healthy and, not to mention, extremely attractive." She grinned wickedly and motioned at the food and drinks on the table like she was a spokesmodel showing off merchandise. "And we've got margaritas and guac. Some seriously good guac. Two of your favorite things." She winked. "So come on, show some life, kid. Dig into those homemade tortilla chips like I know you can and forget about the girl."

"I'll drink but I can't stomach anything to eat. Not right now." Not when Olivia was out there somewhere, undoubtedly lost to her forever. She wasn't yet okay with that, despite Karen's opinions.

If she were being honest with herself, she wasn't sure she ever would be.

CHAPTER TEN

The waiter brought Eve another margarita, and this time she sipped, enjoying the tartness as it mixed with the salt from the rim. She usually relished that fine combination, but everything was still so dull. She took a few more sips, hoping for some color to seep back into her world. The alcohol was relaxing her, but color remained elusive.

As some of the tension lifted, she began to think about climbing out of her funk. That had to be her main objective today. Life hadn't somehow stopped just because she had. It was still spinning endlessly around her, and she needed to jump back on that merry-go-round before she forgot how. After all, she had goals. Ambitions. And she'd always been driven, come rain or shine. That hadn't changed.

"Maybe you're right," she said. "Maybe I need to move on from this."

"You don't sound like you're convinced."

"I just don't know how I'd do it. How can I get her from my mind?"

"Isn't it obvious? You need to do what everybody else does when they need to forget someone. You need to get back on the horse. You need a date."

Eve shook her head. "That's the last thing I need."

"No, it's exactly what you need. A new woman will definitely get your mind off of Olivia. And some seriously great sex, well, that will blow Miss Goody Two-shoes right out of your hemisphere."

Eve frowned, letting her know she didn't like the comment.

"Okay, I'm sorry I called her that. But come on, hon. Hop back on that horse. I've even got someone in mind for you."

"Karen, you don't get it. Olivia isn't just another woman. She's an *experience*. Those precious moments I had with her…let's just say I won't be able to forget her by going on a date or two."

"You say something like that and you *don't* want love? And you don't want to even consider that what you're feeling is headed that way, or that you might possibly already be there?"

"Karen, come on."

"I just want to be sure."

"Love means losing yourself and it leads to commitment. You know how I feel about that."

"So, no love."

"No love."

"Not even with this woman."

"No."

"Then I don't know what to tell you as far as forgetting her. Maybe you should obsess on something else. Work out more. Throw yourself into your fitness."

Eve laughed. "More than I do now?"

Karen shrugged. "It's something you love to do."

"How long have you known me? You know I'm built like a Mack truck. I have my father's physique and I can very easily build muscle."

"Yeah, so?"

"So, look at me. I'm already pretty jacked, Karen. Any more and I'll look like the Terminator. I like classic Arnold and all, but that's a look I'd rather pass on, thank you very much. It just isn't me."

"That surprises me a little. I never thought I'd hear you say that there's a level of fitness that is 'too much.'"

"Yeah, well, I am. I'm happy where I'm at."

"Must be nice." She curled her fingers and pretended to study her nails. "Being all physically perfect and everything. I, of course, wouldn't know."

Eve rolled her eyes and let her continue, knowing she was going to playfully pick on her.

"Most women wouldn't know. But I guess that's what keeps you in business. Keeps you in demand. Our inability to attain perfection."

"Oh, my God."

"And so in you swoop to save the day. Like a superhero. To, you know, help all of us less fortunate souls." She covered her heart with her hand. "What's it like, Eve? To be so wonderful? To make such a difference in so many lives?"

Eve looked at her for a moment with a straight face. "Exhausting."

Karen burst out laughing. Eve joined her with a little laughter herself and it felt good.

Their waiter appeared again, and Karen wiped her eyes.

"Don't mind us. We're just a little happy. And now that you're here, well, we're very happy, aren't we?"

He smiled but looked a bit uncomfortable. "Did you ladies want to order a meal?"

Karen leaned toward him. "I think it's the margaritas. You know what tequila can do to a woman." They were only on their second drink and had been there for close to two hours. She was far from intoxicated.

Eve cleared her throat and gave Karen a stern look before answering the young man.

"No, thank you. We're fine. We're ready for the bill when you get a chance."

Karen ignored her and winked at him. "You get what I'm saying, sweetie?"

He nodded quickly at Eve and hurried away.

Eve kicked her beneath the table.

Karen jerked and squealed. "Ow, what was that for?"

"Can we go anywhere without you verbally accosting the male staff?"

"Oh, come on, he's cute."

"Yes, and now he's scared shitless as well."

"Oh, he's just shy. And I'm just being playful."

"Playful? More like aggressive bordering on harassing. Why don't you just skip the banter altogether and grab his ass?"

"Don't tempt me."

"Karen."

"Oh, stop."

"You can't be so, I don't know, creepy. Not anymore."

"I'm not creepy. I'm just a very friendly, very wealthy, and very lonely older woman."

"Who comes on to younger prospects like a very wealthy, very lonely, very creepy older man."

She reared back. "I'm not that bad, am I?"

"You're getting there."

The waiter returned with their bill and Karen graciously apologized, which still caused a blush. They didn't bother to finish their drinks before they stood. Karen was obviously embarrassed and she tried to make up for her behavior by leaving a sizable tip. More sizable than usual.

They left the restaurant and walked quietly to their vehicles. Eve took in the fresh air, feeling a little better. Her head felt clearer and the world seemed less heavy. A breeze tickled her face and whipped her hair, and she thought how nice a long walk might be.

They came to Karen's white Mercedes convertible. "You feeling any better, sunshine?"

"I am, thanks. And thanks for the drink and the…talk."

"I'm always honest."

"That you are."

"And so are you. Thank you for pointing out my misbehavior."

Eve shrugged. "It's what we do."

Karen slid on her sunglasses. They were large, white, and Gucci. No doubt purposely chosen to match her car.

"I know you don't want to over obsess over your fitness and turn into the Terminator or anything like that, but I still think my other idea is a good one. You should go on a date and meet somebody new."

"Oh, Karen, I don't know. Honestly, I'd probably just compare anyone I met to Olivia."

"But, hon, how long are you going wait for these feelings to go away? It may take months, Eve. You don't want that, do you? You want out of this pit now, right?"

"I do."

Karen patted her cheek. "Then trust me. Mama knows best. I'll set the whole thing up; all you have to do is show up."

"Wait, what?"

"She's fantastic. Gorgeous, driven. Right up your alley. And… she's been single for a while. Which means she's probably hungry for a little monkey business."

"Karen, I—"

"Don't say another word. I'll call you with the details." She grabbed her shoulders. "Now give me a firm embrace and tell me you love me." They embraced, and Karen squeezed her so hard it almost hurt. "That's it, there's nothing like a good bit of bones on bones." She pulled away and kissed her fingertips and then pressed them to Eve's lips. "See you soon, kid. Be good."

Eve closed her door after her. She waved as she backed out and drove away. Eve walked to her vehicle, hoping Karen would forget about the setup. She would've protested more, but she was tired of the fight at the moment. She settled into her Tahoe and dug her phone out of her purse. The screen lit up with a missed call and a voice mail. She started her SUV, muted the music, and dialed in to hear the message. She was looking forward to going on that long, peaceful walk, and she knew exactly where she wanted to go to do so.

But everything came to a sudden and slamming halt as a familiar voice came from her phone.

"Hi, Eve, this is Olivia. You know"—nervous laughter—"from the mountain. I just called to—I was just wondering how you were doing. I've been thinking a lot, and—I don't know. God, I must sound like an idiot. Anyway, if you have time and you want to, give me a call back. I hope you're—you know—doing well. Thanks. Bye."

Eve's heart pounded, and all the sadness and disappointment she'd been feeling vanished, along with her decision to try to forget and move on. All of it was gone, up in smoke, almost as if it had never even existed.

She was aware of what was happening and that she should heed Karen's words or at least take the time to consider them more, but she couldn't. Rational thought and good decision-making seemed to have vanished right along with her sad feelings and Karen's advice.

A new, more vigorous excitement lit her up inside, and that was all she could feel and focus on.

She replayed the voice mail and allowed Olivia's voice to feed the fire of that excitement, to bring her back to life.

When the message ended, she tossed her phone into her purse and sped from the parking lot. She tried to control her speed as she drove, but she was too wound up. She was going home to call Olivia, something that had seemed totally impossible only minutes before.

She couldn't believe it. She couldn't believe that Olivia had called, and she couldn't believe her own reaction.

Women just didn't get to her like this.

But just like she'd told Karen, Olivia was different.

She had more of something in her than any other woman Eve had ever known.

Something that drew Eve in above all else.

Heart.

CHAPTER ELEVEN

Olivia reread the first paragraph of the assigned chapter for what felt like the hundredth time. And still, she got nothing. Nada. Zilch. She hadn't comprehended any of it.

"Ugh!" She slammed the textbook closed and held her head in her hands. "What is wrong with me?" She knew. She totally knew. It had been over two hours since she'd left Eve a voice mail and she was on pins and needles waiting for a response.

She pushed away from the table and stood, carefully putting pressure on both feet, still a little wary about her ankle even though she'd recovered rather well.

She crossed to the living room to relax on the couch.

The silence of her new home had become a steady comfort. Now she was able to sit for hours and read, do all kinds of crafts and puzzles, or just simply lie back and exist. She decided to do the latter and was just about to lean back to close her eyes when her phone rang, startling her.

Eve.

Frantically, she dug in the pocket of her athletic shorts and found her phone. The number was familiar. She'd stared at it for days before getting up the nerve to call.

"Hello."

"Hi, Olivia?"

"Yes."

"It's Eve."

"Oh, hi. It's nice to hear from you. How are—things? I mean, how are you?"

She smacked her forehead.

"I'm well, thanks. How about you? How's the ankle?"

"It's, you know, better. Much better than it was before for sure." She laughed at herself and then closed her eyes in embarrassment.

"So, it wasn't anything too serious, then?"

"No, nothing too bad. Just a sprain."

"That's great. I'm so glad to hear you're okay. I was…pretty worried."

"Sorry I haven't called, I just—"

"You don't have to explain."

There was a pause and they both spoke at once.

"I—"

"Listen I—"

Eve laughed. "Is it me or does this feel a little awkward?"

"It's not you." Olivia exhaled, realizing she'd been holding her breath.

"Thank, God. I thought I was the only one feeling anxious. I usually never have trouble making conversation. People would not exactly describe me as being shy."

Olivia laughed. "No, you definitely aren't that."

Olivia spoke again, before she lost the courage to do so.

"I envy that about you, you know."

"Oh?"

"You're so confident. So comfortable in your own skin. I wish I was more like that."

There was a long silence.

"Honestly, Olivia, I don't know why you aren't. Is it because you don't feel good about yourself?"

Olivia scoffed. "Do you really have to ask?"

She started to laugh but stopped when Eve didn't join her.

"You are beautiful, Olivia. I will say it until you believe it. And then I'll say it some more."

Olivia's cheeks burned with a blush.

"Are you still there?" Eve asked. "Did I scare you away?"

"I'm—" Olivia cleared her throat. "I'm here."

"I mean it. You are. Right now. Just as you are."

Olivia dropped her head into her hand.

"It's just so hard for me to accept. I've never ever thought of myself that way. And the people in my life, they made sure I never would. So, when I hear you, and I do hear you, Eve, I can't help but think you're just trying to be nice."

"I don't say things I don't mean. Never have, never will."

"Never?"

"What would be the point? I'm not into blowing smoke, and I'm not into pleasing people. I say what I mean. So, when I say something to you, you can rest assured that I really mean it."

"Okay, I will take you at your word. But I still don't like my body."

Eve laughed. "Well, I…do. I like your body."

Olivia's heart rate tripled.

"Olivia."

"Yes?"

"Did I make you uncomfortable?"

"No. I'm not uncomfortable."

"Then, what are you?"

"I—" Olivia couldn't process, her brain was not firing like it should be.

"Yes?"

"Flustered."

Silence.

"Why?"

"I don't know—because—"

"Because…"

"Because I don't know what you mean by that."

Olivia could hear Eve breathing softly. She answered, her voice lower and softer and so very alluring.

"I think you do know, and that's why you're so flustered."

Olivia pulled the phone from her ear and stared at it in disbelief. How was she doing this? How was she able to read her so well?

She returned the phone to her ear and closed her eyes. She wanted to ask Eve something. She knew without any shadow of a doubt, though, that she wasn't ready for the answer, regardless of what it may be. But she asked her anyway, unable to resist knowing the answer.

"When you say you like my body…"

"Yes?"

"Are you saying that you are attracted to me?"

She clenched her fist and her eyes, the anticipation almost too much to bear. She strained to hear Eve breathe, to confirm she was still there.

"What if I say I am? What would you do?"

"I don't know." She still couldn't open her eyes.

"Would it scare you away?"

Would it? Wasn't she already scared because of her own attraction and visceral response to Eve?

Yes.

So, Eve confessing that she felt the same…

Oh, God.

That would surely escalate everything. Double it even. Could she handle that?

"Olivia."

"I'm here."

"We don't have to do this. If it's too much…I don't want to pressure you, and yet, here I am, trying to get you to express things you obviously aren't ready to voice or maybe even accept. I'm sorry. I should probably just let you go."

"No!" Her eyes flew open.

"I think maybe I should."

"I want to know," Olivia said. "I do. Tell me. Please. Before my heart pounds too hard for me to even hear you."

"My heart is pounding, too. Because I don't know what's going to happen or where this is going to lead. But mostly my heart is pounding because I am, Olivia. I'm attracted to you. I'm drawn in by everything about you. Not only am I drawn in, but I seem to be completely enraptured."

"Oh, God," Olivia let out, suddenly stricken with a new, more potent wave of emotion and desire. It caused her to stand, and she covered her mouth with a trembling hand.

"I'm sensing that you may be experiencing similar feelings. That's one reason why I've chosen to tell you. The other is because I think you need to know. You need to know that you are truly beautiful and desirable and that someone really…wants you."

"Oh, my God," she said again, on a whisper. She lowered her hand and turned around aimlessly, not sure where to go or what to do. Her body demanded that she move, but where could she go?

"Are you okay?"

"Yes. No. I'm not sure. I feel—God, I'm just so hot." She fanned her face as if that would somehow help. She glared at the ceiling fan, which was already spinning on high.

She tried to focus on calming herself, to see if that would help. But it was impossible. Her mind continued to fly, and an image of Eve came, along with an insatiable curiosity. What did Eve look like when she said those things to her? Was the desire she construed evident in her eyes and on her face?

I bet it is. I bet it consumes more than her eyes and her face. I bet it consumes her entire being. And I want to see. I want to know what it does to her body.

And my God, what would it be like to be under the heat of that stare?

"Can you—" she started. What? Come over? If she opened that door right now and saw that kind of hunger on Eve's face, she'd faint dead away. "No. I mean—"

"Olivia, it's all right."

"No, Eve, it's not." She laughed, so keyed up she didn't know what else to do. "It's really not. It's so not all right."

"Did you—want me to come over?"

"No!" She slapped her forehead for nearly slipping up and asking her to. "No, that's not necessary. I'll—be fine. I'll figure this out and everything will be fine."

"I know what you're feeling, believe me, I know."

"You obviously worked through it."

"I did, yes."

"You found yourself."

"You will, too."

"I'm not so sure if I will or not. I don't know if I'm like you."

"How do you mean?"

"I mean you found out who you are. You found that you're…I mean, I think you came to realize that you're…"

"A lesbian?"

Olivia didn't know how it was possible, but the word alone caused her to get hotter. She was beginning to sweat.

"Are you?" She laughed a little, trying to convince herself that Eve confirming her attraction to women was no big deal. "Are you really, you know…that way?"

"It's not a bad word, Olivia. You can say it and not burst into flames I promise. And yes, I am. I'm a lesbian."

Oh, my dear sweet Lord.

"So, you've been with women?"

"Yes."

Olivia grew dizzy and she worried she might faint whether Eve was at her door or not. She couldn't seem to get a grip and rationally manage the information. She was too overrun with wild, untamed thoughts of Eve with various women, engaged in various intimate acts.

The images caused both extreme jealousy and high arousal.

"Are you sure you're okay with all of this, Olivia?"

"What? Yes, I'm—" She sighed. "I don't know. I don't know anything."

She fell back on the couch like a sack of bones. She felt like she'd just run up that damn mountain again.

"I understand."

"I wish I could."

"You should probably go now and try to relax. I think I've put you through more than enough for one evening, and I would understand if this really is all too much and you didn't want to talk again."

"No, that's not what I want."

"Because even though I know who I am and what I want, I'm flustered, too. I got a bit carried away this evening. You seem to have quite an effect on me."

Olivia looked up at the ceiling and wiped away a tear. She was torn with raw emotion, overpowering yearning, and way back in the corners of her being, the ingrained beliefs of her church and family.

"You have an effect on me, too."

Unbelievably so.

"But you're right. I should go. Not for forever. Just for right now."

She listened to the gentle sound of Eve's breath.

"Okay. Good-bye, Olivia. Please, take care."

"Good-bye." Olivia ended the call and then fell over onto the couch, curled into a ball, and allowed all that was Eve to run free in her mind.

CHAPTER TWELVE

S o, you got a B, it's not the end of the world," Jake said, reaching across the table for Olivia's hand. They were once again sitting under the ramada outside the student union. The day was warm, bordering on hot. Any other day she'd be relaxed, happy to sip her coffee and people watch as Jake went on about his latest date. But worry clouded her mind today.

Jake squeezed her hand twice. "I know being less than perfect is terribly tragic for someone like you, but you really should trust me on this. I'm living proof that the sun will still come up tomorrow with or without an A."

"It's not all about the grade. I'm dealing with something and it's distracting me." She squinted as sunlight made its way through the cloud cover and down through the grated web of the ramada. A cluster of diamond-shaped shadows marked the side of Jake's face. He didn't seem to notice.

"Do you want to talk about it? I don't just have the gift of gab, you know. I'm a pretty good listener, too."

"Actually, you're the only person I would ever dare talk about this with."

"Oh?" A perfectly manicured eyebrow lifted above his shades.

She took a deep breath. "I've been thinking about this for a while, and I haven't really come up with any answers. I mean I go over and over things and it gets me nowhere. I can't stop thinking and I can't seem to concentrate on anything else. I—"

He held up his hand to stop her. "Olivia, why don't you just tell me what it is?"

She exhaled.

"I don't know what it is. That's the problem."

"Well, can you tell me what it's about? It's nothing serious is it? You're not sick or anything are you?"

"No, nothing like that. But it is serious. At least to me it is."

"Okaay."

"I'm…" she sighed. "I've been having these…feelings."

He leaned back. "Go on."

"About someone I recently met."

"Uh-huh."

"A woman."

"A woman."

"Yes." Olivia stared straight at him.

"You're having feelings for a woman."

"Yes."

"You. Olivia. My friend, Olivia. Are having feelings."

She nodded.

He pulled off his shades and studied her long and hard. Then he leaned forward.

"Oh, my dear God."

"Yeah," she said. "I know."

"I know I shouldn't be, not in this day and age, but I'm shocked. Not just because of the way you were raised, but because of who you are. You're so—reserved. I just never ever would've guessed. Not in a million years."

"I still have feelings, Jake. I am human, you know."

"Yeah, but you're just so…vanilla."

"Vanilla? Should I be insulted by that?"

"You know what I'm saying. You're predictable. You color inside the lines and you don't seem to ever veer from that. At least not that I know of or not that I've seen."

"So, I'm boring. Thanks."

He scoffed. "A good girl, yes. But boring? No. No way. You just like to play it safe."

Was he right? Was that why she was having so much trouble in deciding her next move with Eve?

"Have you always had feelings like this?"

She nodded. "Not this intense, but yes, I have."

"In that super-religious and rigid household? I can't even imagine. It's no wonder why you internalize everything. You've probably never been allowed to voice how you really feel. Whether that be about your feelings toward girls or your feelings about what you had for dinner."

"Yeah, Hamburger Helper night sucked."

Jake cracked up.

His laugh faded and he folded his arms on the table.

"So, this woman you speak of. You say you're having feelings, but what exactly does that mean to you? Are you attracted to her?"

She shifted, feeling the weight of change in the conversation.

"I think about her. A lot."

"That's not what I asked you."

"Okay. Yes, I'm attracted to her."

"Do you ever think about being physically intimate with her?"

Her face burned in what was now becoming a familiar way.

"Yes." The admission was huge for her, and she was positive he would react strongly to it, despite the fact that he was gay. He knew her past. He knew what she just said was a big deal. But he didn't even bat an eye.

"Does she know?"

God, bless him.

"I haven't come right out and said those exact words, but yes, she's aware I'm having feelings."

"Does she feel the same about you?"

"Yes," she breathed, recalling Eve's poignant declaration. "Unlike me, she seems to have no trouble in saying exactly what she feels."

He looked perplexed. "If you both feel the same and you're both aware of that, then what's the issue?"

"The issue," she said, lowering her voice and leaning forward. "Is that she's, you know, gay."

"Is that what that's called? When you are attracted to the same sex? To think, all this time and I didn't know."

"Jake. I'm serious. I'm not sure that I am…that way. I don't think I'm…"

"Gaay?"

She looked around, hoping no one could hear their conversation. Jake caught on to her unease.

"Gay!" he said, causing heads to turn. He pointed at her. "We got gay over here!"

"Jake!" She covered her face, afraid to even look through her fingers. She wanted to disappear. "I can't believe you just did that."

"I did and oh, my God, Olivia," he whispered. "It's worse than you feared. Everyone is looking."

"What?" Panic rising, she dropped her hand and looked. No one was even giving them a second glance. In fact, the only person looking at her was Jake. And he had a raised eyebrow once again.

"Are you done being ridiculous now? Because no one gives a fuck, Olivia. They don't care who you sleep with or who you love." He studied his nails. "No, they're far too concerned with their own love lives to worry about anyone else's." He switched hands. "And I know you were brought up to think that being gay, if it was ever acknowledged to begin with, was something that had be kept hush-hush or never spoken of because it was like some kind of disease or perversion. But, the truth is, it's not. So, seeing as how a good portion of the world is now beginning to accept that truth, don't you think it's time you do, too?"

He was right. Her desire for Eve didn't feel wrong. Neither did her small crushes from the past. And she'd never thought anyone else was wrong for their feelings. So, if her desire didn't feel wrong and she didn't see it as wrong in anyone else, why was it so hard for her accept it within herself?

"I've never had a problem with anyone being gay. It just feels different when it comes to me."

"So, it's something you're okay with as long as it's not you?"

"That sounds terrible."

"Is it true?"

"I don't know. Maybe in a way. I guess I'm worried that maybe these feelings aren't really real. What if I delve in headfirst with this woman and realize that, wait a minute, I'm not really into her at all? That the whole thing was some kind of strange fantasy created by a lonely, divorced woman who was hard up for some love and romance?"

"You don't honestly expect me to think that you believe any of that, do you?"

She sighed and held her head as she stared down at the table.

"Granted, it was well thought out and very well said. But it's ludicrous."

She didn't bother to look up.

"You're just trying to mask what's really going on here."

"And what's that, oh, wise one?"

"You're afraid. You're afraid that your feelings are indeed very real. You're worried they're so real and so powerful that once you act on them, you'll lose what very little remaining control you have over your inner self. You're afraid you'll lose that control and fall head over heels in lust and, maybe even in love, and you'll have no choice but to admit you're gay. You won't be able to continue to deny it. Yes, my friend, you are just chicken shit. Plain and simple."

She lifted her head and narrowed her eyes at him. "I thought you were supposed to be like extra sensitive and empathetic and all that."

"Why, because I'm gay?"

"Yes, because you're gay."

"I state the facts, sweetie. I calls them as I sees them. And you, my dear, are so deep in denial that even if I were all sensitive and understanding, it wouldn't do you a damn bit of good. It would only exacerbate your self-torture."

She laughed softly, exhausted.

"Even if all you just said is true, I still have no idea what to do. Knowing that I'm scared doesn't change anything. I'm still scared, and I'm still confused."

"The only way out is through. Haven't you ever heard that? You need to go to her, Olivia."

She shifted even though her position wasn't what was making her uncomfortable.

"I've been wanting to call her."

"Then do it."

"If it were that simple, I would've already done it."

"My God. Grow some serious ovaries and do this for yourself. You don't have to jump her bones or anything. Just spend time with her."

"I've already spent some time with her. That's what started this whole mess. Spending more time with her will only drive me more insane."

He grinned and shook his head. "That's exactly why you should."

She sighed, feeling defeated. "I can't believe I thought you might actually help me."

"Olivia, my precious girl, I've said it once and I'll say it again. You are the most clueless smart person I've ever met." He stood and slung his backpack over his shoulder.

"Wait," she said as he backed away. "What does that even mean in this case?"

"Be brave," he said. "Be bold. You can do it." He gave her a thumbs-up and continued to grin as he walked away.

"That's really all you've got? Some friend you are!"

She watched him disappear and then grabbed her satchel and headed out herself.

God, he was right. She was worried about what might happen when they got together.

She was chicken shit.

She walked toward her car, relenting to the fact that she was going to have to do something to get this madness to stop.

She thought about spending time with Eve, like he'd said, and this time she gave her imagination free rein. She began to picture some of the things that might happen between them, and she got so caught up in the passionate scenarios she tripped over her feet. After she regained her balance and looked around hoping no one had seen, she shook her head and laughed. She wasn't even sure what all women did together during sex, but that wasn't stopping her from fantasizing. And what she could come up with and could imagine got her so hot she ran the last leg to her car.

She climbed inside and started the engine, anxious to get home.

She'd made up her mind.

She was going to spend time with Eve.

She just prayed her poor overworked heart could take it.

Chapter Thirteen

Eve blew past another car and then braked hard and cussed as the traffic light changed. The clock read seven oh two. More anxious than ever, she flipped down the visor and studied herself in the mirror. Her hair still looked good, but she could've done a better job with the little makeup she had on. She'd just been so hurried after oversleeping, which was something she was still having trouble accepting. She never forgot to set her alarm. And showing up late to meet a client? That had only happened twice in the years she'd been fitness training. Once due to a damaged tire and the other because of an accident on the freeway. Showing up late just wasn't her. So, how in the hell could she have spaced and not set her alarm?

It wasn't like her. But then again neither was forgetting the due dates for two of her credit cards or waiting in line for a half an hour at the bank only to blank out and drive right past the teller when it was her turn.

She let out a laugh, knowing exactly what, or rather who, was causing the unusual mayhem in her life. It was the same person who had also elicited the sadness and crankiness she'd felt before. And she was most likely sitting at the park right now, rechecking her watch, wondering why the hell she'd agreed to meet with Eve.

Seven oh four.

"Fuck."

Eve breathed a little easier as she pulled into the parking lot. But her gut clenched when she first saw Olivia's car, and then again when she saw her sitting at a nearby picnic table.

She cussed and scrambled from her Tahoe. She had the urge to give herself another once-over in the window, but she was too concerned about Olivia having to wait. So instead, she took a deep breath, hoped she looked okay in her Adidas track pants and matching tank, and crossed the wet grass to her. She smiled and tried not to react to the way Olivia looked with her thick brown hair and large liquid eyes gleaming in the bright sunlight.

"I'm so sorry I'm late," Eve said as she slid onto the seat across from her. Olivia smiled in return while resting her cheek in her hand. The usual storminess of her eyes appeared more tranquil today which allowed Eve to see just how deep the gray in them was. They were soulful and tempting, and Eve had to find other things to concentrate on. She moved on to Olivia's light purple V-neck. It was snug and short-sleeved, showing a new, slightly bronzed look to her arms and chest. The curve of her ample bosom and the harbored strength she had in her arms and shoulders just waiting to be brought out, left Eve overexerted though she hadn't moved at all. She just kept imagining how strong Olivia would look if she actually worked those muscles.

"No problem," Olivia said.

"It is for me. I'm usually very punctual. So, again, I'm sorry. I promise it won't happen again."

Olivia cocked her head. "You're flustered. Just like you were at first on the phone. I never thought I'd witness it in person."

"I'm not really flustered."

Who was she kidding?

"I just don't like to be late."

"I don't either," Olivia said after watching Eve closely for another moment. She seemed to be amused and Eve wasn't sure what to say. She'd never had a woman be so interested in her behavior.

Thankfully, Olivia continued.

"I was actually afraid I was going to be late, too. I changed outfits like five times."

Eve had changed three times, tearing off clothes like they were on fire while willing the bedside clock to reverse.

"You, too, eh? We are some pair."

"I think we should talk about that," Olivia said. "I didn't say much when I called to ask for this meeting because I thought it best to do it in person. Although, now seeing you, it's not going to be as easy as I'd hoped."

She focused on the tabletop and rubbed the back of her neck.

"I—want to do this. I want and need your help in getting fit. But I—need to, for the time being at least, keep my feelings in check."

"I completely agree." Eve had been mulling over the same thing after Olivia's call. While she was thrilled to hear from her again, she soon realized that if she took her on as a client, it would have to be on a professional basis only. Which was good and bad. Good in the sense that she would get to see more of Olivia, but bad in knowing that she couldn't act on her attraction to her. "I take my work very seriously and I want to give you my absolute best."

"Good, I'm glad we're on the same page, because I'm also hoping that this will be a good way to get to know you. To, you know, spend time with you, without all the craziness of emotion."

"That may not be easy," Eve said softly. "With that craziness you speak of. If, say, some feelings became noticeable or overwhelming, or if one or both of us actually crossed that line, then we would have to stop our professional relationship."

Olivia exhaled and straightened. "Okay."

"Yeah?"

"Yes."

Eve stood. She thought about shaking her hand but hesitated, not quite sure that they should touch. They would of course have to in working out together, but at that moment, with what they'd just discussed, Eve thought it best not to.

"Great, let's get moving, shall we? We can go over the details as we walk."

Olivia joined her and Eve led them to the path that circled the park. Eve moved at a slower pace than she normally would have in consideration of Olivia's ankle. Olivia had said it had healed, but she wanted to be sure.

They discussed Eve's fee and what days Olivia was able to meet her. Olivia sounded eager and excited, and she readily agreed to doing some work on her own time as well. They touched on diet, and Eve was glad to hear that Olivia was doing pretty well on that front. She wasn't a vegan, like Eve, but the majority of her clients weren't.

Some had chosen to become vegan after hearing her knowledge on the subject, but it wasn't for everyone and she respected that. Eve would give Olivia the same basic information she gave everyone on the matter, but she wasn't going to touch on that until later. There was no reason to talk to her about drastically changing her diet in any form right now. She was doing well already and Eve had learned she was studying nutrition, so she obviously had an avid interest in what food did for the body and probably was quite knowledgeable on the subject. So there was no need to press her further about food. Giving up the diet drinks, however, would likely be the hardest thing she had to do. A lot of her clients seemed to have a diet drink addiction of some sort, and Eve often considered them to be like some sort of hard drug, the kind you'd buy on the streets. Her clients were that addicted to them and they fought her on it constantly. Olivia, however, seemed to be okay about it so far, but Eve knew she might eventually think she could have one or two a day. But they'd deal with that when it arose.

The sun grew stronger and breathed upon their skin and the freshly watered grass, causing it to glisten. The day smelled fresh, like citrus blossoms, and Eve took it all in, really enjoying the morning with Olivia by her side, giving her a sneak peek into her life, past and present.

Eve was surprised to learn that, despite her strong build, Olivia had never played sports. They didn't interest her, and she'd only ever exercised as an adult to try to shed weight. And even when she'd done that, her attempts hadn't lasted very long. She'd never lifted weights and when Eve inquired about her discomfort threshold, Olivia again surprised her by being completely honest. Most people often fibbed a little about that, or tried to mask it while hoping to somehow persevere once it came time.

"I hate the way pushing myself feels," Olivia said, shaking her head. "Like more than anything. It's awful and it hurts and I can't get my mind past that."

"What about endorphins? Have you ever felt those?"

"I have. Yes. For a very short while. But they weren't enough to keep me from feeling like I was dying. Like, you know, when I ran up that mountain."

Eve laughed softly. "That's because you actually *did* almost kill yourself. Anyone with any remote ability to feel would've stopped after an attempt like that. I would have."

"Really?"

"Hell, yes. What you have to do is slowly build up your strength and stamina. Get those endorphins working for you. If you'll let me, I'll soon have you actually *wanting* to work out. Actually, wanting to run."

"Ha. Right. I'll do what you say and all, but I'm just not made that way. I cannot ever imagine wanting to torture myself like that."

"You'll not only want to but you'll feel like you need to."

"What? No way."

Eve laughed again. "For the time being, let's forget all that. How do you feel right now, after walking this track a few times?"

"I feel good."

Eve stopped them and checked her pulse. She was right where she wanted her to be. "You feel good, your heart's pumping, everything is circulating, and you're breathing just a little faster than usual."

"Yes."

"No pain."

"Nope."

"Just awake, alert, and alive. Energized. You know you've exercised, you can feel it, but you're not overwhelmed with pain or exhausted."

Olivia smiled at her like she'd somehow read her thoughts. "Yes, exactly."

Eve smiled in return. "What you're feeling right now, it will only get better from here."

Olivia looked at her in disbelief. But Eve stopped her before she could speak.

"Yes, there will be discomfort and there will be moments when you really have to dig deep and push yourself. But I will train you so that when you reach those moments, you'll be able to push through, you'll want to push through. Not just for me because I told you to, or for those amazing endorphins. You'll do it for you, Olivia. For yourself. Because what you'll soon learn is that this journey is not only about your body, it's about all of you, inside and out." She placed her hands gently on her shoulders, and then dropped them as Olivia looked into her eyes, the moment suddenly feeling more intense than it should.

This arrangement is not going to be easy.

But she wasn't about to change her mind. "So, what would you say to starting off with walking like this every day?"

"That's it, just walking?"

"For cardio, yes. That's all I want you to do for now. You do realize we just walked well over a mile?"

"No way. I didn't even—it didn't feel like exercise."

"That's what I want. I want to ease you into your cardio, not only because of your ankle, but so you will feel good and start to enjoy those endorphins. I want you to enjoy all of this. So, what do you say? You ready to give this a shot?"

"Yes. I can't wait."

They were smiling at each other, and Eve could once again feel that current of energy between them. Olivia seemed to sense it too because she was the first to glance away. Eve ended the tension by leading them back toward their vehicles.

"I'll text you a schedule and we'll get you started on weights. We'll start off light, like the cardio. I don't want you to be so sore you can't move."

"Thank you, Eve. You really are a very nice person."

Eve was touched, but she hid it with humor. "Oh, I don't know. There will be moments when you'll think I'm the devil himself."

"I can't ever imagine thinking that about you. But even if I do, I'll get through it, right? And I'll like you all over again."

Eve resisted the urge to wrap her arm around her and pull her close. She'd liked walking with her like that on the mountain, even though Olivia had been injured. She knew it was probably selfish of her to feel that way considering Olivia's condition, but having her so close and feeling the curves of her body, it had been invigorating, and Eve realized just how much she wanted to embrace her again.

Olivia looked over at her.

"I think no matter what happens, now or in the future, I'll always like you."

Eve stared off toward the horizon and knew it was useless to try to be less than truthful.

"Me too, Olivia. I think I'll always like you."

More than you'll probably ever know.

CHAPTER FOURTEEN

No, Auntie Liv, you can edit and filter your photos on your phone," Olivia's niece, Molly, said in exasperation.

"I realize that, but my phone can only do so much. I want to do more to my photos."

Molly rolled her eyes at her and took her phone. She was eleven going on fifty, and Olivia swore she'd come out of the womb that way.

"You just need an app," Molly said, elbows propped on the dark red tablecloth, thumbs attacking the cell phone screen. "I'll download three awesome ones for you. They're what I use."

Olivia smiled and looked at her brother, Aaron, who was busy winding spaghetti around his fork. He was fresh from work as a mechanic, wearing his standard uniform shirt with his name on one side and the dealership on the other. Though he often wore latex gloves and he'd recently scrubbed his hands, his fingernail beds were still stained black. It was from years of working on engines of all kinds. Aaron had been as into working with his hands and fixing things as she had been into reading and learning. They were polar opposites in nearly every way, yet they'd always gotten along. And now, as adults, they remained close, able to understand each other unlike anyone else.

He caught her stare and grinned as he chewed. They were eating at Streets of New York, a popular chain of small Italian restaurants located throughout the greater Phoenix area. This particular one, closest to the dealership where Aaron worked, was Molly's favorite place to eat. They'd talk and munch on garlic bread nestled at a back table, surrounded by classic black-and-white images of New York on the walls and flat screen televisions silently playing the latest ball game in every corner.

When she was younger, Molly used to beg to eat there because, according to her, it was dark and cool and smelled good. But that was Molly. Always noticing and appreciating things others didn't. She reminded Olivia so much of herself at that age.

Olivia took a bite of her turkey sandwich and sipped from the second Diet Coke she'd allowed for the day. Technically, in agreement with Eve, she was supposed to only have one, which she usually had in the morning. And that allowance of one was supposed to come to an end today. But she was dreading tomorrow and every day thereafter when she couldn't have any. With that in mind, she'd been unable to resist another when ordering and she'd told herself it was okay because they were eating out. She wondered, however, what Eve would say, if she ever dared to tell her.

It probably wouldn't go over very well.

"So, you're working with a trainer now?" Aaron asked, sipping from his mug of beer. "How's that going?" He absently brushed back a lock of hair from his forehead. He was a handsome guy with thick brown hair like Olivia's which he wore combed back away from his face. Loose strands often fell forward by the end of the day, despite his heavy use of hair gel. His eyes were also like Olivia's, only a shade lighter. And they, in combination with his hair and square jaw he inherited from their father, got him a lot of attention from the ladies.

"We're just getting started, so I really can't say yet. I'm meeting with her tomorrow for weightlifting. Kind of nervous."

"Weightlifting? You? What's the world coming to." He laughed and cut into a large meatball.

"She's making changes, Dad," Molly said, setting down the phone. She forked some of her pasta. "Don't give her a hard time."

"I'll say," he said, directing his comment to Olivia. "You're making so many changes, I'm having a hard time keeping up. Do you know something we don't? Is the world going to end?"

She gave him her best "ha ha very funny" look. "I just got sick and tired of the rut I was living in. And I realized I didn't want to waste another second wallowing in it."

They hadn't spoken a lot about the changes she'd made in the past year or so, and she was surprised he was bringing it up now. He'd been supportive, of course, with each decision she'd made, but he hadn't pushed her for her reasons why. But that was how they'd always been. In her family, you didn't talk about your feelings or anything very deep. So she and Aaron had grown up side by side this way, just always supporting the other with a quiet presence. The only thing they ever discussed in depth was their relationship with their parents. That was a topic they both had a lot to say about.

"I understand," he said. "You weren't happy. I know being married to Kenny wasn't easy. I'm not, as you now know, a big fan as far as he is concerned. So, I totally get you needing to leave. Even if Mom and Dad don't."

She'd always suspected that he didn't like Kenny. She could tell by the way he behaved around him. Now, she wished she'd asked him why. Maybe if they'd talked about it, she wouldn't have married him. Maybe if they'd talked about the way she felt toward his ex-wife he never would've married her. But then they wouldn't have Molly. And she knew no matter what Aaron had experienced with Gina, he'd go through it all again in a heartbeat for Molly.

"Why are Grandma and Grandpa so old-fashioned? Why would they want Auntie Liv to stay married to a grumpy jerk like Kenny? I don't get it." Molly didn't bother to look up from her food. She just forked another bite.

Olivia laughed at her reference to Kenny. She'd heard her refer to him as such once before, on the day she moved out and Molly and Aaron had come to help.

"They don't believe in divorce, Molls," Aaron said. "It goes against their faith."

"So, you're just supposed to be unhappy?" She shook her head. "We have faith, Dad. So does Auntie Liv. Why don't Grandma and Grandpa have any common sense like we do?"

"Their beliefs are a little different than ours. A little more intense." He glanced at Olivia and sipped his beer.

"Yeah, I know that. You guys tell me stories all the time. I just want to know why. Why would anyone choose to live like that?"

"People just do. They choose to believe what they want. When you grow up, you may decide to believe something other than me."

"I'll never believe in staying married to someone who makes me miserable. That's for sure."

She was so smart and insightful. She amazed Olivia every time she saw her.

They ate in silence for a while before Aaron spoke again, directing his words to Olivia.

"Have you spoken to them lately?"

Olivia put down the remainder of her sandwich, suddenly unable to finish it.

"Mom called a week ago. She didn't bring up the divorce or anything, just filled me in on the little church she and Dad found and proceeded to complain about it, but said they would keep going regardless."

"I got the same," Aaron said. "Only then I got grilled about your life."

"Why doesn't she just ask me?" Olivia said.

"Come on, Olivia, you're the smart one. You know how Mom and Dad are. They don't talk about anything personal and they insist they don't want to know anything personal. But that's total crap. Mom has an obsession with wanting to know. She's just sneaky, or in her case, not so sneaky, in the way she tries to get information. Hence her never asking us anything about our lives directly."

"Have you noticed that her questioning and curiosity skyrocket when she suspects we're doing something she doesn't approve of?" Olivia rubbed her forehead. "She must be absolutely riddling you with questions about me, then. Since I'm a divorced woman and all. I'm so sorry."

"Don't apologize for what she does," Aaron said.

"She's just, she drives me nuts."

Molly laughed and Olivia realized what she was doing in talking the way she was.

"I'm sorry, Molls, I shouldn't say this stuff in front of you. You have a good relationship with your grandparents and I don't want to taint that."

Molly laughed again. "It's okay, Auntie Liv. I pretty much already know they're crazy."

Olivia blinked at her in disbelief and then looked at Aaron.

Molly just shrugged. "I know I'm a kid, but come on, you guys. I have eyes and ears."

Aaron cleared his throat. "That may be so, but you shouldn't call them crazy. It isn't nice."

"What about nuts then? Like Auntie Liv said. Would that be nicer than crazy?"

Aaron laughed but tried to cover his mouth. Olivia tried too but was unable to hold it in.

"It's okay, you guys are allowed to laugh," Molly said. "Why do you still act like you're going to get in trouble or something? They're far away in Mexico; they can't hear you. And you're adults now so it shouldn't matter anyway. My gosh, live a little."

"Where is this coming from?" Olivia asked. "Has she ever talked about them like this in front of you?" she asked Aaron.

He shook his head, still trying to control his laughter.

"Really, you guys?" she asked. "I've always known they're nuts. It's kind of hard to miss how uptight they are. I just never said anything because I didn't think I should. No one says anything in this family." She took another bite and Olivia took her observation to heart. Things needed to change, especially for Molly. They should talk. The three of them. Like this, like now. And they should do it more often.

Molly took a drink and looked to Olivia.

"After the way they acted when you left Kenny, I really knew they were crazy, then. I mean, I'm only eleven and I could see that he was a mean jerk. You had to leave, Auntie Liv. If a kid can see that, then there's no excuse for them not to."

Olivia stared at her for a long moment. "I love you, Molls. So very much."

Molly smiled at her and took a bite of garlic bread. "I love you, too, Auntie Liv. And I for one, think you should do whatever it takes to be happy."

Olivia smiled as her words reached her in a place Molly couldn't see.

"I'm getting there, sweetie. I'm getting there."

CHAPTER FIFTEEN

U-Fit was stuffy and loud, but far less crowded than usual for a Wednesday afternoon. Eve was grateful, hoping Olivia would feel comfortable amongst a smaller mass of muscle heads rather than the larger mass that often accumulated and clogged the modest gym. These people were her friends, but even she could see how someone could be intimidated by all the sweating and groaning and grunting.

"Hi."

Eve turned and found Olivia looking a little nervous with a white-knuckle grip on the gym bag slung over her shoulder.

"Hi." Eve stepped over the weight bench and took her bag. "I would ask how you are, but you look a little…"

"Freaked out?"

"Freaked out, really?" Eve encouraged her to sit and she joined her, straddling the bench to face her. "Nervous is okay, but freaked out worries me. Can you tell me why?"

Olivia stared ahead seemingly off in the distance somewhere. Eve couldn't help but admire her perfect profile, which was more accentuated with her hair back in a tight ponytail. She didn't seem to notice Eve's entrancement and she rubbed her palms on her thighs while her legs bounced with nerves. Tight black shorts hugged her curves, and a sleeveless peach colored T-shirt hung loosely off her upper body. Her running shoes appeared to be new, and she had on a Fitbit which Eve assumed was new as well. She looked like any other gym rat, but her nervousness set her apart, and a few of Eve's friends eyed her curiously as they walked by.

"Olivia?" Eve said softly, touching her arm.

"Yes? Oh." She smiled, but it seemed to fall flat. "Everyone is so ripped. I feel ridiculous." She plucked at her T-shirt while looking at it with contempt. "I stick out like a sore thumb."

"No, actually, you don't."

"It's so obvious I don't work out, though. I'm—"

"Olivia, stop. No one is thinking anything bad, I promise you."

"How do you know?"

"Because I know almost all of them and they are good people. And besides, they are body builders, they're way too busy looking at themselves in the mirror to worry about you."

Olivia laughed.

"So, try and relax, okay? We all have the same mission in mind. We want to better ourselves."

Eve stood and patted her shoulder. "Now, let's get you warmed up on the treadmill."

Olivia followed her, and after ten minutes of brisk walking, Eve led her back into one of the smaller weight rooms, showed her how to stretch, and then gave her a pair of eight-pound dumbbells. She eased her into the proper stance, told her to watch herself in the mirror, and then had her begin arm curls.

"How does that feel?"

"Fine." She was pumping her arms quickly. "Doesn't really feel like I'm lifting anything, though."

Eve grabbed a pair of ten-pound dumbbells and had her switch out.

"Try these."

Olivia started again and did the same thing.

"Try to slow down a bit."

Olivia did, but Eve could tell nothing had changed.

"You should be feeling the weight. It should be getting more difficult."

Olivia finished a set of twelve.

"I'm not feeling anything."

"Okay." Eve knew Olivia looked strong, but now she was seeing firsthand just how strong she really was. She grabbed the twelve-pound weights and handed them over.

Olivia took them and started again.

"Better?" Eve asked.

Olivia nodded. "Yes. I can feel it some now."

Thank God. She didn't want to go any higher, not on the first damn day. She didn't want her to be overly sore. She watched her closely and recalled that there had only been a few other women she'd worked with who'd had the strength to begin with a higher weight. One of them was herself.

Olivia finished three sets of twelve and only began to fatigue near the very end of the third set. She was, indeed, very strong.

Eve took the weights from her and Olivia massaged her biceps.

"Is it supposed to burn like that?"

"Yes."

"Good to know I'm not a freak or anything."

Eve laughed. "No, you're just like everyone else, I'm afraid." She had her sit on a bench and brought her the ten-pound weights again. She sat next to her and showed her how to rest her elbow on her inner thigh to do isolated bicep curls. Olivia began and Eve watched, curious to see if she was now too fatigued to continue with the twelve-pound dumbbells. She got her answer when Olivia once again lifted the ten-pound weights like they were nothing.

"I can kind of feel it," Olivia said. "But not a lot."

"Jesus," Eve said aloud this time. She went back for the twelve-pounders and traded them out.

"Something wrong?" Olivia asked. She began to lift again as they talked.

"No, not at all. You're just really strong. Especially for someone who has never lifted before."

"Is that bad?"

"Why in the world would that be bad?"

"I don't know. Women aren't exactly supposed to be strong, I guess. It's not feminine."

"Where in the hell did you hear that?"

Olivia looked at her like she was crazy. "That's what I've always been told. Women should be petite and dainty. You know, really feminine. I've always been too tall, too big, too muscular."

"Is that why you hate your body so much? Because someone has filled your head with crap like that?"

She shrugged.

Eve watched her quietly as she finished with the isolated bicep curls. Again, she didn't fatigue until the very end of the final set.

Eve took the weights and had her stand for hammer curls. This time she didn't bother to go back down in weight.

"I now know what our biggest challenge is going to be with you," Eve said. "It's not going to be anything physical. It's going to be the way you think. We're going to have to reset your brain, so to speak."

Olivia pumped through two sets and then finally began to struggle on the third. Eve stood in front of her and spotted her. She talked her all the way through with Olivia crying out on the last two curls. Eve quickly took the weights and then massaged her arms.

"Wow, was that hard," Olivia said, laughing with what sounded like disbelief. "My arms are shaking."

"It's normal. Nothing to worry about." She smiled at her and tried to ignore how soft her skin was and how her thick muscle was trembling beneath her fingers. But when their eyes locked and they both seemed to realize that they were touching, Eve quickly stopped and moved on.

"How do you feel?"

"Good. It's weird though. I feel like I'm feeling my biceps for the first time ever. Like I just got them or something. Like they're this new part that's been installed in my body, never used before."

"I've never quite heard it put like that before," Eve said, amused.

"But I'm still normal, right?" She laughed and Eve was glad to see her enjoying herself.

"Yes. You are still very human, Olivia. You don't get your freak card yet."

Eve led them to a pulley machine, set the weight to the level she'd started at, and pulled down the hanging rope handle. The handle was split, like an upside-down V, one side for each hand with a wooden ball at the ends to keep the hands from slipping off.

"Now we're going to do some tricep pulldowns," Eve said. "Or some people call them tricep pushdowns, whichever you prefer. In case you're a stickler for correct terms and such."

Olivia laughed. "Yep, you got me."

Eve demonstrated the exercise for her by getting in the proper stance. She reached up, gripped the two handles, and pulled down.

When her arms were at a ninety-degree angle at her sides, she spoke to Olivia. "This is your starting position." She then extended her arms down, until they were perpendicular to the floor, engaging her triceps. "Think you got it?

Olivia nodded and took Eve's place.

"Okay, good." Eve rested her hand on her lower back helping her with her stance. "Now lean your torso forward, just a bit more. Good. Leaning forward like this, instead of standing straight, engages all of your tricep, including the long head."

"Sure. Okay. I'm obviously clueless."

Olivia grabbed the rope handle and, as Eve had instructed, pulled downward to her starting position. Then she extended down.

"Good, now back up slowly to your starting position and then extend down again."

Olivia continued.

"The tricep has three different bundles to it," Eve explained. "The long head, medial head, and lateral head. Doing this exercise the old way, where you stand straight up, only works two of those. Whereas this position works all three."

"I believe you, but I'm not feeing it. I think it needs to be heavier," Olivia said.

"Do a few more for me." Eve crossed her arms over her chest and watched in amazement. Olivia was breezing through the exercise quicker than she had the bicep curls. "Okay, hold up." Eve adjusted the weight and backed away. "Try it now."

Same thing. Olivia shook her head.

Eve couldn't believe it. She adjusted the weight one last time. "Now you're at the weight I use now for my workouts."

"Seriously?"

"Yes. But rest assured, still no freak status reached."

"You promise to let me know, right?"

"The second it happens."

Olivia began again, and Eve could see her triceps come to life as she worked. Her form was close to perfect, and all Eve had to do was teach her how to breathe. She finished without the struggle she'd experienced at the end of her bicep sets.

Eve led her back to the free weights and picked up a twelve-pound dumbbell. She showed her how to position her fingers to hold the end of the dumbbell and lifted it back over her head. She then lowered it vertically, straight down between her shoulder blades and brought it straight up above her head until her arms were fully extended.

"Got it?"

"Yep."

They switched positions and Olivia began.

"It feels a little light, too."

"Your arms are shaking quite a bit, though. So, I'm worried about your stability. If we go heavier you might drop the dumbbell."

"Okay."

"Just continue what you're doing. Nice and slow. Concentrate on your breathing and on the individual muscle you're working."

"I can feel it now. More than the last one. The whole back of my upper arm is burning."

"Women love this exercise for that very reason. It's great for firming up that area."

"You mean I'm not the only one with flab?"

Eve rolled her eyes. "No."

"That makes me feel better."

"Whatever gets you there, I suppose. Although, I've got news for you, and this might devastate your well ingrained maudlin beliefs about yourself."

Olivia finished her set and set the dumbbell in her lap to rest. She questioned Eve with her eyes.

"You're not flabby."

"Yeah, right, okay." She held her arm out and squeezed while looking in the mirror.

"I don't see any flab, Olivia. You just need to work your muscles a little, like we're doing. Once those muscles grow and harden with strength, you're going to be beyond tight. In fact, you're probably going to be a bit etched."

Again, she gave Eve a disbelieving look. "Okaay."

Eve laughed. "We've got a long way to go on that head of yours."

"Does that mean we're going to be working together for a while, then?"

"In knowing what little of your mindset I do so far, I'd say yes."

"Because I'm a head case. And stubborn."

"Yes, I'm beginning to realize. The way you seem to ignore everything I've told you about your body, I'd say that stubbornness might surpass anyone I've ever worked with."

"So, in a way, I am a freak." She grinned.

Eve palmed her forehead. "Oh, my God."

"What?"

"Will you stop? You're not that different from everyone else. You're just sensitive and intelligent. There's nothing wrong with you. Not anything. And I seriously want to kick anyone's ass who's ever told you anything different."

Eve could feel the heat in her face as she spoke. But she couldn't help it. Olivia didn't deserve to feel the way she did about herself. She was incredible, and the more Eve learned about her and the more time they spent together, that became more and more obvious.

"You're upset."

"I'm fine." But she wasn't and she knew she didn't sound fine. "Go ahead and finish your sets."

"I was kidding around. Trying to make things a little less tense, I guess. I didn't mean to upset you."

Eve pushed out a breath, but she couldn't look at her. "I know you're not just kidding around, Olivia. Not totally. You do feel that badly about yourself. But you're not why I'm upset. You didn't make me feel this way. You make me feel—" she stopped herself and closed her eyes to get a grip. "Very far from upset. And please don't ask me to explain further. Because I can't and won't say any more than that."

Olivia turned and finished her sets quietly while Eve watched her form in the mirror.

She wished she could tell her exactly the way she made her feel.

But even if she could, she wasn't sure there were enough known words in the universe that could explain something like that.

In the meantime, she'd try her best to show her by helping her any way she could.

CHAPTER SIXTEEN

Hey, Mom, it's me," Eve said as she scrambled inside carrying several fabric grocery bags and a twelve-pack of citrus flavored soda sweetened with Stevia. She kicked the door closed behind her and hurried to the kitchen where she managed to set it all on the table before anything fell. She began putting things away, scowling as she opened the fridge to find it nearly empty. The pantry wasn't as bare, but it wasn't up to her standards either. Her mother couldn't survive on an old head of lettuce, a few yogurts, and boxes of minute rice alone. Why did she seem to be the only one who understood this?

"Evelyn," her mother said from behind.

Eve turned with a box of penne pasta in her hand. Her mother smiled softly at her, and Eve relaxed some, noting that she was looking less gaunt than she had the week before. She appeared to have gotten a little sun, and her hair had been cut and colored. Eve gave her a gentle embrace and caressed the familiar fabric of her worn terry cloth robe. It was what she always wore while at home, regardless of the temperature or what she had on underneath. It was her soft, faded pink comfort. Like a child with a security blanket.

"What brings you by today?" her mother asked. "You didn't need to do all this."

Eve inhaled the scent of Dove soap from her skin and pulled away to continue to unpack the food.

"I know, I just wanted to," she said, downplaying her concern and visit. They did this dance of denial every week or so when Eve came by to check on her. Her mother would feign needing anything at all, and Eve would feign having any concern for her at all. "I was at Trader Joe's and saw a few things you might like."

"That's really nice of you, but you know I don't need all this."

"I know, Mom. But I like to do things for you, okay?" She held up a bag of ginger snaps. "Look what I found."

Her mother took the bag and her eyes lit up. "Oh, my goodness. Ginger snaps. I can't even remember the last time I had these."

Eve finished putting everything away and then filled a glass with ice and cracked open a can of the citrus soda. Her mother had turned her nose up at the Stevia sweetened soda when Eve had first bought it for her. As she did most everything healthy Eve brought home for her to try. But the soda, she'd liked. The whole wheat and gluten-free pastas, she had not. Still, Eve took what she could get and she often brought her mother new, healthy alternatives to try. She poured the drink as her mother fumbled with the cookie bag.

"Here, let me." Eve traded her the glass for the snaps and they walked into the dim living room where her mother sat on the couch. Eve opened the blinds to let in some sunlight and joined her. She opened the bag of snaps and placed it next to her mother who quickly bit into one and grinned. She then moaned her approval and leaned back to enjoy it.

It was nice to see her happy. That was something Eve had rarely seen as a child.

"How have you been feeling?" Eve asked. "You look well. I like your hair that color."

"Oh, yes. Bethany did it for me. You know how she dotes on me."

Eve wanted to roll her eyes at the mention of her older sister. It was true, she did tend to her mother's hair and clothes and other things involving her appearance, but would it kill her to check the damn fridge for food when she came? Bethany came twice a month at best, which, granted was more than Eve's other three siblings, but Eve knew her sister could still do more. And why it seemed to be solely up to her and Bethany to look after their mother was beyond Eve. Her brothers were nearby too and just as capable. But apparently, they thought calling their mother was sufficient enough.

"It looks nice," Eve said, easing back to cross her legs. The house was quiet save for the grandfather clock in the corner. Eve made sure to wind it every week, knowing her mother loved hearing the chime every quarter of the hour. It used to drive Eve mad, but now the ticking and the chimes felt nostalgic, confirming she was really home.

"I see you've gone completely blond now," her mother said, biting into another cookie. "I like it. It brings out your eyes."

"Thanks." Eve ran her fingers through her hair. She'd just had it done, having finally decided to throw some caution to the wind and ditch the highlights she'd worn for years for full blond. She felt good about it, glad she'd made the change, but also glad she'd resisted the urging from her hairdresser to go even lighter than the shade she'd chosen. This was enough of a change for now and she was pleased. The nice comment from her mother added to that feeling.

Compliments from her used to be few and far between, and there had once been a time when Eve would've killed to hear one. She would've killed for any attention at all growing up in their overcrowded household. But being the youngest of five, she was often left to fend for herself or rely on her brothers or Bethany for everything. Their father had worked long hours, or so that's what she'd always been told. She wondered now if he just didn't want to come home to all the chaos. Chaos that had only grown worse after her mother had been diagnosed with lupus.

Eve stared into the dark green wingback chairs across from the coffee table. The throw pillows were covered in bright pink flowers to match the print of the fabric on the couch. The living room was also decorated in pink and dark green, colors her mother loved. Though she had always referred to the pink as mauve, correcting Eve anytime she slipped up and called it pink.

Though the color scheme and the furniture were very outdated, everything was still the same, and Eve both liked and hated it. Each visit was different, bringing out one feeling or the other. Today, she hated it. Because she was frustrated with Bethany and the apathy of her brothers, and that put her in a mood where she didn't want to think about the past.

"You remind me a little of a Hollywood starlet now. Not quite Marilyn Monroe but similar," her mother said. "Only you are more sporty than any of those women from that era. A tomboy. You always have been though, haven't you? I suppose growing up with three brothers will do that to a girl." She studied Eve closely. "You were always strong. Very independent. Not at all like I was. I was always so proud of you for that."

"I had no idea," Eve said. She was touched yet confused. Why hadn't she ever said so? Eve had desperately needed to hear things like that growing up. But instead she'd been surrounded by bickering and complaining or worse, sometimes nothing at all. As if she didn't exist.

"I should've told you a long time ago," her mother said, sipping her soda. "I should've done a lot of things. But I think I was just so caught up in the struggle of being a mother of five with little help from your father, well, I think I was overwhelmed." Her focus shifted to somewhere beyond. "And tired. I remember just always feeling so tired. Every day, I'd wake up with these big plans for you kids for the day and by midmorning, I just ran out of steam. I just couldn't do them."

Eve could see the regret on her face and the heavy sadness settling over her body.

"You were sick, Mom. It couldn't have been easy." There were many things Eve wished she could change about her childhood, and her mother had made mistakes, but nothing was done out of malice and there was no way to go back, so it was pointless to dwell on it. Her mother really had been sick, with bad days often outnumbering the good. And where the hell had her father been? Her mother was right; she'd had very little help.

"That's no excuse," her mother said, almost to herself. "I want so badly to make it up to you kids. Especially to you." She looked at Eve with tears in her eyes.

Eve leaned toward her and held her hand. "You are making it up to me, Mom. Right now. By saying the things you're saying."

"You come every week," she said. "And you had it the worst of all."

"Don't cry," Eve said as emotion began to tighten her throat. "You're going to make me cry, and you know how I hate that. We'll just both end up being a blubbering mess. What good will that do?"

She squeezed her hand and then released her to sit back once again. "We've got stuff to do, things to take care of. Did the pool guy check the chlorine last time he came?"

But her mother only looked at her with the same sadness in her eyes.

"Do you have anyone special, Evelyn? Who you care about? Who cares about you? You never say and I never ask. But that doesn't mean I don't want to know. I think about you and your life quite often, you know. And I find myself wondering, is she alone?"

Eve uncrossed her legs and repositioned, truly surprised by her mother's interest.

"I—date, here and there. Mostly there." She laughed at her own joke. Her mother's gaze was intense and so filled with love Eve had to look away. She wasn't used to seeing that, wasn't used to any of this.

"No one special?"

Eve stood and brushed down her shirt and navy shorts as if they were wrinkled or dirty somehow. She tried to change the subject.

"How are you on medication? Do you need me to run to the pharmacy?"

Obvious disappointment clouded her mother's face.

"You don't want to tell me, I understand."

Eve sighed. "There's nothing to tell, Mom. There hasn't been—anyone."

"No one?"

"No."

"But why? You're a beautiful young woman. Very kind and strong and independent. How can anyone pass you up? Are they blind? Stupid?"

"Mom." She massaged her temple.

"Why don't they want you? I don't understand."

"It's not that they don't want me. Oh God, how did we get into this?"

"Then what is it?"

"I—I'm happier being on my own."

"Oh, I see." Her mother set her glass on the coffee table. "It's you who doesn't want them. Why, Evelyn?"

Eve didn't respond. She didn't want to be dishonest and she didn't want to discuss it.

"Have you been hurt?" her mom asked.

"Mom, no." If she told her the truth, that commitment and family life and sacrificing yourself and your dreams terrified her, mostly because of her childhood, it would crush her. She already blamed herself enough. Eve didn't want to cause her any more pain.

"Is there really not anyone, Evelyn? Not even now, after all these years?"

Eve was about to say no when Olivia's face flashed before her eyes. She straightened as if something hot had run up the center of her back. Olivia was definitely the someone her mother was referring to. Someone she truly liked. Someone who truly moved her. Not wanting to explain her feelings about commitment was understandable, but with Olivia, she literally didn't know how to explain what was happening with her. She was crazy about her, and Olivia had also confessed similar feelings for her, yet they weren't together. It didn't make sense, not even to her. It in no way would make sense to her mother, so she didn't want to go into detail about it. Olivia, and the way she felt about her, was a topic she was trying like hell not to overthink on, even within herself.

Her mother, however, didn't seem to need an explanation. She looked as though she could read it on her face.

"There's someone, isn't there? That's one thing about you, Evelyn. You've never been very good at hiding your feelings. You're used to verbalizing them. So, when you don't want to you try to hide them. But you're too easy to read and the look you have now, well, it's as beautiful as it is obvious." She smiled and it reached her eyes. "I hope someday you'll tell me about her. Because I'd love to know all about the woman who causes a look like that to come over my daughter."

Eve almost put a hand to her heart she was so moved. But she knew if she gave in to the rising feelings inside, she'd soon be overcome by them. She didn't like to lose control and she didn't like to cry. It had never felt good to her. It had never eased her pain or made her feel better. It only ever made her a mess, inside and out. So, she wasn't about to break down now. Not even with her mother.

She knelt and kissed her cheek.

"I'm going to go check the chemicals in the pool and then run to the pharmacy for you. I know there's at least one medication you need refilled." She headed toward the kitchen for the back door but stopped just short of the doorway. She turned, suddenly needing to reach out a little in return to her mother, because she was now finally reaching out to her. She gave her what little of herself she could at the moment. "I hope so too, Mom. I hope that maybe someday, I'll be able to tell you all about her."

Chapter Seventeen

Olivia sat on the park bench, plucked the water bottle from her hydration belt, and quenched her thirst. She was halfway finished with her walk and had no further plans for the evening, so she'd decided a short break might be nice. The sun had settled in for the evening, and the park was mostly quiet with only a few people walking the cemented path. She enjoyed her time here almost as much as she did on the mountain at Thunderbird Park, which she still visited frequently for early morning hikes.

She checked her new Fitbit and saw she'd already put in two miles. She could quit now if she wanted to, but she liked the way she felt and really liked the fact that she was improving steadily, both in stamina and speed. Eve had been right. When she got her heart rate up, like with the walking and the weightlifting, she felt great. Like her whole body was thrumming with a powerful music she couldn't hear but could somehow feel.

Her breathing began to slow, along with her heart rate as she sat back and relaxed. The overhead lights flickered to life, and thoughts of Eve drifted into her mind, where they, especially lately, seemed to have taken up residence. Thinking of Eve was second nature now and just as natural and involuntary as breathing in and out.

She wondered what she was doing right now. Was she home? Was she alone? Was she by any chance thinking of her?

She took another swallow of water and noticed the tight feel of the muscles in her arms. Just about every muscle in her body had been isolated and worked, leaving her keenly aware of each one. She was sore, some days more than others, but not overly so. Eve was being very careful in the way she was working her, making sure she didn't over stress her body. Olivia was grateful, preferring not to feel like death warmed over every day.

She honestly hadn't thought that Eve could train her in a way she enjoyed. She'd thought for sure she'd be in pain and agony and hating every second of it. But, to her sincere astonishment, she was actually liking everything Eve had her doing. And when she examined her bicep now and saw the bulge, she smiled, a little bit of pride breaking through. The shame and worry of looking too masculine was fading.

Things were definitely changing. Good things were definitely happening.

And Eve seemed to be the common denominator in almost all of it.

"Hey, you," a familiar voice said from behind.

Startled, Olivia turned. She blinked in disbelief. Eve was standing there in the deep blueberry of twilight wearing a white, form fitting shirt and dark blue shorts. She seemed to radiate, even in the dim light, with her broad, beautiful smile and her surprisingly new blonder hair. Her skin, which was now deeply tanned, seemed to be shimmering and Olivia was so stirred she had the urge to graze her fingertips along her forearm, curious as to how it would feel.

Would she feel as soft and silky as she looked?

"Mind if I join you?"

"Please." She scooted a bit and Eve sat and rested her arm across the back of the bench. She crossed her legs, which were, as always, well moisturized and so toned Olivia could see the individual muscles flex as she moved.

"I thought I might find you here," she said. "You'd said you might try walking twice a day."

Olivia forced herself to stop staring at her mouth even though she was almost certain that Eve had just applied lipstick. For a split second, she wondered if she'd done so for her.

"Did you need to see me?" Olivia asked, her eyes moving from her mouth, down her incredible body to her shoes. She wasn't wearing socks, just a pair of white canvas Vans. There was a casualness to her look, but she was still chic and well put together. Olivia could see that her shirt was designer and the mid-rise cotton shorts she wore with a thick belt probably were as well. Everything about the way she looked at that moment turned Olivia on, and she realized she'd never seen her outside of their workouts before. It was no wonder her entire being was on fire. She was seeing the personal side of her. Eve in everyday life. Everything suddenly became so much more tangible.

"No," Eve said slowly. "I was just in the neighborhood."

"Oh?"

Eve chuckled and Olivia swore she heard nervousness in it.

"My mother lives two streets down. I was visiting her and thought I might swing by to see if you were here. I'm not bothering you, am I?"

"What? No, of course not."

"You can tell me. I know you weren't expecting to see me."

"I'm surprised, yes. But pleasantly so."

A light breeze teased Eve's hair and carried her scent to Olivia.

"God, you smell—" Olivia stopped. "Sorry."

"I smell?" Eve made a face. "The way you said it sounded like that sentence was going to end well, but now I'm not so sure."

"I was going to say that you smell nice."

"I smell nice."

"Yes. Like you always do." Olivia glanced away, embarrassed.

"Thank you," Eve said after a short silence. She plucked at her shorts, but Olivia was pretty sure there was nothing there to pluck.

Could she be as anxious as I am?

They'd been doing great at keeping things professional and light-hearted. But Olivia was still struggling to control her attraction, and she honestly didn't know how Eve didn't seem to notice. Olivia caught herself staring at her every chance she got. Sometimes she wished she could just take her picture so she could look at her all she wanted whenever she wanted.

"You look like you're somewhere far away," Eve said. "You're very cerebral, aren't you? Probably a lot smarter than I even realize. I know you're going for your degree, but I sense there's more. You're a bit of an egghead. Am I right?"

Olivia laughed. "I like to learn. Like to read."

"Always?"

"Yes."

"I thought as much."

"What about you?" Olivia asked. "You're obviously educated. You're very articulate."

"I did the whole university, live in a dorm, nearly starve to death thing up at NAU. I thought about going for my master's, because, like you, I've always liked learning and liked school, but I got into fitness instead."

"Do you think you'll ever go back?"

"For my master's? Possibly."

"Would you go back to NAU?"

"Uh, probably not. I love Flagstaff and really loved my time there, once I got over freezing my ass off that first year, that is. But Phoenix is, well, Phoenix is home."

They both grew quiet, and Olivia stared out into the park, lost in the sheen of silver the lights cast upon the grass.

"I know what you mean," she eventually said. "I love it here."

"I don't get why people complain so much about the heat. It doesn't matter to them that it's dry; they still hate it. They say it's like walking into an oven. Well, you know what? I hate humidity. That feels like walking into a swamp. Not to mention how it fucks up my hair and ruins my makeup."

Olivia laughed. "I wouldn't really know. I've never been that far outside of Phoenix. The only humidity I've ever felt is August during monsoon season."

"Even that much bothers me," Eve said. "But I'd take Phoenix over anywhere, I think. The good far outweighs the bad."

"How so?" Olivia asked. "I mean, I know why I like it here. I want to hear why you do."

"Oh, there are so many things." She thought for a long moment. "I like the way the desert smells on a cool spring morning. And the way the endlessness of the big blue sky makes you feel so free. And of course, there's the relentless sunshine, and the fact that I can look in almost any direction and see the majesty of one of those purple serrated mountains."

"Mm, I feel the same."

"What about you?"

"Oh, I like weird things."

"Like?"

"Like the way a gallon of sun tea looks brewing in the sunlight. I used to sit and stare at that as a kid. It was so fascinating to me."

"What else?"

"The chlorine smell of a pool, along with the smell of sunscreen. Both of those bring back good memories for me." She laughed. "My brother hated it, but I liked how the pool felt like bath water by the time July rolled around. And how the deck got so impossibly hot we either had to sprint as fast as we could into the pool or splash the water all over the deck to try and make it bearable enough to walk on."

"Which doesn't always work," Eve said.

"No, it doesn't, does it?" She smiled to herself. "I love the monsoons. Love watching them move in. You know when the sky turns midnight blue and the lightning flashes and veins out in different directions. And I love how, when the storm closes in, the wind picks up and you can smell the dust and the rain. Like they're mixed together. I don't know. There's just something about those storms that makes me feel…alive."

"Those things aren't weird, Olivia."

"Oh, they are."

"You're just perceptive. I think you notice things others don't."

Olivia thought for a moment. "Okay, but this one is definitely weird. I love those first few seconds of sitting in a hot car after spending hours in frigid air conditioning."

Eve laughed and clapped. "Yes! Oh, my God, I've never heard anyone say that before. It feels so good sometimes I don't even want to start my car. I just want to sit there for a while."

"It makes burning your hand on the door handle to get in so worth it, right?"

They both laughed and Olivia was really enjoying herself. Good, hearty laughter hadn't exactly been a staple in her life.

"And don't even get me started on Mexican food," Olivia said. "I could go on about that for hours."

"You and me both. Maybe one day we'll get you to Mexico for some seriously authentic food. Get you to venture out of Phoenix some."

"That sounds nice."

Really nice. So nice I won't sleep tonight thinking about being alone with you on a Mexican beach.

But that fantasy was quickly overshadowed with something else pertaining to Mexico.

"My parents live there," Olivia said. She heard the sorrow in her voice as her words faded. "They retired there recently. Just outside of Rocky Point."

"You don't sound like you're too happy about that. Do you miss them?"

"Oh, no, it's not that. In fact, it's sort of the opposite. I don't really miss them at all." It pained her to say it, but it was the truth.

"You aren't close then?"

"We were a tight family when I was a kid. But in looking back, it wasn't because we were connected or close. We were tight because my parents wanted total control and very little outside influence. And now, I'm realizing, I can't really relate to them at all." She stared off once again, contemplating. Eve remained quiet and Olivia could feel her watching her. She was giving her time, giving her space, graciously waiting to see if she wanted to share more. It was very considerate and exactly what she needed. "Sometimes I think who I was as an individual never mattered to them. All that mattered was what they believed and that I conformed to it."

Olivia met her gaze. "They're very religious."

"I see." There was a soft kindness to her face. "So much about you makes sense to me now."

"Great," Olivia said, joking. "I don't think I want to know what you mean by that."

"Nothing bad, silly. You're…torn. It sounds like you're questioning everything that you've ever known to be true. You're making new discoveries. Even about yourself. Searching for your own truth. That can't be easy."

"One second, I feel free and excited and so full of passion I feel like I might burst. And then the next I feel so guilty and scared it sometimes hits me right in the gut. You know the funny thing is that dealing with the rigidness and deep-seated beliefs of my past isn't nearly as overwhelming as dealing with my feelings toward you—" Olivia clamped her mouth closed. "I'm sorry."

"It's okay. You can tell me."

"No, we have an agreement and I need to honor it."

"Olivia—"

But Olivia stood, needing to put some distance between them.

"I should go."

"You didn't do anything wrong. Stay. Please."

Olivia breathed deeply and her chest shook.

"I want to, Eve," she said. "You don't know how badly I want to."

"I do, actually," Eve said softly.

"That's all the more reason why I should leave."

"Look at me," Eve said. "Olivia."

Olivia did, and the way Eve looked against the backdrop of the night sky and under the soft glow of the tall lights left Olivia completely speechless and she couldn't, no matter how hard she tried, tear her eyes away from her. She absolutely radiated.

"Please, don't let this thing between you and me eat you up inside. Guilt of any sort does not belong in this equation."

"What about fear?"

"Oh, Olivia." She palmed her chest, as if Olivia's words had penetrated. "Hearing you say that, and knowing you feel that way, it makes my heart ache. Are you sure you want to continue with this? With our working together? Are you sure it's not too hard on you right now?"

"No, I'm not sure about any of that. But there is one thing I'm sure about."

"What's that?"

"I can't stop seeing you."

Eve didn't move and she didn't speak. She just stared right into Olivia's eyes.

"Don't make us stop," Olivia said in a throaty voice. "I need to see you. I need you in my life. Even if it's just to be near you. Please. Don't take the most meaningful experience I've ever had away from me."

Eve stepped toward her, but then stopped. She moved her mouth to speak but instead shook her head as if she were truly conflicted inside. Finally, she managed to say something.

"Okay."

Olivia smiled, but it wasn't big or bright or full of happiness. It was a smile of relief, of gratefulness.

"You have no idea how much being with you means to me," Olivia said. She turned to walk away before she confessed anything more. "Good night." She was already several steps away when she heard Eve answer.

"Good night, Olivia."

CHAPTER EIGHTEEN

"Okay," Eve said as she led Olivia to one of the full-length mirrors at U-Fit. "This is the last exercise of the day."

"Oh, thank God," Olivia said. "You're killing me today."

She wiped her brow with her hand towel and tossed it on the bench. Sweat moistened her hairline, and a few strands of hair were stuck to her red face. She quickly tore off her tank top and tossed it on top of her towel, and Eve tried not to stare at her chest, which was also scarlet and glistening with sweat, or her abdomen, which had tightened nicely and was now hinting at the beginnings of definition.

The changes in her were becoming more and more noticeable, and Eve was rightfully and expectedly proud, but those weren't the only things she was feeling. Every time she touched her or got to see more of her body, like now, she was overcome with lust and wanting. Which was why she was trying to avoid having to touch her, so she wouldn't feel the hardening of her physique or the way her muscles moved beneath her fingers. And she hoped every day, that Olivia would wear a shirt over her sports bra, so she could remain focused on their workout. But when she didn't or later took it off, Eve couldn't help but secretly thank the stars above, because the sight of her was so fucking eye pleasing and arousing that her mouth would actually begin to water.

"I tried to warn you," Eve said, "about wanting to kick my ass at some point."

"Are you kidding? How can I do that when you just literally kicked mine? And here I was worried about plateauing," she said.

"Oh, no. That won't happen with me." She grinned.

"Yeah, no shit. I got that loud and clear today. You could've at least warned me of your plans to switch things up, you know?"

"Why would I do that? You know you'd only worry and stress."

"But I would've been prepared."

"You are prepared. You're more than ready for this next level. You just don't feel like you are because these exercises are all new to you. You'll adjust. Just like you did before."

Eve looked at her and chuckled.

"Do you realize what you just did?" she asked her.

Olivia looked confused.

"You just cussed."

Her eyes widened. "I did, didn't I?"

"I haven't heard you do that since the day you sprained your ankle on the mountain. I figured that had been just a strong response to the pain. I didn't think the day would ever come when you cussed casually."

"It kind of felt good," she said.

"I bet it did. I couldn't imagine not being able to say what I want. Or to hold back my true voice in reaction to something that moved me. Maybe you should do it more often. Let yourself go a little."

"I remember the first time I took the Lord's name in vain. It just slipped out. And I felt so awful and ashamed. But saying 'Oh, my God' isn't tragic. It's just an expression. So, maybe I should let myself go a little more."

"Who knows? There may come a day when you sound a lot like a dirty old sailor, like me." She gave her a playful shove.

"Don't terrify me, now. I would like to keep *some* intelligent articulation in my wheelhouse."

"Just for that, I'm going to make you do two more exercises."

"What?"

"Yep. Come on, let's go." She stood next to her. "Stand with your feet shoulder-width apart." Olivia did. "Now shift your weight to one leg and bend that knee a little. Okay, now bend forward at your hips and extend that free leg all the way back." Olivia did so and she wavered a bit, struggling with her balance. Eve quickly supported her. "Now lower that leg and do it again, this time squeezing your glutes, legs, and abs." Olivia did, and she lost her balance again and reached out. Eve grabbed her hand and forearm and stabilized her.

"I'm too unsteady."

"I've got you."

"Don't let go."

"I'm right here and I won't let you go. I would never do that." Eve cleared her throat after the fading of her voice, after the realization of what she'd just said settled in.

Olivia lowered her leg and looked over at her. Eve could see that the words had reached her some place deep as well. And though the deeper meaning was originally unintended, the connection that Eve felt with her as they locked eyes confirmed the significance of what that meaning represented now.

"Promise?" Olivia asked.

Eve swallowed. "I promise."

After a long silence, Olivia readied herself again, refocusing on her position.

"I want you to give me eight more," Eve said, still feeling the gravity of what had just transpired.

Olivia was quiet as she finished her set and started in on the last two. Then, Eve had her switch legs and begin again. She held her carefully, ensuring her balance and couldn't help but notice the glide of her muscles beneath her smooth, satin-like skin. And when Eve checked her form as she extended her leg, she had to close her eyes every now and then to try to keep herself calm after observing the hypnotic dance of her rounded glutes as they shifted in constriction and release.

"I'm finished," Olivia said as she straightened. "My legs and butt are toast."

Eve kept hold of her and eased her onto the bench. "Here, sit down for a few." Her legs were trembling from the extensive lower body workout she'd gone through today, and Eve wanted to rest her hands on them to help her relax, but she knew it wouldn't be effective and would probably only make matters worse for the both of them. But the need to do so, to touch her and comfort her, remained, regardless.

"You'll be a little sore tomorrow. Comes with the territory, I'm afraid."

"I'm sure those words will be a great comfort when I scream in pain as I sit to pee in the morning."

Eve couldn't help but laugh. "If it makes you feel any better, the same thing still happens to me when I go hard on my lower body."

"Even now?"

"Even now. It's not awful though. And it shouldn't be for you either. That's why we warmed up and stretched more than usual today. To help prevent that toilet sitting trauma you referred to."

"Funny."

"I thought it was pretty clever."

Olivia rubbed her quads. "Anything else I can do? Like when I get home?"

"You could take an ice bath."

"Ugh, oh my God no. No thank you."

"Don't like cold water, I take it? You'd only have to be in it for ten minutes."

"Um, no, won't be doing that."

"Well, be sure to drink plenty of water, just like always. And later tonight, a few hours from now, you can use a heating pad."

"That sounds so much better." She stood and stretched some. "Okay, bring it on. Let's get this over with. What's next?"

"I was kidding. We're done for the day."

"Oh."

"Don't tell me you're disappointed. First the cussing and now disappointment over our session coming to an end? You can't shock me like this twice in one day, Olivia. I don't think my heart can take it."

Olivia put her towel and tank top in her gym bag and zipped it closed. A quietness seemed to have come over her again.

"I am disappointed, Eve. Just not for the reasons you think." She slung her bag over her shoulder and drank from her water bottle. "And your heart? Well, if it's anything like mine, then you're in trouble. Because mine is so overused and overloaded sometimes I think just one more heated look from you, or one more smile, or one more touch of your hand might literally send me into cardiac arrest and kill me. And you know what? I'd die with the biggest, happiest, dopiest grin on my face I've ever had."

She moved to walk past her.

"Does that sound anything like your heart?"

Eve didn't respond, wasn't sure how to, and Olivia moved on, headed for the front entrance.

"Olivia, wait up." She hurried after her, but Olivia had parked close and she was already climbing into her car. Eve knocked on her window, but she seemed to be ignoring her and she started her ignition. Eve grew desperate and rounded the vehicle to open the door and climb into the passenger seat.

"What are you doing?" Olivia asked, appearing a little astonished.

"I'm trying to talk to you."

"I don't think that's a very good idea right now." She stared straight ahead through the windshield.

"Why? What's going on? Talk to me. What you said back there—"

"What I said back there was stupid. And I apologize. Again. For saying stupid shit. For going against our agreement."

"Hey." Eve reached out and lightly touched her arm, unable to resist the urge to ease her pain. "What you said to me back there and the other night in the park, Olivia, you, you just have no idea of the power of your words."

"I do, though," she said. "Because that's how I feel. And what I feel for you is that powerful."

"Olivia."

But instead of answering her, she closed her eyes and breathed deeply.

"Eve, you really need to move your hand."

"I don't want to."

"Please."

"I don't want you to hurt. I can't stand to see you hurting like this."

Olivia looked at her then with such intensity and emotion, Eve's breath caught in her chest.

"This isn't me hurting, Eve. This is me trying my damndest not to come over there and take your mouth with mine and devour you vehemently, like you are the only thing, the only thing left on this earth that will feed my body and my soul and keep me alive."

Eve couldn't think. She couldn't breathe. Her heart was either beating beyond her awareness or it had stopped altogether.

"Olivia," she whispered. She touched her face and felt the burning of her cheek. Olivia closed her eyes and sighed and then ran her hand along Eve's arm to cover hers. She opened her eyes and Eve leaned toward her, desperate to capture her lips with her own. But Olivia gripped her wrist and pulled her hand from her face.

"Don't," she rasped. "We can't."

Eve searched her eyes, needing more than anything, to kiss her, to connect to her, to fucking meld together with her.

But Olivia remained firm.

"We can't. I don't think it would be smart."

Eve leaned back, completely weak and devastated from the rush and downfall of emotion. She opened the door, her throat too tight to speak.

"Eve," Olivia said.

Eve looked at her once more.

"I'm sorry."

"Don't be," she managed. She smiled, but it was weak, just like the way she felt. She crawled from the car and closed the door. Olivia drove away, leaving her standing like a rag doll, ready to collapse. "There's no need to be sorry."

But inwardly, she really did wonder how much more either one of their hearts could take.

Chapter Nineteen

"Y ou don't understand," Eve said as she quickly sorted through a rack of Adidas T-shirts, one after the other, causing the loud, ear-gouging metal on metal scrape of the sliding hangers. "I have never, ever been more turned on in my life."

"Why? Because a seriously prude woman told you her heart ached for you?" Karen was at the next rack, doing the same as Eve only with Under Armor tees. They were inside Dick's Sporting Goods at Arrowhead Towne Center, and thankfully, because it was midmorning on a weekday, no one was nearby to overhear their conversation.

"It was so much more than that," Eve said. "She actually told me she wanted to act on her feelings. And the way she said it…my God, it was like lightning surging right through me."

"Yeah, okay, sure. If you say it was hot, then it was hot. Who am I to judge?"

"Precisely. Who are you to judge?"

Karen held up a T-shirt for examination. "She just sounds so God damned puritan."

"And there went the no judging right out the window," Eve said as she, too, held up a T-shirt. It was light pink with the white Adidas stripes on the sleeves and, not only was it her size, it was on sale. She draped it over her forearm and continued. "Puritan or not, she gets me hot. Beyond hot. I'm talking burst into flames hot. I mean every single cell in my body goes haywire."

"Uh-huh. I'm pretty sure Hester Prynne had that same effect."

Eve rolled her eyes.

"Will you quit? I'm trying to tell you that she's different."

"So you've said."

"She's got layers to her, and every time I see her, I swear she pulls back another and shows me something unexpected. She's very intelligent and the way she expresses herself, she's like a poet. An incredibly eloquent romantic poet. I would love to curl up next to a fire and read her all night long."

"I bet you would. But not because you're such a diehard romantic."

Eve laughed but continued with her point.

"She's confirmed to me that she's never been with a woman, yet she's somehow able to convey all that burning passion and insatiable yearning that women feel when they desire another woman. It's like she already knows what being with a woman feels like. I can't imagine what she would be like when she really did make love with a woman." She cocked her head. "Actually, you know what? I can. I think about that all the time, and let me tell you how it's wreaking havoc on my sleep at night."

"Well, you sure sound smitten, like you're two star-crossed wannabe lovers. But didn't she cancel your session yesterday?"

"She said she had to meet her group for a class project."

"Do you believe her?"

"I have no reason not to."

"Eve, it's summer. Is she even enrolled in a class right now?"

Eve's stomach fell. "I would assume so. That's what she said she was doing."

"You don't think maybe her poetic confessions of desire scared her back into her shell?"

"God, I hope not. I hope she's not freaking out to the point of avoiding me. I don't know what I'd do if she is."

"What could you do?" Karen started in on the opposite side of Eve's rack.

"I've tried to pull back a little with her. Tried to keep things less personal and more professional. After our conversation in her car and how she insisted we keep things status quo, I thought maybe that would help."

"Has it?"

"I don't know. We didn't talk a whole lot. We focused on our workout."

"I don't know how you're doing this. You're up and down and all over the place with this woman emotionally. And you've told me more than once that your libido is so high you're practically pelvic thrusting when the wind blows."

"Yeah, well, I can't deny that. It's more than true."

"And the ol' vibrator's not cutting it anymore?"

"No."

She tsked. "That's a crying shame."

"You're telling me."

Karen finished with the shirts and winked at her. "So, are we done here? Did you get enough goodies to last you a while?"

Eve held up the five T-shirts and three pairs of shorts folded over her arm.

"I think I'm good."

They walked to the register and paid for their clothes, then headed for the interior of the mall with their bags in tow.

"I don't know about you," Karen said. "But I'd blow my ex-husbands twice right now for a soft pretzel."

"Ugh, Jesus, thanks so much for that image. I think I just threw up in my mouth. I could've gone for a pretzel too, you know."

"Oh, get off it. You've heard worse from far better."

Karen nudged her as they continued on, now with the pretzel stand as their unspoken destination. Eve inhaled the smells that only a mall could bring and stared up into the bright light beaming down through the skylights.

"I worked here in high school," she said. "Hard to believe that was more than ten years ago, now."

"Ha, talk to me when it's been thirty, kid." She shook her head. "So, where did my little Evie-Eve work?"

"Dairy Queen and PacSun."

"No kidding? Huh. You probably made about a million Blizzards for me."

"It's possible."

"You guys put crack in those things, don't you?"

"What?" She laughed. "No, there's no crack, Karen."

"Don't fuck with me, Monroe. I can't handle being accountable for my issues with ice cream at the moment. My blood sugar's dropping and I can't even smell the pretzel place yet."

"We're almost there."

"I'm obsessing already. Should I have the cream cheese with my pretzel or the nacho cheese?" She shook her head. "You're going to say neither if I want to keep my girlish figure."

"You know me better than that. I'm not going to say a word."

"Maybe I need you to. Help keep me in line."

"No. I know very well you're capable of making decisions about food on your own."

"Yeah, well, not here. Walking through the mall with all these smells and temptations, it's like going to the God damned state fair. Fuck the rides, the games, and the cute little farm animals. I go for the food."

Eve cracked up as Wetzel's Pretzels came into view. Karen sighed with apparent relief as they stood at the counter and looked at the menu. After Karen finally decided on her cheese preference, they ordered and then took their food and drinks to search for an empty bench. They settled into one next to a large silk plant, and Karen busied herself tearing her pretzel apart to dip it in nacho cheese.

"You're still going to go Friday night, right?" Karen asked just before taking a bite.

"Hm? Oh, you mean for drinks?" She shrugged. "I guess."

"Good, because you know, I'm bringing that friend of mine. The one I told you about."

Eve forced down a swallow. "No, Karen. Don't. Oh, God, I would've said no if you'd told me that sooner. You know I would have."

"Which is why I didn't tell you. I probably shouldn't have told you now. But I'm not a total schmuck, so I thought I should let you know."

"I'm not up for meeting anyone."

"You may not want to, but you need to. At the very least to just enjoy the company of another lesbian. And it wouldn't hurt if it led to a little sex now, would it?"

"Karen." Eve looked at her, ready to fight it out.

"You owe me, Monroe," she said. "I hate to call it in for something as trivial as this, but it seems I have to."

Eve sighed as she recalled Karen saving her ass on a double date they'd gone on over a year ago. Karen and her date had hit it off, but Eve's had been a nightmare. She couldn't totally recall why it was a disaster, but she did remember that the woman was overly loud and obnoxious. Eve had been so turned off she'd been willing to chew her own arm off to escape. Thankfully, Karen saved her by claiming that she felt ill. She'd insisted Eve take her home and they'd left. Karen, however, had yet to let it go.

"You're wrong," Eve said. "You are a schmuck. A big, giant schmuck."

"I may be, but I'm also your friend and I care about you. So, be there, Friday night, eight sharp."

Karen popped in another bite and Eve sipped her drink, hating both Karen and her life at the same time. She rubbed her temple, unable to find a way out of the arrangement. She finally sat back and crossed her ankles, the fight in her unwilling to even spark. She thought about the date and realized that she'd never dreaded an oncoming Friday night before. Fridays were supposed to be fun, light-hearted, and a promise to a wonderful weekend ahead.

But not this one.

This one, Eve knew, was going to be anything but fun.

CHAPTER TWENTY

Olivia wound her way through occupied tables, following the bubbly young hostess who had greeted her at the door. Jake, who had made the reservations, was already seated and studying a dark red menu so intently, she wondered just how special the sushi was there. He didn't even bother to look up when she sat and opened her own menu.

"I'm fine, thank you, and yourself?" She waited for a response, hoping her rib at being ignored was successful. She even raised an eyebrow, mocking the way he often did it to her. He didn't notice.

"Hello, Olivia, how are you?" he said dryly, eyes still trained on the menu.

"I've been better. Not that you really care or anything." She scanned the list of food and then realized it was pointless. She knew what she was going to have. It was what she always got when Jake insisted on sushi.

California rolls and miso soup.

"You still wigging out?" he asked. When she didn't say anything, he finally closed his menu, rested his cheek in his hand, and looked at her. "You are, aren't you?"

Olivia took in his perfectly styled hair, his fashionable eyeglasses he wore just for show, and his perfectly pressed dress shirt. His blond hair and white shirt contrasted nicely with his newly tanned skin. He almost…radiated. A sense of familiarity flooded her mind, nearly carrying her away, as she remembered the way Eve looked that night at the park.

"Yeah, you're definitely wigging on me."

She sipped her water and cleared her throat.

"Did you see her yesterday?" he asked.

"Yes."

"And?"

"Everything was fine." She gave the well-practiced smile she'd always used to convince everyone that she was fine. But lately she was having a hard time pulling it off. Especially with Jake.

"I call bullshit."

"What do you want, Jake? Do you really want to hear how we could hardly look at one another? Or how we gave awkward, forced, polite smiles when our eyes did meet, or that the uncomfortableness between us was so heavy it was hard to breathe? Or how about how she spoke to me? Soft and quiet, like I was fragile and about to break. Which, I can only surmise, must also be the reason why she wouldn't touch me. At all, Jake. Not even when she should have, like to help me stretch or spot me."

"Sounds like she's wigging out, too."

"Yes, and it's because of me. Because of all that stuff I said to her. I broke our agreement. And now she's only continuing to see me because I practically begged her to and she's being polite. Because that's how Eve is. She's nice."

"Olivia, stop, take a breath. Rein your drama llama a little."

"I can't. I'm freaking out. I think about never seeing her again and I literally freak out. And, Jake, I've never freaked out before. I don't know what to do with myself."

"Of course, you've never freaked out before. You want someone. You feel for someone. For the first time in your life. And did I forget to mention that she's a woman? Sweetie, to be honest, I'm surprised you haven't freaked the fuck out sooner. About any or all of it. Because it's overwhelming, especially for someone who's never experienced this kind of emotion before. And now you tack on your fear of losing her and everything she encompasses and you're about two seconds away from a complete meltdown."

"So, what do I do?"

"Well, for starters, you can breathe. In and out. Nice and slow."

Olivia slowed her breathing, but it only made her dizzy. She still continued to try, though, really preferring not to pass out in a crowded restaurant.

"Okay, what else?"

"You can stop all the assuming."

"Assuming?"

"Yes. You don't know for sure what she's thinking or feeling, or why she's still training you. If you ask me, and oh yeah, silly me, you did, it sounds like she's trying really hard to control herself around you. That means she has strong feelings for you, Olivia. She's probably still helping you because she wants to and because she wants to be with you, too. My guess is, she doesn't want to give up your time together either, so she's being very careful not to fuck things up on her end."

Her heart lifted.

Could that really be it?

She sipped more water and stared at the crowded bar in the distance as she seriously contemplated what he'd said. A woman with blond hair caught her attention and her eyes trailed downward to a tight black dress on a fit and tanned body.

No, it can't be.

The woman turned and Olivia saw her profile.

It was Eve.

"Oh, my God."

"What?" Jake followed her gaze and turned to look. "Do you know someone?"

"It's her," Olivia said, trying to suck in air.

Eve was sitting near the end of the bar, and for a brief moment, Olivia's eyes were solely trained on her. She watched as Eve brought a glass to her lips and smiled just before taking a drink. Then she nodded and said something. Olivia didn't want to. She didn't. She was terrified at what she would see. But the need to know made her look to the person sitting next to her.

It was a woman. A very attractive woman.

No.

Please, no.

She was smaller in stature than Eve, with short, close-cropped auburn hair. Her dress was red and form-fitting, showing off a petite body. She laughed at something Eve said.

Olivia wanted to look away. Knew she should look away. But she was frozen, unable to even blink. Acid churned in her gut, like it was trying to eat right through her. Her heart was racing, like it was completely out of control, and a fierce heat rushed to her face as anger and hurt and betrayal began to build.

"I think you're wrong about Eve and her intentions with me," she said.

"What makes you say that?" He turned again to look at the bar.

Olivia stared at Eve and her companion so hard she thought for sure they would feel it. But they kept chatting, oblivious to the hell coming to life inside her. Eve spoke again, and the woman laughed and this time rested her hand on Eve's forearm, where it remained. Eve didn't push it away.

Olivia felt the sting of tears and the tightening of her throat.

"Because she's into someone else." If words could take physical form, the ones she'd just spoken would've been sharp and jagged and designed to cause serious harm. She knew because they'd literally just torn her apart as they left her body.

"Who, her? The one in the red dress? Olivia, that doesn't necessarily mean anything. They're probably just friends, meeting for a drink."

"I would never wear a dress like that to meet with you," she said. She looked down in disapproval at her black stretch capris and teal Henley top. She didn't look anything like Eve or the woman in the red dress.

Her growing hell continued as Eve took another sip of her drink and glanced around at her surroundings. Olivia panicked and tried to lean to hide behind Jake. But Eve caught sight of her and she honed in and moved so fast, she had ditched her drink and was already crossing the restaurant toward them before Olivia could even speak.

"Olivia, hi," Eve said, coming to stand next to them.

Olivia was staring at the table, willing herself to disappear.

"Hi," she said, glancing at her fleetingly. Eve was smiling at her like she was happy to see her and she looked sincere. She also looked drop-dead gorgeous in the black designer dress and full makeup. She smiled at Jake and stuck out her hand.

"Hi, I'm Eve," she said, shaking his hand.

"I'm Jake," he said, giving Olivia a look that told her she was being rude. "A friend."

Eve looked back to Olivia. "It's a nice surprise to see you here," she said.

"Yes, it's been a surprise for me, too."

Jake looked up at Eve and gestured with his thumb toward the bar. "Are you here with a friend, as well? Would you two like to join us?"

Olivia felt her eyes widen and she clamped her jaw, wanting to ask him through her clenched teeth what the hell he was doing. Jake noticed but he didn't seem to care.

"Actually," Eve said. "I haven't known her for very long. It probably wouldn't be a good idea."

"Oh," Jake said. "More like a date-type thing." He glanced at Olivia, and his concern for her was obvious.

Olivia looked down at the table again, unable to even glimpse at Eve as she answered.

"Uh, I'm not really sure what you would call it," Eve said. Her nervousness was palpable and very unusual for her, which, to Olivia, made the fact that she was on a date all the more evident.

Someone kill me. Please, just put me out of my misery.

Eve was doing her very best to downplay the whole thing. But Olivia wasn't sure if that was because she was trying not to hurt her or because she felt guilty. At the moment, it seemed like it was the latter.

"Well, I don't want to take up anymore of your time," Eve said. Olivia could feel her focusing on her, waiting for her to engage, but Olivia didn't dare.

Instead, she stood and slung her purse over her shoulder.

Jake stood along with her. He appeared stricken. She almost laughed, because that had been her mere seconds ago, when she'd first realized Eve was with a woman and then again when Eve bumbled over herself, trying to deny that she was on a date.

Well, she was no longer stricken. Not anymore.

"Don't worry about taking up our time," Olivia said. She glanced at Jake. "I'm going home. I'm not hungry." Then she looked back to Eve but didn't bother with her well-practiced "I'm fine" smile. "Eve, it was nice to see you. I hope you enjoy your evening."

She turned away just as a crestfallen look came over Eve, leading her to wonder once again if the motive for her trying to hide her date from her was concern or guilt. She didn't stick around to find out.

She hurried from the restaurant and nearly ran through the parking lot to her car. She fumbled with the door, climbed inside, and burst into tears as she started her engine. The new inner resolve she was growing accustomed to was totally disintegrating now. She was, as Jake would put it, in full-on meltdown mode. Her Prius jerked into reverse and she peeled away leaving Eve and the mystery woman behind.

Her eviscerated heart, however, which she wished she could've left behind along with Eve and her date, remained inside her, beating unbearable pain into her veins.

CHAPTER TWENTY-ONE

Eve walked up the cemented path toward the front door. She double-checked the address on her phone and stopped to compose herself. She didn't know what she was going to say or what she was going to do to make things right, but she knew she had to do something. The way Olivia's face had gone from panic to pain to a hardened apathy had devastated her. She'd started to go after her, but Olivia's friend, Jake, had stopped her. They'd spoken and when she answered his questions, he'd buried his head in his hands and told her she needed to go to Olivia. He didn't say why, and he didn't offer any insight. He'd only given her Olivia's address.

Eve had left almost immediately, after she'd told Sharon, the woman Karen had set her up with, good-bye. She didn't take the time to explain nor did she feel a need to do so. She'd just wanted to get to Olivia.

She rang the doorbell and waited. No answer. She backed up to look in the front window, but the blinds were closed. She rang the doorbell two more times, waited again, and then, finally, knocked.

"Come on, come on." She thumbed her phone to life again to call her. The only reason she hadn't was because she knew Olivia probably wouldn't answer. And she didn't want to leave a voice mail or a text. Whatever she was about to say, it needed to be done in person.

A lock disengaged and Eve dropped her phone in her purse. The door opened, but only slightly.

"Olivia—"

"I'm sorry," she said, cutting her off, completely confusing Eve.

Her voice was weak and strained, like she'd been crying, long and hard. It shattered Eve to think of her in so much pain.

"I had no right to behave the way I did." She wiped away a tear. "If you don't mind, I'd like to be alone now." She started to close the door.

"Olivia, wait, please." Eve pressed her hand against the door, worried she would try to close it again. "We need to talk." When she didn't say anything, Eve continued. "It's crucial that we talk. And we need to do it now."

"I don't want to. I—can't."

"Then let me talk. All you have to do is to listen."

"You have every right to date and do whatever you want. But I will never be able to see or hear about it. So, please, if you care about me at all, just go." She tried to close the door, but Eve wouldn't let her.

"Can't you see that's why I'm here? Because I do care?"

Olivia looked away from her and Eve knew she didn't believe her.

Though she was fraught, Eve remained determined, and tried again.

"Just let me say what I have to say, and then I'll leave. I promise."

Olivia was quiet, obviously contemplating. Eve kept her hand against the door, terrified to let it close.

What Eve was experiencing was beyond desperation and she didn't know where it was coming from and had no idea how to handle a panic like this. All she knew for certain was that she was willing to go to hell and back for this woman. To lose her now would be detrimental and she wasn't about to let that happen.

Eve wasn't sure if Olivia sensed her boundless distress, or saw it in her face or eyes, but for whatever reason, she eased the door open. The interior of her home shed light upon her, revealing an anguish Eve couldn't fully see before. Tears of mascara trailed down her cheeks, and she was hugging herself as if she were cold. And as Eve stepped inside at the silent invitation, she could see that she was trembling.

"Oh, God, Olivia." She reached for her to pull her close, to pull her tight, but Olivia recoiled like Eve was a striking rattler. "Okay, I won't," Eve said, quickly dropping her hand.

Olivia closed the door and they stood there, just inside the entryway of a modest living room where a small lamp glowed from an end table next to a blue couch. Sitting in front of that was a coffee table with neatly stacked books and magazines. There was a television, but it wasn't large, and it didn't appear to be a newer model. It was nestled in an unassuming entertainment center along with a dozen or so DVDs. A large clock finished off the room, hanging on the wall near what Eve thought might be a dining area. She could hear the faint ticking of the second hand from where they stood.

"I like your place," Eve said, feeling comfortable there, despite the limited decoration. "It feels warm. Welcoming."

Olivia closed her eyes as if she were gathering strength. "Thank you."

"May I put down my purse?"

"Sure."

Eve set her purse on the coffee table and then smoothed down her dress, trying to calm her nerves. She was going to try to explain and plead and hope that Olivia would believe her. But with the way she currently felt, so panicked and desperate and willing to do anything in the world to keep Olivia in her life, she knew she was going to have to say things that crossed their agreed upon boundary.

"Olivia." This was it. What she feared was her only chance. Olivia appeared fragile and Eve knew speaking to her was going to be a delicate act. "Will you please look at me?"

Slowly, Olivia lifted her gaze. She looked so lost and so broken, it took all the strength Eve had to just continue talking.

"I'm not interested in the woman you saw me with tonight."

Olivia startled her with an immediate response.

"But I saw you tonight, you looked—" She stopped and massaged her forehead like she was struggling to find the right words. "And the way you've been behaving around me during our last couple of sessions, I guess I should've had a clue. I shouldn't have been so shocked to see you with someone."

She tried to glance away, but Eve got in her line of vision, making sure she didn't.

"I've been acting that way because I'm scared. And that doesn't happen to me very often. And when it has, it was never because of anything like this. What you said to me at the park and in your car, left me tossing and turning, night after night, aching for you, without any way to quell it. But I had to keep seeing you, so, I had to do something to continue to remain professional. I did the only thing I could think of. I tried to distance myself from you. Hoping that it would help us both. But in doing so, I came off like an insensitive ass. I just didn't know what else to do. I'm sorry, Olivia. I never ever meant to hurt you."

Olivia hugged herself tighter.

"Then why did you go on a date, if you have all these feelings for me? Was that another attempt at distancing yourself from me? I don't understand."

"I was with that woman tonight because my friend Karen wanted to set me up with her. I never had any interest, and initially, I refused. But Karen insisted, said she'd already planned it, and she called in a favor I owed her."

Olivia's brow furrowed, and Eve saw the hurt she'd seen at the restaurant building in her once again.

"So, you what? Got all dressed up to go on a date you didn't really want to go on?"

"I got all dressed up because Karen was supposed to go too. The plan was to have quick drinks with this woman and Karen, then tell the woman good-bye and go out for a nice dinner with Karen, just the two of us. But Karen, being the pain in the ass that she is, didn't show. She hung me out to dry. What's worse was she'd already sent the woman a photo of me, so I was recognized before I even realized Karen wasn't coming."

"But you were having a good time, I could tell. And there's nothing wrong with that. You deserve to be happy. You—"

"Olivia, I only stayed as long as I did because I soon learned that I knew her sister. She was a client of mine a couple of years ago. So, I decided to have a drink while she updated me on her sister. Then, I was going to politely say good-bye and drive over to Karen's house to kick her ass. I was not in any way interested in her. Okay?"

"Maybe you should be," Olivia said. She grabbed a tissue from a box on the end table and wiped away the black tear tracks on her face. "I have no right to get upset with you, and that's what makes it hurt even more. You're so beautiful and wonderful and full of life and love, but you are in no way mine. I wish you were, yes, I do. It's so clearly obvious to me now. But I've been so inconsiderate to you by blurting out my desire and feelings only to then keep you at arm's length. And even now, after telling you I want you to be mine, I can't promise you anything because I have no idea what any of this means and I have no idea what to do about it. You just, you deserve so much better, and I'm so sorry I'm such a big mess and—"

"Olivia, stop." Eve couldn't take anymore.

"But I—"

"Stop." Eve crossed to her, and before she could say another word, she gently cupped her jaw and kissed her.

CHAPTER TWENTY-TWO

Olivia's lips were soft, salty from tears, and impossibly hot. They were, by far, the best lips Eve had ever tasted, and once she started, she couldn't stop, enveloping them again and again, until she felt the surprise and stiffness fall from Olivia's body. She went limp so suddenly, Eve had to embrace her quickly and back her to the door for support.

Eve held her tight and stared into her, wanting to make sure she was okay.

"Why did you stop?" Olivia asked. Her eyes were wild and searching.

"I wanted to make sure you were okay. You can't even stand, and—"

"I don't want you to stop."

Eve felt Olivia grip her waist. She pulled on her, inching her closer. Eve felt the warmth of her breath, and she swore she could still feel the soft plump of her lips against hers.

"Did you hear me?" Olivia breathed.

"Yes."

Their mouths connected again, and Olivia came to life, first with a noise of helplessness and then with the aggressiveness of her own kisses. Lips encased lips, fervent and fluid, as if they were melding together with every touch. Eve groaned in surprise when Olivia slid her fingers into her hair at the base of her head. And when she fisted those fingers and slightly tugged, pulling her away, wrenching her mouth from hers, Eve became so aroused she thought she might come where she stood.

"I don't ever want you to fucking stop," Olivia said. "Please, don't you ever fucking stop again."

She forced Eve's mouth back onto hers and kissed her hard and deep, exploring and conquering with a slick, eager tongue. Olivia's hunger felt so good Eve moaned in sheer pleasure and answered with her own tongue. Their kiss became a dance, and they seemed to be made to perform it together.

Eve blindly pulled up on her own fitted dress, unwilling to break their connection. She raised the hem above her thighs to better maneuver. Then she pressed her leg between Olivia's and felt the heat of her on her bare skin. Olivia broke their kiss, and a redness plumed on her cheeks and chest. She didn't speak. She just slowly lowered her hands and smoothed them over Eve's ass. Then, tentatively, she began to deliberately move against her thigh. The pleasure seemed to penetrate instantly, causing her eyes to initially widen and then narrow and glaze over.

Eve got lost in her, infatuated with her expressions and the way she was able to show the pleasure coursing through her. But the sight of that stirred her own desire into a potency she could no longer ignore. She leaned in and nibbled the delicate skin behind her ear.

"I've wanted you so badly for so long, there's no way in hell I'm going to stop."

Olivia gasped and drove her hips purposefully, obviously craving the friction from the weight of Eve's thigh. Eve began to move with her, giving her what she wanted. She devoured her neck, lightly sucking and tasting the sweetness of her perfumed skin. Her noises grew louder and rode the coattails of her sighs. She clawed her way up Eve's back and sank her nails into Eve's shoulder blades. She tilted her head, offering more of her neck.

"Did you hear me?" Eve asked, tracing the outline of her ear with her tongue. Olivia jolted and Eve felt the gooseflesh erupt on her skin.

"Mm." Her eyes were closed and one of her hands returned to tangle in the base of Eve's hair.

Her eyes flashed dangerously, and her lips slightly parted, beckoning. She was silently relaying a desire Eve would've willingly killed to see had she known it even existed.

"I've never seen anything like you," Eve said softly, hypnotized. "I can see everything inside you. Every emotion. It's all coming up out of you and right into me. I can *feel* it. Feel you."

Olivia's stare dropped from Eve's eyes to her mouth and back up again.

"Touch me," she said.

"Is that what you want?"

"Yes."

"Where?"

Olivia was quiet, still seemingly captivated by Eve's mouth.

"Tell me," Eve said. "Tell me where you want to be touched. I want to hear you say it. I want to hear you say what it is you want."

Olivia took her hand and slowly brought it down her body. She pressed it between her legs.

"Here," she said. "I want you to touch me here."

She was hot and moist against Eve's hand.

"Right here?" Eve began to rub her through her pants, loving the full, pliable feel of her flesh.

"Ah, oh my God," Olivia said. "Yes. Mm. Yes. Right there."

"You sure?" She kept rubbing, increasing the pressure and speed. "Because I can take my time and start somewhere else. Like maybe, here." She skimmed the fingers of her other hand across Olivia's breast, awakening her nipple through her clothing. "I can slowly and carefully remove your bra and touch you here, just like this, with my fingers. I can get your nipple hard and play with it, running my fingers over and over it and then pinch it ever so slightly, to get you to cry out. And then, when you arch your back and whisper for more, I can tease you with my tongue, get your nipple all nice and wet and flick it and breathe upon it until you're writhing and begging. And then, I can send you through the ceiling by taking the entire aching center of your breast into my mouth to suck you off."

Olivia groaned and covered Eve's hand with her own, encouraging her continued movements.

"Is that what you want? Do you want me to take you to your bed and unwrap you slowly and deliberately like you're the best fucking present I've ever been given?"

"Mm."

"Huh? Because I can." She stilled her hand and Olivia's eye widened and her hips jerked.

"No!" She pushed into Eve's hand, desperate for movement. "No, I need it now. I have to have it now."

Eve was burning alive for her and she, too, couldn't wait. She wanted her now. Right then. Right there.

"I'm going to give it to you now, Olivia. I'm going to make you come."

Eve felt her jolt and she looked at her and spoke, but only a single word.

"Please."

Eve hurriedly unfastened her capris and teased the skin just above her panties.

"Close your eyes," Eve said. "Now, let everything go and… feel."

When Olivia did as requested, Eve carefully eased her hand inside her satin panties and slid her fingers along her slick, hot flesh.

"Oh, fuck," she said, sucking in a quick, ragged breath and rising to her tiptoes.

"Yes, that's nice, isn't it?"

"God, yes."

Eve sought farther, sinking her fingers into her folds.

"Ah, Eve, oh my, God!" Olivia clasped Eve's wrist and tossed her head back against the door.

"Wait, there's more," Eve said. "It gets even better."

She found her engorged clit and began to tease it with delicate strokes.

Olivia jerked in spasms, her whole body on edge.

"How can it—be so good? How can I—want more? Oh, God, I do. I want more."

She clung to her wrist and to her waist, moaning and jerking with her eyes clenched and her lips pressed firmly together. She was beautiful and untamed, her reactions visceral and raw. Eve could've watched her for all eternity, but she, too, wanted more.

"Look at me, now," Eve said as she continued to stroke her.

She did and she started to speak, but then crashed again into short, powerful moans.

"Look at me, love. That's it. I want to look into your eyes as I make you come." She dipped into Olivia's warm, silky excitement and then glided along the sides of her clit, trapping it between her fingers, working her up and down and side to side.

"Oh, my fucking God," she called out, short and loud and gripped Eve harder. Her mouth fell open with brasher sounds and rapid breaths.

"Eve," she said. "Eve, help me. It's so good. It's too good. Oh, dear God, help me."

"Just take it, love. Take it all. Every last bit." Eve kept on, leaning in every few seconds to taste her lips, kiss her jaw, and speak into her ear. Olivia's eyes remained open, but Eve could tell it was difficult by the way she continued to throw her head back against the door, the way she bit down on her lip, and the way she began bucking against her hand. Eve fastened on to her neck, nibbled her skin, and gave to her quick and hard and then slow and deliberate. She teased her like that until Olivia was so overcome and wound up, her knees were buckling and she was crazed with excitement, eating Eve alive with her gaze.

"Yes, oh God, yes. Eve. I didn't know. I just—didn't know. It's so—fucking—good."

She was close. Her flesh was full and heavy.

"Are you ready to come, my dear, sweet Olivia?" Eve asked.

"I don't—Oh, Jesus. Don't—stop. Please—Eve—" She angled her head back one last time, dug her fingers into Eve's wrist and waist, and thrust uncontrollably into her hand.

Eve whispered one final request.

"Oh Christ, yes, Olivia. Come for me. Come for me now."

Olivia's entire face crumbled then, just before she cried out with deep, primal emotion. Not once, not twice, but three times, each one longer than the first.

"Oh, Olivia, yes. Feel it, love. Feel how magnificent it is." Eve continued to give to her, bestowing all the passion she had with her hand, luring the orgasm to surface and then loving the feel of it as it consumed her body. She could see it in the pulsing veins of her neck and feel it in the growing moisture on her skin. It saturated Eve's fingers as Olivia rode them shamelessly, claiming all the satisfaction that she could, until the last of her climax left her in abrupt, body-rocking bursts.

Eve held her limp form in her arms and smoothed her hair away from her face. She was trembling all over again and looking at her with a new, sentimental serenity. The gray in her eyes was vibrant and clear, like the cloud cover of the usual storm had passed.

"Hey," Eve said, grazing her cheek.

"Hi."

Eve smiled at her and Olivia, once again, did something she didn't expect.

She fell into her and cried.

CHAPTER TWENTY-THREE

"You're serious," Eve said. "You'd never…" She paused, repositioned herself on the couch, and crossed her extraordinary legs.

Olivia shook her head and wiped her cheeks again, ensuring the tears that had fallen were gone.

"Never."

Under any other circumstance, she would've been embarrassed to admit such a thing. But considering what they'd just done, or rather, what Eve had just done to her, it was a little late for shyness.

"Your reactions were rather…remarkable. Not to mention unforgettable. As a matter of fact, I don't think I'll be able to concentrate on anything else for quite a while. But I just thought you reacted the way you did because you hadn't been touched in a long time or touched in that way. And I had no idea you'd never been brought to orgasm before. Didn't you ever touch yourself?"

Olivia felt herself blush despite their recent intimacy.

"There were a few times when I started to, but I didn't have a clue what I was doing or even totally understand what an orgasm was. And you have to understand, I was always told not to do such things. So, if you take my innocence and a heck of a lot of shame and guilt and toss them together, well, I guess I never had a fighting chance."

Eve couldn't seem to believe what she was hearing.

"What about with your husband?"

Olivia scoffed. "Yeah, okay, right. He didn't make me feel anywhere close to the way you just did."

Eve reached for her hand and massaged the top with her thumb. She was warm and attentive, and any awkwardness that had ever been between them was gone. Olivia felt at ease with her, safe, cared for.

"It's no wonder you cried," Eve said. "All of that pent-up emotion and passion. Orgasms can be very powerful and sometimes they open the floodgates to the heart."

"Have you ever cried after having one?"

Eve stared at her for a moment and then shifted, as if she were uncomfortable.

"No, that's never happened to me and I doubt it ever will." She plucked at her dress, like maybe she had a tiny piece of lint or something, like she had at the park. But Olivia now knew that it was more of a nervous gesture.

"Why?"

"Hm?" She looked back up at her, and she seemed surprised Olivia was asking further.

"I've never been that moved by an orgasm before. And even if I had been, I wouldn't have cried."

"Why?" Olivia asked softly.

"Olivia," Eve sighed.

"I want to know you," Olivia said. "All of you."

She smoothed her dress and closed her eyes for a few seconds.

"I don't like to cry. I don't like the way it feels. So, I don't cry."

"Ever?"

"Not in a very long time." She took a big breath and slapped her hands on her lap. "Let's get back to you, shall we? I find you so much more interesting." She smiled coyly. "I wish I'd known, you'd never come before. I would've done some things differently."

"Like what?" Olivia didn't understand. What had just happened was well beyond anything she'd ever experienced before. She was still flushed with heat and the knot of nerves between her legs was still twitching. Not only from what she assumed was exertion, but from a remaining hunger as well. It was why she kept crossing and uncrossing her legs. The slightest pressure made her want to move her hips again.

She uncrossed her legs again and scooted a little closer to Eve, who, she suddenly noticed, was watching her intently. A sly, knowing smile spread across her face and she traced her fingertips along Olivia's hand to her thigh, where they teased in an up and down motion.

"Well, as I said before, I would've taken things a bit slower. I would've kissed you softer and longer. Touched you lightly, like I am now, to awaken and tease you. Undressed you slowly, kissed your body with my eyes, and then again with my mouth, careful and deliberate, avoiding your erogenous zones."

Olivia swallowed the rising lump in her throat. The flush of heat that was still pressing against her skin began to burn hotter and it shot down to that hungry knot between her legs, and a collision occurred, causing her to lift slightly from the couch.

Eve moved closer, almost completely up against her. The heady perfume she wore, the one that had been driving Olivia wild, floated to her once more, and Olivia grew dizzy once again.

"Then I would lie next to you on my side and put voice to my desires for you as I lightly touched all those areas I had avoided. I would tease them to life and watch as you arched up into me and began begging me for more. And then, finally, when I could no longer resist, I would work my way down your body and kiss those places again and again and relish in your cries and pleas for more. I would do that until you quivered and shook and sweat broke out on your skin. Then, I would fasten my mouth to your most delicate place and make love to you with my hungry lips and heavy tongue."

Her fingers walked up her thigh to her epicenter of nerves where they caressed and teased. Eve leaned in and spoke, her jaw pressed against Olivia's.

"And then, my sweet Olivia, I would make you come."

A sizzling shudder ran through Olivia, and Eve laughed devilishly as she intensified the massage of Olivia's flesh.

Olivia whimpered and gripped the couch for control. But it was useless, she was too far gone. She eased back and let Eve completely take over, just as she had before. And once again, she seemed to know, even through the fabric of her pants, just how to play her.

"You're still thrumming, aren't you?" Eve asked. "Despite coming in my hand mere minutes ago."

Olivia's hips kicked to life at the behest of an insatiable need to come all over again.

"You're trying so hard to hide it, but it's pointless. I know exactly what's happening."

"Is this how it is?" Olivia asked. "Wanting it so soon again?"

Eve laughed. "Yes, Olivia. You're a woman. Multiple orgasms, some of them right on top of the other, are one of those perks you've sadly been missing out on." She cocked her head. "Sad for you, yes, but selfishly I'm really enjoying being the first to give these gifts to you. For me, this is better than any damn Christmas I've ever had."

Olivia jerked, unable to help herself as Eve hit the bull's-eye of her sensitive clitoris again and again with the continued rubbing of her hand.

"Me too," she said. She took in quick hits of oxygen as her eyes threatened to roll back in pure pleasure. "Oh, fuck."

Eve laughed again. "A woman cussing has never been so sexy before. You make it seem so naughty. I'm seriously corrupting you, aren't I?"

"Mm, I think so. But I'm—I'm loving every single second."

Eve looked at her with a fresh, fierce hunger. "Christ, what you do to me," she said. "You have no idea. You just have no idea." She stopped her hand dead center and then moved in small circles, her focal point deliberate and very obviously mischievous. She was sending Olivia through the roof, the assault of her clitoris now direct and relentless. She knew what she was doing. Olivia had no doubt.

The corner of her mouth lifted, confirming Olivia's belief.

"Ah, ah, Oh God." Olivia reared back, unable to hold any of this pleasure in, and lifted her hips off the couch. "Eve. What—are you doing?"

"Didn't we already establish that? I'm totally and completely corrupting you, and apparently, I'm pretty good at it."

Olivia tried to laugh, but the pleasure was accumulating.

"You know what?" Eve said, stilling her hand. "Forget all that stuff I said about taking it slow. I want you again. Now."

Chapter Twenty-four

I mean it. I want you right now," Eve said, sliding off the couch to sit on her knees and unfasten Olivia's capris.

Olivia grabbed her hands, the world once again spinning madly around her.

"What's happening?" she asked.

"I'm going to make you come again, Olivia. With my mouth."

Oh, dear God.

"Here? At this very moment?"

"Why? Don't you want me to?"

Olivia's entire body was pulsating with her heartbeat.

"I'm—nervous."

"I know," Eve said gently. "You don't have to do anything you don't want to."

"What about you? Are you sure you want to?"

"Oh, Olivia, I've never wanted anything more. And I think, I can honestly say, at this point, I would kill to do this to you. I would absolutely, without a doubt, fucking kill to taste you and to feel the silkiness of your most sensitive skin beneath my lips and tongue."

The impact of her words hit Olivia hard and fast, causing her desire to rise to a critical level. She'd never craved touch like this before. Eve's incessant massage had her want rivaling what she'd first felt with her by the door, where she'd sworn, as Eve was awakening her, that nothing could ever be more powerful or feel any better. But there she sat with a new need, this one dominating and incessant and so much stronger than before. She was sure she was going to die if she didn't get it.

Oh, yes, she wanted it.

And she wanted Eve to give it to her.

God, did she ever.

"I want it," she said, her voice sounding raspy and coarse. "I want it bad."

Eve didn't move. Her stare was poignant.

"Even when I dreamed of you saying things like that and wanting me like this, it wasn't nearly this good."

Olivia was speechless.

Eve, too, was quiet once again. With their gazes locked, she lowered Olivia's zipper and tugged down her pants. She removed them from her feet and tossed them over her shoulder. Then she did the same with her panties. She gently parted Olivia's legs and carefully inched her forward.

Olivia sat perched on the edge of the couch, staring down at Eve as she breathed upon her skin, each teasing breath causing a flamethrower to go off inside her.

She trembled helplessly, trying to control her movements as Eve planted soft kisses on her inner thighs.

"It's going to feel good," she said. "Really amazingly fucking good. I'm telling you because I don't want you try to control yourself. Do what you did before. Just let everything go, and feel."

Olivia nodded and swallowed against a dry throat.

Eve gave her inner thighs another round of kisses.

"You're going to like it, love. But not nearly as much as I am."

She licked and teased where she'd just kissed. When she finished one leg, she did the other, and then rested them on her shoulders, cinching Olivia closer to her, opening her farther. She took hold of Olivia's hand and placed it on the back of her head. Olivia instantly knew why when Eve finally lowered herself and breathed upon her aching flesh for a few torturous seconds before she snuck out her tongue for a taste. The sensation of both arched Olivia's back, and suddenly, she was digging her fingers into Eve's hair.

"Eve. I—Oh, God."

Olivia watched like a lustful, starving being as Eve tantalized with her teasing tongue and then pushed farther in, fully attacking with it.

"Oh, my dear sweet God," Olivia hissed and fell back to stare up into the ceiling. She felt Eve continuing, licking and swirling, saturating Olivia's flesh with wet, heated pressure. The pleasure it elicited was heavy, like a thick flowing lava, Eve's tongue working some kind of inexplicable magic. But she didn't care that she couldn't fathom it. She just knew it was good. Great. Fucking insane. She was looking down at Eve and crying out with cuss words one second and then the next, gaping up at the ceiling, praising God almighty the next.

And just when she thought the pleasure couldn't get any greater, Eve tugged her even closer and fastened herself to her, moaning with obvious delight as she kissed her flesh just like she'd done her mouth. Olivia nearly screamed as more pleasure racked her body and she knotted her hands in Eve's hair, desperate to tug her away because it was too much, and desperate to hold her tightly in place because it was so damn good. It was so incredible, that it began to take over her body. Her hips began to move, urging her flesh into Eve's mouth in a hungry rhythm.

"Oh, fuck, Eve. Oh, my God. Oh, dear God, yes." She held fast to Eve and circled her hips unabashedly. The sight and feel of Eve's head bobbing between her legs added to her growing ecstasy, along with her own purposeful gyrations into her. Layer upon layer, the pleasure mounted and Olivia became keenly aware of what she was doing.

She was fucking Eve's face.

And she was loving it.

Eve groaned her approval as if she knew of Olivia's revelation. Knowing Eve was loving it too made Olivia move faster. Soon she was pulling Eve away, teasing her, as this new, naughty feeling took charge. Eve looked up at her with questions in her eyes the first time, and then thereafter, she only laughed and tried desperately to return to her flesh as Olivia tried to hold her back. It was an erotic battle between them, one they both seemed to thoroughly enjoy.

They continued to dance in perfect rhythm, Olivia fucking and Eve feeding, until Olivia was damp with sweat and so ready to burst, she worried she might actually hurt Eve when she came.

"Eve," Olivia breathed.

"Yes, love?" Sweat moistened her face. Her lipstick had long ago smeared, and Olivia could see her own excitement around her mouth. Olivia cupped her jaw, beyond moved at the sight of her.

"Tell me," Eve said, reaching back to bring Olivia's hand to her mouth. She kissed her inner wrist.

Olivia's legs shook.

"I'm going to come," she said.

Eve grinned. "That is the plan, you know."

"I'm going to come hard, Eve. Really hard. I can feel it and I don't want to hurt you."

"You won't," she said. "You can't. Not while you're coming. Because even if you did manage to do something that was painful, I know I wouldn't feel a fucking thing. I'll be too caught up in you. So, relax and go crazy. Lose control. I *want* you to."

She kissed her wrist once more and then kissed her way back up her thigh.

Olivia tangled her hand in her hair and hissed once again as the sensation of Eve's hot mouth against her flesh shot through her. She moved her hips as Eve moved her tongue, and they quickly fell back into their beautiful dance. Pleasure reignited and soared up to its previous level in seconds.

Eve moaned and sucked Olivia into her mouth.

Olivia began to jerk as Eve thrusted and circled her tongue against her flesh. She tried to pull Eve away, but she fought her harder now and she kept sucking, literally tugging on her.

"Eve—I—"

Olivia grit her teeth, the pleasure far too intense, her flesh far too sensitive. But Eve didn't stop. She kept on with her maddening assault, and Olivia squirmed and pleaded and pulled at her hair. But still, Eve kept going.

Olivia couldn't take it. Her head was going to explode and her heart was going to implode. Her body jerked wildly and then, to her shock and amazement, a wave of pleasure burned from her flesh all the way out to the tips of her fingers. Burned so damn good.

"Oh, God—Oh fuck—Oh, Eve."

Her hips started moving and her body bucking, and she was fucking Eve all over again. The pleasure mounted along with that naughty feeling, and Olivia massaged Eve's head, encouraging her along.

"Oh God, Jesus. Eve. Fucking give it to me. Make me come again. I want it. I want it so bad. Yes, that's it. Oh my God, oh my God, Eve, baby you're making me come."

She dug her nails into Eve's scalp, forced herself into her face and grunted and groaned and spasmed as she was rocked with orgasm. Her body was gone, just completely gone from her grasp, totally free from any control she'd still kidded herself in having. She writhed and then shuddered. An endless stream of animalistic cries came from her. Her voice caved before she finished, leaving her pulsing with a silent, open mouth. Her climax was so long and so intense, she was just about convinced it would never end when, finally, the last glowing ember floated away, leaving her desperate for breath and looking down at Eve.

She tugged on her head and Eve left her flesh with an audible smack.

"Hi," Eve said, grinning up at her.

Olivia shook her head. "What did you just do to me?"

"What I wanted to."

Olivia couldn't help but laugh.

"Do you always do what you want?"

"Mm, you were a bit of a toss-up. I actually doubted that I'd ever be able to do what I wanted to you."

"Well, now that you've done what you wanted, what's next?"

"Oh, who says I'm done?"

"What? You can't be serious."

She straightened and held Olivia's face. She was close enough to kiss her. "I'm deadly serious."

"Eve, I can't possibly take any more. Not now, not tonight. What you've done to me, my God. You have seriously just upended my entire world."

Eve touched Olivia's lips with her finger. "You can take more. Yes, even tonight. I'll take you to your bed and show you. And then, you'll take even more. Because we have so much more than just tonight."

Olivia stared at her, completely bewildered. Everything felt so surreal, including Eve herself.

"Where did you come from, Eve Monroe? Who are you? You can't be real."

Eve stroked her face.

"I am, love. I'm very real. And I'm the one who wants to continue to upend your world."

CHAPTER TWENTY-FIVE

Eve stood in the middle of the park, enjoying the feel of the midafternoon sun. She widened her stance and bent forward, placing her palms on the warm grass.

She stayed in that position, relishing the stretch and the heat from the sun. She exhaled long and slow and closed her eyes. This particular park was a new location for her. She'd chosen it because it was closer to Olivia's home and she'd wanted to make things a little more convenient for her since she usually had to drive farther than Eve to their workout locations.

She opened her eyes and straightened to rest her hands on her thighs.

It was Monday and she'd left Olivia on Saturday morning, after making love to her nearly all night long. Once they'd connected with that first kiss, Eve had been hopeless. She just couldn't have stopped. And leaving her on Saturday, while she slept like an angel, her beautifully nude body tangled in her sheets, had been more difficult than she'd expected.

Just thinking about her and their steamy encounter was getting her hot, which combined with the heat of the day, was suddenly too much to bear. She crossed to the shade of a nearby tree and sipped some water.

"Hi." A hand pressed into Eve's back and Olivia came to stand before her.

"Hi." Eve was breathless though she had yet to exercise. The effect of Olivia's presence was immediate, and it quickly progressed as Eve scanned her body and recalled how her curves had felt beneath her fingertips, with their gentle dips and smooth inclines. Even in a gray T-shirt with a maroon Sun Devil trident and dark mesh shorts, she was stunning.

Olivia looked like she was trying to read Eve's thoughts, studying her closely, seemingly oblivious to her hair whipping across her face in the warm breeze. She must have finally deciphered her thoughts, because she glanced away like she was embarrassed.

Eve sensed that old familiar shyness was back.

"What's wrong?"

"Nothing. I—"

"I know something's bothering you." She touched her arms. "Tell me, please."

Olivia shrugged, with her arms extended, palms to the sky. "I don't know, okay? I mean, I know I should be happy, but then I think about now and our professional relationship and what comes next and—"

Eve gently squeezed her arms.

"Everything is okay. Come sit and talk with me." Eve led her to the base of the tree, and they sat with their backs against the large trunk. "What do you want to have happen next?"

Olivia squinted from the brightness of the sun, despite being in the shade. She drew her knees up and hugged them.

"I want to be with you. To spend more time together. And I want Friday night all over again."

Eve felt her heart lift and she smiled, able to tell that the confession hadn't been easy for her.

"You got me. What else?"

She seemed surprised at how quickly she'd accepted and concurred with her wishes, and she hesitated a little before she shared her next concern.

"Well, what about our workouts? I don't want to stop, and I don't want to work with anyone else."

"I will no longer charge you and you will no longer be a client."

"But—"

Eve held up a hand. "That doesn't mean we can't still work out together. I can still share with you all that I know. Things just won't be as regimented."

Olivia still didn't return her smile. Something was still bothering her.

"Spill it," Eve said. "It's all over your face."

"I'm just wondering how we're going to get any work done when we feel like we do about each other."

"Oh, I see. Well, that's an issue that's been on my mind too. How am I going to be able to control myself around Olivia? Hm. I've thought long and hard about it and, I gotta tell ya, I got nothing."

"Nothing?"

"Nope. Nada."

"Great."

"Now that I'm here with you, though, I've come to the realization that we should probably work out somewhere where there are a lot of people around."

"Like here," Olivia said. "That makes sense."

Eve grinned and picked at the grass. "Only, there aren't any people here at the moment."

Olivia grew quiet. Her cheeks tinged with color.

"People could come though at any moment," Olivia said, obviously trying to keep the building desire between them carefully reigned. But even as she said the words, she was staring at Eve's mouth like she was captivated.

Try as she might, Olivia couldn't hide what she wanted.

Not from Eve.

"I'm not thinking about people coming. I'm thinking about you coming."

The color in her cheeks deepened.

"I can't see that hunger in you right now, Eve. It'll make me want it again. It'll make me want you again. God, I already do." She rubbed her forehead.

Eve touched her chin and turned her face toward her own.

"What's wrong with that?"

She looked at Eve like she'd lost her mind.

"We're in a park. In the middle of a park!"

"There's no one around," she said. "Not anywhere. We're at the far edge of a small neighborhood. No houses are facing us. The street in front of us leads to a dead end so no one probably uses it. And we're under the dark shade of a tree. We won't be easy to see."

"Are you really trying to convince me to get it on with you in public?"

"We're allowed to kiss, Olivia. To make out. Even pet a little. You know that, right?"

"I'm just not exactly in a good frame of mind. My mother called today. You don't understand how she is."

"You can try and tell me," Eve said softly.

"She has this way of making me feel judged and ridiculed without having to say very much at all. She'll ask me how I am and what I've been up to, and I'll tell her, and instead of saying that's great or whatever, she just sits there in silence. And if I try to get her to say something, she gets critical and lets me know, in no uncertain terms, that she disapproves."

"And her disapproval bothers you."

Olivia didn't have to answer. Eve knew.

"I know she makes you feel like you're still under her control, but you're not. You're a grown woman. A woman who's not only kind and beautiful, but intelligent and insightful and caring. And if that alone doesn't make her happy as a mother, well, I'm not sure anything ever will."

"Thank you. That was—I've never heard anyone say something like that about me before."

"No need to thank me. Just please believe it. And as for your mother and pleasing her, it's probably a lost cause. And it's not something you need to try to do."

"I think I'm coming to realize that," she said. "I tried to tell her about school and how I just finished for the semester and how excited I am and what I'll be able to do with this degree. And, as usual, she got real quiet. Then she started up again about my divorce and how I was alone now, and I shouldn't take such risks like student loans when I didn't have a man to pay them off."

"Really?" Eve touched her shoulder. "She's that archaic in her thinking?"

"Oh, yes. A woman without a man, well, she's doomed, isn't she? My mother can't imagine a woman in a worse position. And a woman who actually chooses to be in such a position? Well, she's suspected to be something that usually isn't even whispered about."

"Yikes."

Olivia laughed. "Now *I'm* that woman. I've chosen to be alone without a man. And I know what she must be thinking and fearing. She's just not saying it aloud, probably too damn scared to do so. Afraid I might actually admit it."

"If she ever did bring your love life up…what would you do?"

"I don't know. A part of me is angry and resentful, but there's also that part of me that's still afraid."

"You mean of being gay?"

"Actually, I'm not really afraid to accept that about myself so much now. The time spent with you and the way I'm feeling, and of course, there's Friday night to consider. Don't think that wasn't a huge eye-opener. What I'm more afraid of is what my family will do if I declare I am. I'm afraid that they'll cast me out. I hate that I feel this way, but being cast out by my parents is scary to think about even though they drive me crazy."

"You love them. That's understandable."

"I love them even though I don't agree with their beliefs and often times their behavior. So why can't they love me the same? How can we love so differently?"

"I don't know." Eve touched her cheek, hurting for her and her obvious pain.

"I worry about my brother, Aaron, too. We're pretty close, but I don't know how he will feel about Molly knowing. Will he ask me to hide who I am or maybe bring her around less? Or not let me see her at all? If that happened, I'd be devastated. It would kill me. Without him and Molly I really would be alone in the world."

"Oh, Olivia," Eve said tenderly while delicately brushing away loose strands of hair from her face. "You're not ever going to be alone."

"You don't know that."

"I do. You're way too special. You will always have people wanting to be in your life. People who really care about you and love you for who you really are."

"I wish I could believe you."

"You'll get there," Eve said. "Things will eventually settle."

They stared into one another, and Eve ran her thumb over her bottom lip and felt her quiver. The reaction, just as all her previous ones had done, turned Eve on, despite the sadness she'd just seen in her seconds before.

"Eve, we can't," Olivia said. But the adamancy to her words had vanished.

"Oh, yes, love, we can. Just a little."

"I don't feel like what we're doing is wrong. I don't. Nothing with you ever feels wrong. But other people…"

"I know."

What she'd just told her about her mother and her parents in general, made it evident that she had a ways yet to go as far as freeing herself from caring about what people thought.

"But I'm here with you and I'm not afraid. I think that's one of the reasons you're drawn to me. The fact that I'm not afraid and I don't care what people think."

"You take risks I would never dream of taking. I don't know how you do it. I don't think I'll ever be able to."

"Oh, I don't know. Look how far you've come already."

"Being intimate with you doesn't count."

"It doesn't?"

"No. Because you're too persuasive and you know exactly what you're doing when you're touching me. And the way you look at me and the things you say. It isn't fair. Isn't fair at all. I don't stand a chance. I don't think I ever did."

"You shouldn't have told me any of that," Eve said, drawing closer. "Now I know that you can't tell me no. Oh, the power. Just think of all the things I can do with that."

"Yes, but not now. Not here." But her voice was weak and she visibly swallowed. "Eve, we can't."

"I'm not asking you to jump out of a plane with me, Olivia. I'm just asking for a kiss. Just a little kiss." Eve inched closer and held her face. She felt the burn of her skin. When Olivia didn't protest any further, she dipped in and kissed her. Olivia made a noise, but she remained still, her lips pressed together, unresponsive.

Eve backed away, the smell and feel of her skin quickly arousing her, despite her lack of a reaction. But she wanted Olivia to want it too. But she was just too nervous.

She looked serene, with her eyes still closed from the kiss, as if lost in her own wonderful world. Even though Eve wanted her more than she could ever express, she put her feelings above her own, something she didn't often do when it came to those she dated.

She knew it meant that she cared about her. More than she'd even been aware of. But the revelation didn't hit her as hard as she'd expected something like that to. But rather, it settled over her, like a warm blanket on a chilly evening. It was almost comforting, and it felt…right.

Olivia was doing more than moving her beyond what she thought even possible.

She was changing who she was.

And Eve didn't seem to mind.

CHAPTER TWENTY-SIX

Olivia squeezed the lemon slice into her iced tea and took a sip. It wasn't too bad with the lemon juice, but she was still getting used to drinking tea without the artificial sweetener. She took another drink and smiled as Aaron slid into the booth across from her.

"I can smell the soap," she said.

He raised his eyebrows as he drank his Coke. His forearms still glistened from where he'd just washed them in the restroom.

"Did you order yet?" he asked.

"Yes, and she assured me we would get our food quickly."

"Yeah, they're pretty good here. A lot of the guys come here for lunch. Meet their ladies." He grinned.

"What about you?" she asked.

"Me? Ah, hell no."

"Hell no?" She laughed.

"Women are the last thing on my mind right now."

"It's not like you have to go looking, Aaron. They usually come to you."

He shrugged.

"They still do, don't they? You've never had any trouble getting a date."

"Every now and then someone will show some interest. I'm just not interested in return. I'm tired of the dating game, I guess. Tired of the three- or four-week hot and heavy relationships that end when things get a little too real. It seems like everyone wants things exactly their way and when they don't get it, they aren't willing to compromise. They just bail." He stirred his Coke with his straw. "I want the real deal Holyfield here. I can't continue to have women coming in and out of my life with Molly. That's why I try to keep my dating away from her until I'm sure I know it's something stable."

"Which is why you leave her with me."

"Yes. But it's too much. Even though she doesn't know about them, it takes up too much of my time. I just don't think it's worth it anymore. I'm tired, Olivia."

"I'm sorry." She hated hearing that he was unhappy. It tore at her, just as it always did. "I know you want to give up, and I don't blame you, but I really think someone will come along who wants what you want. She'll be strong and she'll be crazy enough about you to want to stick around and compromise. Because she'll see you, and she'll know that you're worth it. Just like I do."

She played with her straw as her own words struck her. She was relaying what it was she wanted. She'd been thinking about it more and more, and she couldn't help but imagine Eve as being that person in her life.

"You look distraught," Aaron said. "You deserve someone like that too, you know. You deserve it more than anyone."

The waitress brought their food and she and Aaron both started in on their minestrone.

"So how have you been?" he asked. "Looks like you're still working out a lot. You're getting some serious guns."

She touched her bicep, which was quite noticeable in her short-sleeved shirt. She was, indeed, showing some definition. Eve absolutely loved it, and she wasn't shy about saying so or in showing her just how much it turned her on. It didn't seem to matter where they were, she'd get that look and Olivia would know what she was thinking, and she'd ready herself for a sneak attack. Eve would walk behind her, touching her quickly along her waist or ass and whisper something provocative in her ear. Then she'd move away, leaving Olivia melting on the spot in the middle of whatever store they were at. Last week it had been the farmer's market, where Eve had shown her how she shopped and what she ate. And then she'd done it again at the bookstore. Though her doing things like that in public still made her worry some, even though Eve was always quick and discreet, she couldn't help but react. Because, like it or not, Eve set her afire with her looks, her words, and her touch. It didn't matter if it was one or all of those things at once, Olivia was vulnerable regardless.

"You're gone again," he said. "Where are you?"

She refocused. "Sorry, I just have a lot on my mind."

"Care to share?"

She was quiet, unable to come up with anything quickly enough.

"You know you can talk to me, don't you?"

"Yes."

"Then why don't you?"

"I do."

"About Mom and Dad, yes. But not anything else. You didn't even talk to me about Kenny or you being unable to have a child. And I know that affected you. You were so sad and withdrawn."

"I didn't want to burden you with it." She spooned a bite and then changed her mind and returned the full spoon to the bowl.

"Well, you should've, Olivia. When I ask you questions about how you are, you should really tell me. You keep way too much in and it's not healthy."

"I don't understand what you want from me."

"I want to know how you are, Olivia. For *real*."

"Fine. You want to know? Right now, I'm happy and I'm conflicted. I'm the happiest I've ever been, but I'm conflicted about it."

"Why?"

"Because I don't know what I should do."

"What you should do? About what? Your happiness? Why can't you just enjoy it?"

She sighed and propped her elbow on the table to palm her forehead.

"Because it's not that simple. The situation is complicated. And the deeper into it I get, the happier I get, and that scares me because it's causing me to want more."

There it was. She'd said it aloud. She wanted it all. The whole thing. The white picket fence. She always had, even as a young girl. She was a romantic at heart, and a long-term loving relationship with someone special had always been her dream. So, wanting it now didn't surprise her. She just hadn't expected to want it with someone specific anytime soon. When she'd thought about love it was always in the future, after she'd finished school and settled in a new job and her new life. But in walked Eve, and now she was reeling with these quickly evolving feelings. It was like she was on the greatest roller coaster of her life and she was coming up too fast on the loops and hills that made it the ultimate ride. And there didn't seem to be any way to slow it down.

"You're seeing someone."

She looked up at him, startled. She thought she'd done a fairly good job at being vague.

"It's okay, I'm not going to push you for more. You obviously aren't ready to tell me or you would've already. I'm just glad you shared what you did. It's a start."

He continued to eat his soup. "Eat. You don't have to tell me any more about it. I'm backing off. For now." He winked at her and she laughed a little and took another bite. "How's the house? That faucet isn't still giving you trouble, is it?"

"No, everything is fine."

"You sure you're okay with furniture and stuff? You don't have very much."

"I'm okay. I kind of like not having a lot. It's simple and makes me appreciate what I have and what it is I really need."

"You're a minimalist," he said. "You always have been."

"Maybe."

"You don't have cable or Netflix. That in itself is highly unusual for this day and age."

"I know, it's tragic. People really freak out when I tell them that."

"That's because they can't figure out what it is you do with your time. They can't imagine their lives without those things."

"Yeah, well, it shouldn't bother them that I choose to live without that kind of stuff. And why do they care what I'm doing at all?"

"You know why. It's different, and some people still have a hard time accepting differences. Look at Mom and Dad."

"My God, sometimes people act like I'm living in the sixteenth century."

He laughed.

"I am a little surprised your neighbors haven't kidnapped you and taken you to the town square for stoning."

"Ha, if only the villagers knew what all I was really up to." She felt her face flush as she realized what she'd said. Aaron was studying her, and she continued to eat, hoping he hadn't noticed or read into anything.

"Molly doesn't seem to mind your lack of digital entertainment. I think she likes that you guys do other things."

"We still watch movies. We get them from the library, and she loves picking them out. She likes the older movies, too. She's pretty well rounded."

"Yes, she is. And I appreciate all the time you've spent with her. You're a wonderful aunt and a very big influence on her. She adores you."

"I love her like she's my own." She started to get choked up, so she sipped her tea to try to hide it. "I would die if I didn't ever get to see her."

"Why would something like that ever cross your mind?"

She closed her eyes, once again having said too much.

"I don't know. I'm just a little overwhelmed right now I think."

"You must be because that's one of the most ridiculous things I've ever heard you say."

"I seem to be blurting out all kinds of crazy things these days."

"I guess Molly gets it honest."

"Funny."

"Her birthday's coming up. She wants to have a small party at the house with some friends."

"That sounds like fun."

"Well, Mom and Dad are coming."

"Oh, right."

"Anyway, I thought you might want to bring your new...friend."

"What?" She pushed her bowl away, finished. "No. That won't be happening." She pinched the bridge of her nose and closed her eyes. "Oh, my good God," she said laughing to herself. "I can't even imagine."

"Why? Mom and Dad?"

"Just, it's not a good idea."

"Okay. But you are welcome to if you change your mind."

"Thanks."

"Can you tell me just one thing?" he asked. "Can you please tell me that they are nothing like Kenny?"

"Aaron, I can guarantee you that you have nothing to worry about in that regard. That is one thing you can be certain of."

Kenny doesn't even come close to comparing to Eve Monroe. He's not even in the same solar system.

And that was something she was very thankful for indeed.

CHAPTER TWENTY-SEVEN

Are you sure you want me to?" Eve asked her with an obvious sincerity to her voice.

Olivia didn't even have to think about it.

"Yes. I want to feel you inside of me."

They were in her room, and Eve's face was illuminated by the small lamp on the dresser. It was quiet, save for the hypnotic click from her ceiling fan. Olivia was sitting on the side of her bed with Eve standing before her, in a white deep V-neck tee and olive colored shorts. Her hair was clinging to the damp skin of her neck and in some places along the sides of her face. Her lipstick had long ago worn off, and Olivia could see a small dark mark in the crook of her neck, and she knew it was from her. Eve was doing things to her now that caused her to act like some kind of ravenous creature. Like giving to her until she was just about to explode in climax and then easing off at the very last second, forcing her to wait. She was being driven to the brink of sanity and often left covered in sweat and panting with exhaustion, but still so frantic with need she couldn't stop.

"Only—I want you to take off your clothes. I want to see you. All of you."

They'd been making love for over an hour, beginning on the couch which had soon led to the floor. Then they'd hurried to her bedroom.

Eve started to move, but Olivia stopped her.

It had been weeks since they'd first made love, and in all that time, Eve had been the one in the lead, insisting only on pleasing Olivia. She hadn't ever completely undressed, and she'd only allowed

Olivia to touch her some, but not in her intimate places. Eve didn't want her to feel any pressure when it came to reciprocating. And at first, that had been fine. Olivia had been way too caught up in new discoveries and overwhelming, relentless orgasms to give it much thought. But lately, she'd not only been thinking about touching and exploring Eve, she was even having dreams about it.

"Please," Olivia said. She gathered the bottom of Eve's shirt in her hands and carefully lifted it off over her head. Then Olivia helped her with her shorts. Eve stood silently in a matching white lace bra and panties. "You're just—so—Eve, you're so beautiful. No," she said, correcting herself. "Beautiful doesn't even come close. You're absolutely stunning and you're fucking flawless. And, dear God, help me, sexy as hell."

"Come closer," she demanded, pulling on her hips. She ran her fingers up her abdomen to her ribcage and to the back of her bra. She unhooked it and slowly eased the bra from her breasts and body. She tossed it aside, totally captivated by the creamy, round fullness of her breasts. She'd never seen a naked woman in the flesh before. And even if she had, she knew no woman would've been comparable to Eve. She was carved from marble by a master artisan.

"I've never seen anything like you," Olivia said, barely able to speak. "Not even in books." She was on fire and so turned on her body shook as she exhaled. What she felt was an urge and a desire, yes. But what she wanted now was to be the one doing the touching. She wanted to touch her so badly, her clitoris twitched, as if it, too, was desperate to reach out and stroke her.

"I want to feel you and see you with my hands. I want to do that until I know you so well I'd be able to sculpt you blindfolded if someone asked me to."

She glanced up at her and saw that Eve, too, was flushed and breathing hard. "Can I?" she asked. "Touch you?"

"Yes."

Olivia's mouth watered as she skimmed the back of her fingers up Eve's abdomen and then up over her breasts, causing the cores to bunch and pucker. Olivia shuddered along with Eve at the sight and feel of her gathered pink skin. She did it again and again, loving how the firm buds of her nipples moved against her fingers.

"Eve." She was so excited she was tempted to rub herself against the edge of the bed.

The feel of her overcame Olivia, and she quickly turned her and pushed her back onto the bed, holding her arms above her head. She forced her legs open with the press of her thigh, and she could feel the moist heat of her through her panties. It sent her into an involuntary frenzy, and she couldn't wait any longer. She had to get to her. To where all that was Eve came together in a nucleus of nerves, where her most deeply rooted needs and desires could be awakened, accessed, and experienced. She had to get the very heart of Eve.

She lay on her side next to her and held her wrists together with one hand and lowered her other down her torso to her panties. She rubbed her mound up and down through the lace, and her eyes narrowed as she felt the meaty pulp of her for the first time against her fingers. Eve stirred beneath her and made a noise of sweet desperation, like she was helpless with longing.

Olivia came to the top of her panties and dipped her hand inside.

She gasped and Eve called out as she slid into her hot, wet flesh.

"Oh, God help me," Olivia said, closing her eyes. "You feel so fucking good."

She was going to pass out, she knew it.

"So, fucking good," she said again, struggling to speak.

Eve writhed and made small noises.

Olivia responded with her own barely audible noises.

She kept her eyes closed, her focus intent and heavily concentrated on Eve's pleasure. She touched her delicately at first, light caresses and teasing skims, causing a steady progression to Eve's movements and cries. At some point Eve moved and Olivia opened her eyes as she freed herself and tried to grip Olivia's wrist. But Olivia resisted and quickly pushed her desperate hand away. Eve lifted her head and silently beckoned her to give more. But Olivia held back, choosing instead to increase her pleasure in another area. She slid down to suck on her breast. Eve hissed and dug her fingers into Olivia's hair, massaging and encouraging. Her pleas were strained and wordless. Olivia circled the bunching around her erect nipple with her tongue and then re-centered to lick and flick her nub. Then she took it all into her mouth and sucked, making Eve shout and knead her scalp. She released her and refastened to do the same to her other breast, all while she continued to carefully arouse her with her hand. And she did so until Eve, panting with excitement, pulled on Olivia's head, insisting she look at her. She didn't say anything, just swallowed and tried to catch her breath. But her gaze was heavy and brimming with an unmistakable yearning.

"Say it," Olivia said. "I need to hear you say it."

Olivia started moving her hand again, trying to tease the words out of her.

Eve pressed her lips together.

"Mm. Olivia."

Eve touched her face and her hand drifted down to her neck and then back into the nape where she reattached to her by clutching her hair. She tightened her grip and tugged, pulling Olivia back and holding her firmer than before.

The move was adamant and dominating.

A demand.

And it got Olivia so hot she almost gave in.

"Say it," she said again.

"Touch me," Eve finally said.

"Tell me more, Eve. Tell me how. Tell me what you want."

Eve tugged on her again. "Harder."

"Like this?" Olivia increased her pressure.

"Yes," Eve said, lifting her head. "Ah, fuck, yes. But harder. Harder, baby. Please."

Overcome by her passionate request, Olivia kissed her and held her bottom lip captive as she slid into her flesh fully, gliding her fingers along her folds. Eve cried out and tried to move, but Olivia held her prisoner, biting softly into her lip, knowing that she couldn't move, *loving* that she couldn't move as she pleased her. When she finally did release her, Eve gasped and forced her into a searing kiss with the powerful hold she still had on her hair. Her tongue met Olivia's and she moaned, her gratification apparent. Olivia dove into her mouth continuously as she played with her, quickly learning what she liked by her audible responses and the short kick of her hips. Eve seemed to love it when she paused to coat her fingers in her slickness and then began again, gliding knowingly throughout her contours. She seemed to love it even more when Olivia began focusing more on her clitoris, slipping and sliding across the exposed bulb, causing sudden quakes to rush through her. And soon their kisses began to mirror the intensity of her pleasure, slowing when it was tolerable and then becoming heavy and immediate when it was extreme. Olivia was equally as affected, especially when they were at the extreme, and she found herself taking claim of her pleasure by plunging into both her mouth and sex with unrelenting aggression, until they were both about to climb the ceiling.

"Tell me when you're close," Olivia said, finally having no choice but to pull away so they could catch their breath. Her hand, however, kept giving.

"I'm close. So close—but—"

She tried to clench her eyes as another obvious surge of heat bolted through her, but Olivia wouldn't let her.

"Uh-uh-uh." She stilled her hand until Eve forced her eyes back open. "That's it. Look at me. I want you to look at me."

She started in again and Eve squirmed and writhed, but she made Olivia stop by gripping her wrist. Olivia looked at her in confusion.

"Let me go inside you," she said. "Let me fuck you while you touch me."

She let go of her and Olivia shifted, rising to her knees.

Eve grazed her hand up Olivia's thigh and sank into her core, into her excitement. They both groaned, and in a blink of an eye, Eve slid up into her, filling her and fucking her with fingers that felt like searing shafts made solely just to satisfy her. She looked down, almost uncertain that what she was feeling were Eve's fingers alone. But all she saw was her arm, moving and fucking with a hand that disappeared between her legs.

How could it feel so good? How could fingers alone be doing this to her when intercourse with a man had not? But the thought was lost as Eve quickened the thrust of both her hand and her hips.

"Does it feel good?" Eve panted.

"God, yes."

Eve did something inside her then. Moved her fingers somehow, pressing them against her in a fiery new place and then rubbing them up and down, fucking her again. Olivia nearly screamed and she held onto Eve's arm, suddenly needing support.

"How 'bout now?" She kept driving into her, rubbing that same fucking spot.

"Yes."

"Yeah?"

"Mm-hm, yes. Fuck, yes." She saw the blatant desire in Eve's face and the slight sway of her breasts. Seeing Eve's incomparable nude form, the look on her face and the way her arm was moving as she fucked Olivia, were all strong enough to send Olivia over into ecstasy. But it was the added pleasure of being able to feel her wet, heated lusciousness beneath her hand as she got her off that totally and completely launched Olivia into orbit.

"I'm going to come," Olivia said with astonishment. "It's happening. It's happening so fast."

"Sweet Olivia," Eve said. "Come, love. Come with me."

The words penetrated resolutely, just like her fingers.

"Oh, God. Yes, I am. I am, Eve. I'm coming. For you. With you. Oh, God—I'm coming."

Eve fucked her harder and stared directly into her eyes just before her face and entire body shattered. Olivia crashed into convulsions herself and they came together in a wild fit of fucking and rubbing and insatiable gyrations. Olivia let out a series of low screams, her climax hitting her incredibly hard and deep, raging through her with a vengeance, while Eve called out in softer, though no less powerful, quicker cries. Olivia watched as best she could, the sight of her coming making her own orgasm all the more tremendous. She watched her like a voyeur, captivated and spellbound as Eve pulsed in unison with her cries as the swells of her orgasm passed through her. Her ride of pleasure lasted longer than Olivia's, which enabled Olivia to take her in as she finished, her focus completely on Eve. And though she didn't speak or make noise when she calmed, Olivia knew how vehement her orgasm had been. She'd witnessed it firsthand and now that she had, she knew two things for certain. She knew she would never ever forget it and she knew she would want to see it again. That she would no doubt obsess over seeing it again.

She studied her in the continued silence, still completely awed by her. Sweat glistened on her face and chest, covering the red tint of desire kissing her skin. Her mauve lips were thick and full, as if engorged with blood and begging to be sucked, much like Olivia knew the flesh between her legs to be. And her hazel eyes were deep and darker than usual as they danced in the low light, as if hidden depths had been stirred to life.

What Olivia had seen moments before was Eve in the throes of passion.

This, however, was Eve in the afterglow.

And Olivia couldn't decide which was more beautiful and compelling.

"Eve," Olivia said quietly.

"Yes?" She gently removed her fingers from Olivia and pulled her down to lie next to her. Olivia then carefully moved her hand, which was still nestled between her legs, up Eve's body to rest on her heart.

Olivia warmed as she felt the soothing thud of her life force.

Everything she'd ever known to be true was vanishing.

In its place was this. This moment.

This woman.

And this expanding and singing in her own heart.

She drew her closer and nuzzled her neck.

She inhaled her scent and closed her eyes.

And she said the only thing she knew to be absolutely true.

"I love you."

CHAPTER TWENTY-EIGHT

Eve opened her eyes and listened intently. She was spooning Olivia who was fast asleep in her arms, breathing softly. They were nude with Olivia's backside against her front. Her soft skin was hot, like it was still on fire with their lovemaking.

She kissed her shoulder and released her to roll onto her back. She lay spread eagle under the fan, begging for its cool caress. She lightly ran her fingertips across her nipples, causing them to firm. The touch reawakened the passion she'd felt with Olivia, and she lowered her hand between her legs and sank into her creases. She inhaled, stunned at how warm and wet she still was considering she'd even climaxed with Olivia this time.

How can I still be so turned on?

She was like a live wire, twisting and writhing and sparking, seeking some sort of connection. She longed for that connection to be Olivia, but she didn't want to entirely overwhelm her with her insanely raging libido. Climaxing with her tonight had been a wonderfully erotic and beautiful first step. But it had also been momentous. Not just because it had been so all consuming and completely conquering that she'd had to nearly clench her jaw, along with every muscle in her body, to keep from screaming and thrashing. But because it had obviously been just as astounding and meaningful to Olivia, leading her to confess her love.

Eve could still recall the way she'd sounded when she said the words.

She'd been serious. The confession heartfelt.

And Eve's heart had been pierced. As if Cupid's arrow had torn right through her. She could still feel the hot blood from the wound spreading throughout her body.

She closed her eyes and moaned softly as her fingers got lost in her flesh. Hunger collided with something different as she slid along her swollen shaft. It was beyond lust, beyond want, beyond need. It was deeper. Stronger. And unexpected.

I love you.

It was Olivia and her words.

Olivia and her love.

"Oh, God," Eve whispered. She lengthened her strokes and held her clit firmly between her gliding fingers. She'd touched herself after making love to Eve, many times now. But this current desire was turbulent and more demanding, as if her earlier climax had been nothing but a tease. A test to see how her body reacted to Olivia's touch. Now her body seemed to know, and it was insisting on being fed to full satiation and at the hands of Olivia. But Eve didn't want to wake her, and again a part of her still worried that these cravings would be too much. And then there was the love confession. God, those three little words had such power and they had infiltrated her with an indescribable warmth and acceptance, and she'd had an urge to say something in response, but she'd stopped herself, afraid she'd get carried away and move beyond the boundaries she'd set for her life so long ago.

She pushed her concern away and quickened her hand, allowing it to take her away to a beautiful oblivion. But even though what she was doing felt wonderful, and had begun to grow, the pleasure wouldn't edge beyond a certain point. She groaned, both in longing and frustration.

"Hey." Olivia stirred next to her and turned. Her voice was heavy with sleep and deeply sexy. She felt for Eve in the dim light and Eve froze. Olivia found her arm and traced it downward.

"Are you—touching yourself?"

"Hm? Uh, yes."

"Why?"

"Why?" She panicked. Was she upset? Would she be upset?

"Yeah, why would you do that when I'm right here and dying to do it for you?" She sounded husky and intrigued, and her hand grazed over the top of Eve's. She splayed her fingers between Eve's so she could feel her through the gaps. She wasn't upset. Not at all. She was aroused.

"Olivia, you don't have to—"

"Let's do it together," she said. "Show me how you touch yourself."

"Olivia, you—"

But Olivia silenced her by dipping her head to take her nipple into her mouth.

"Oh, my God." Eve arched into her, unable to help herself.

Olivia sucked her, gentle at first and then harder.

"Olivia—Jesus."

"Mm." She released her. "You like that? Was it too much?"

"No. Yes. I mean, I liked it." Why did she sound so flustered? How did this woman have such an effect on her?

Olivia bent again and kissed both breasts like she'd done before, swirling and teasing and then taking and pulling. Eve squirmed and ran her fingers through her hair. Her hips began to move on their accord as the invisible string leading from her nipples to her clit ignited and surged, forcing the electricity to flow between the two.

"You want more?" Olivia asked, breathing against her neck.

"Mm."

She moved her hand and sighed when Eve responded to the feel of her touch gliding along the winks of her flesh.

Too turned on to resist, Eve pulled her hand out from underneath Olivia's leaving Olivia's directly on her.

"I thought we were going to do it together," she said into her ear.

"I want you to do it," Eve said. "It feels so much better and I would love a repeat of what you did to me earlier."

"You liked it."

"Oh, hell, yes, you know I did."

Olivia responded by urging her hand even lower.

"Yes, get yourself wet and slick with me," Eve said, so eager to come again she could hardly get the words out.

Olivia did so with a throaty groan, like she'd just discovered her and was fascinated. Then she slid her hand back up to her cleft.

"Keep talking," she said. "Tell me exactly what to do."

"It's turning you on?"

"You wouldn't believe how much." She knelt and licked her nipple.

"Oh, believe me I do. It's getting to me, too. Ah, fuck."

"What would you like me to do now?"

"Move your hand all around. Saturate me with my juices." She jerked as Olivia did what she was told. "That's it. Yes. Slip and slide all over me."

Eve arched, her neck strained. "Oh, Jesus."

"You feel so fucking incredible," Olivia breathed. "Like silk. Like hot, slick silk. How can touching someone else make me feel this good?"

Eve relaxed fully onto the bed again and clenched the bedsheet with one hand and began to massage Olivia's scalp with the other.

"Because we're women," she said. "We get off in giving pleasure almost as much as we do in getting pleasure."

"Oh, my God. You're right," she said. "Because I swear, right now, I'm so excited, I think I could come without you even touching me."

"Make me come and you'll feel so good and come so close to climaxing it'll blow your mind."

Olivia closed her eyes like she was deeply moved.

"Do you have any idea what those words just did to me?"

Eve laughed. "Yes I do. Your words have been doing the same to me for weeks now. You've been making love to me with your words and you never even realized it."

"Oh, I realized it. Maybe not at first, when I was just reacting to what I felt. But very soon thereafter, when I saw the flicker of desire in your eyes and the quickening of your breath and the way you sometimes bite your lower lip, like you're trying to control yourself, I knew. I was then very much aware of what I was doing and what I was saying. And I meant every damn word, wanting, more than anything, for each one to reach out and touch you somehow. I wanted to make you feel the way I do when you so much as look at me."

"You did. I don't think I can explain how much you affected me. And—ah—right now, you're doing a pretty damn good job, too."

Olivia changed the movement of her hand. She began to go in circles, directly pressing on her clit.

Eve stiffened and made a noise of helplessness.

"I want to do so much better than good, Eve. I want a fucking A-plus."

"Dear—God—you've turned into such a bad girl."

Olivia only laughed and quickened her hand as she took her bunched nipple into her mouth and sucked.

Eve cried out and urged her hips into her hand and watched in erotic bliss as Olivia sucked her hungrily, first one breast and then the other, until Eve was clawing at her scalp and thrusting up into her hand.

"Olivia." She kept exhaling her name. Again and again.

"Fuck. Oh, God. Oh, my fucking God." She was trying desperately to hold back, to control the raging inferno inside. The raging inferno this woman, this virginal woman had somehow set aflame and was somehow feeding those flames far better than any other woman ever had.

How did she seem to know what she was doing?

Why did the two of them together erupt and enflame like gasoline poured on a fire?

"Fu-ck!" Eve cried out.

She bucked harder and faster, all the while staring into Olivia.

And then she came. And it was so astounding and so deep, dark, and hot, she danced wickedly into Olivia's stroking hand and cried out in a low, throaty voice, "Oh—hell—ye-es."

She rode it out long and hard, enjoying, taking, and milking every last fucking drop. It was so delicious and lasted so long, she laughed at the craziness of it with her back and neck arched, lost in the spinning blades of the ceiling fan. She heard Olivia imploring her, talking dirty, naughty, all while she continued to massage the sweet bliss into her flesh.

Olivia.

She was so fucking beyond belief.

Olivia.

Eve calmed, jerked twice, and then went completely still. She eased her back onto the bed once more and looked at her.

Olivia didn't have to say it. She didn't have to voice it. She'd just shown her with her mouth and with her hand.

And she was showing her now with that look.

She was telling Eve that she loved her.

Eve yanked her forward and enveloped her into an impassioned, meeting of the souls kind of kiss.

When Olivia groaned, Eve held her tighter and continued, harder and deeper, needing more, more, more. And when she moaned with what sounded like mercy, Eve wrenched her away and looked into her once again, breathlessly.

Olivia.

Dear, sweet, fucking insanely insatiable Olivia.

She affects me like no other ever has.

And...she loves me.

What the fuck am I going to do?

CHAPTER TWENTY-NINE

Auntie Liv!" Molly said just as Olivia stepped inside the front door.

"Hey, you!" Olivia gave her a big, one-armed squeeze. "Happy birthday!" She produced the sizable gift she had perched against her hip.

Molly took it eagerly and wrapped her arm around Olivia's waist. "Thank God you're here. They're insane and it's so embarrassing."

"Oh, no, already?"

"Yeah. And a lot of my friends aren't even here yet." Molly placed her gift next to a few others on the old pool table, the one Aaron had insisted on keeping when their grandfather passed away. Olivia could still remember how he'd taught them to play when they were barely tall enough to see over the top.

Aaron appeared at the entryway to the kitchen. He leaned against the wall and eased his hands into the pockets of his black Dickies shorts. A Fox Racing T-shirt and low-rise black Chucks completed his ensemble. She could smell his aftershave and feel just a hint of stubble as they embraced.

"Thank God you're here," he said as well, causing her to laugh.

His trademark loose strand of gelled hair fell onto his brow. He looked exhausted.

"Ma and Pa already making themselves known?"

"Do you even have to ask?"

"So are the Dudleys and the Grahams," Molly said, her disdain more than evident. "I thought this was supposed to be my birthday party, not theirs."

"But you have friends coming, right, hon?" Olivia asked, stroking her hair. The Dudleys and the Grahams were long time friends of her folks, and they'd been to many family celebrations throughout the years. She wasn't totally surprised they were there. But she felt bad for Molly.

"Only two are here so far," Molly said. "And Mr. Dudley keeps telling them to put away their phones."

Molly was obviously upset, and seeing her that way never failed to tug at Olivia's heartstrings.

"I'll try and keep the adults occupied, okay?"

"Thanks, Auntie Liv." She squeezed Olivia tight and took off through the kitchen to the living room and hurried out the back door.

"Auntie Liv to the rescue," Aaron said with a grin. "Again."

"Why haven't you done anything?" Olivia asked. She and Aaron had become a team, especially lately, unified in their mission to protect Molly from the rigidity of their parents.

"You think I haven't tried? All they want to talk about is how kids today are lost and corrupt and completely morally bankrupt. And how technology is the gateway to hell itself. If I even go near them, they hone in on me asking me what I plan on doing about Molly and her quote unquote obsession with her phone. As if she is, along with the phone, the devil. It's taking all I have not to light into them all."

Olivia rolled her eyes.

"I guess we deserve it though," he said. "After all, we *are* lost, corrupt, and morally bankrupt." He chuckled but Olivia didn't find it funny. She knew damn well that's exactly what her parents, especially her mother, had been thinking about her since she'd left Kenny. And they'd probably have it tattooed on her skin if they knew about her heated affair with Eve.

A sense of anxiousness overcame her as she thought about Eve. She still couldn't believe she'd told her she loved her. But she just hadn't been able to help herself. She'd been so caught up in the moment and in Eve herself, doing so had just felt right. But still, even though she really felt like she was hopelessly in love with Eve, she wished she'd kept that tucked away inside. She already felt exposed and raw enough with their intense lovemaking and sensual connections, she didn't need the added vulnerability that her admission of love added. Because even though she felt it, and she meant it, falling like she was for another human being was as brand new to her as the wildly passionate sex. She hadn't been in love with Kenny nor had she, even in her fantasies about love, ever imagined she could ever feel so deeply and so completely out of control for someone. And that was fast becoming the front and center of her concerns, on its way to surpassing the whole gay thing. Admitting she was a lesbian was one thing, a huge thing, but being able to trust someone with her heart? She hadn't even given hers to Kenny and he'd still managed to stomp all over it and crush her insides. Who's to say what would happen if she actually, truly, let someone in?

And then there was Eve and her lack of response, her face giving away just a tiny sliver of fear before she recovered. What did that mean? And what did her continued silence and newly growing distance mean?

Olivia wasn't sure she wanted to know.

Aaron's brow furrowed in obvious worry. "Hey, what is it?"

"Huh?"

Everything.

God, Aaron let's just go. Let's just go into the backyard and dig all the way to China like we used to try to do in our sandbox as kids, desperate to escape. Maybe we can really do it now. Maybe we can finally get away from all this…madness.

But she only shook her head. "Nothing."

She crossed into the living room, needing to face the storm head-on, before she chickened out and actually ran out into the garage to search for a shovel to dig with. Like it or not, she was going to stick around. She owed it to Molly, and she'd promised to distract the party poopers. This was Molly's day after all. It wasn't supposed to be about anyone else. But as she came upon the old familiar faces of her childhood, those old familiar feelings of anxiousness and dread began to wash over her.

Well, not today. Today she was going to try something new. Why? She really wasn't sure. She didn't have any plans beyond the next few seconds. She just felt…different.

"Hello, everyone." Her voice sounded weaker than she'd expected, and she chided herself. She thought of her long talks with Eve about taking back her power with strength and courage, and she realized that maybe that was what was fueling this new fire. As things stood, however, she knew it was going to be easier said than done. Just being in their presence alone was proving nerve-racking.

Her mother rose but didn't smile.

"Olivia," she said, offering her cheek for a quick kiss.

"Hello, Mom." Olivia kissed her and noted that she looked relatively the same, with her long, graying hair worn in a tight bun, which always accentuated the classic features of her face. She never chose to highlight her beauty, though, and today was no exception. She wore very little makeup that Olivia could see.

Femininity, according to her mother, should be delicate and more of an undertone. No woman should ever overdo with makeup or fashion. And she was apparently continuing to stand by that belief today, in an unremarkable long denim dress and jewelry that was simple and sparse, consisting of a tiny gold pair of earrings and a matching necklace with a cross. The whole ensemble was simple and sparse, yet it made Olivia feel overheated and stifled. She was glad to put her attention on her father, who now stood alongside her mother.

"Hello, Dad." He gave her a small smile as she went to her tiptoes to kiss his cheek. He wore his all-gray hair slicked back away from his face, just like Aaron. His jaw, however, lacked the spicy scent of aftershave despite being baby smooth from a fresh shave.

"Hello, dear," he said, resting his hands on her hips. She'd always been closer to him than her mother. Even more so now, as an adult. He just seemed more relaxed than her mother and oftentimes, even happy.

"How's Mexico?" She smoothed the shoulders of his light blue button-down shirt, even though it appeared to be sharply pressed, along with his khaki Dockers.

"Hot," he said.

"Hotter than here?"

"Where we just were? Yes. Jungle heat is different," he said. "You wouldn't believe it." His blue eyes twinkled. "You really should go, sometime," he said softly. "Chichen Itza is a sight to behold. Your mother didn't exactly love it, but I know you would."

Olivia smiled, moved by his comment. As a kid she'd loved history and ancient civilizations, but her parents had never encouraged her interest. They'd always been reticent for her and Aaron to learn about other cultures who didn't share their beliefs. She would've never guessed that he would want to visit a place like Chichen Itza. There was obviously more to him than she had ever been aware of. Why hadn't they ever shared these things?

Her father sat, saying nothing more. Her mother, whose eyes matched Olivia's, were deep and searching, just as they often were with Olivia lately. She was obviously sizing her up, trying to seek out truths that Olivia had yet to share or maybe was even completely unaware of. It made Olivia uneasy, more so than usual, and irritated. So, she bent and quickly embraced the Dudleys and the Grahams, hoping to distract herself from those feelings.

"You're looking very well, Olivia," Mrs. Graham said. "Fit as a fiddle. And you even have a little color to you. What are you doing differently?" She was perched perfectly upright, with her hands resting on her thighs. She, like her mother and Mrs. Dudley, wore a long dress.

"I'm working out," Olivia said. "Spending a lot of time outdoors." It was nice of Martha to notice and nicer still that she'd said so with such kind words. Olivia wished, to this day, that her mother could be more like Martha.

"I guess so," Martha said. "From the looks of you, you must be exercising quite a bit."

"Five days a week. And sometimes, on an off day, I still go for a long walk."

Mr. Graham whistled. "That's dedication."

"Are you lifting weights?" Mr. Dudley asked. His interest seemed genuine and she recalled he used to lift years ago. Though no longer as bulky or cut, much of his brawn still remained.

"I am."

Her mother fingered her throat as if she were rattled. "I hope not too much." She looked away suddenly as if Olivia's appearance were something offensive.

Olivia felt her stomach clench, not just with fear and uneasiness like usual, but with anger and resentment at being judged and criticized. They were relatively new feelings, and she'd only ever experienced them while away from her mother, like while on the phone with her or in talking things over with Eve. But never while face to face.

She opened and closed her fists as these emotions rose up through her with the old familiar fear trying to hold them back. It was a battle. An all-out war going on inside her. How she wasn't mirroring the chaos inside by ranting and raving and throwing furniture around like a mad woman, she did not know.

"What's that supposed to mean?" Her voice, though whisper quiet, was laced with venom.

Her mother did a double take, obviously shocked by her confrontation.

Aaron, who was suddenly beside her, stepped in. "Olivia's working with a personal trainer," he said. "She's working hard and doing everything she says."

Olivia almost laughed at his oblivious attempt to smooth things over.

"Oh, I am," she said, staring into her mother. "I'm doing *everything* she says, everything she asks of me."

Like coming for her.

Again and again.

In her mouth.

Aaron laughed nervously and squeezed her tight, almost as if he somehow knew.

If only they did know.

They'd die a thousand deaths.

Mr. Graham stood and eased up the sleeve to her snug fitting T-shirt. "My, my, my. Look at that bicep. Very impressive."

Her mother looked away again, obviously disliking what she'd seen.

"Aren't you impressed too, Mom? I'm pretty strong now." Her mother flat-out refused to look at her. Olivia hated that she still yearned so badly for her mother's approval. Would this craziness ever end? "Why can't you just tell me you're proud of me?" Not just for her current state of fitness or her success in school, but for everything, for anything. She'd settle for one thing. Just one.

Aaron laughed again and forced a smile at everyone before he refocused on her.

"How about a drink, sis? You look thirsty. I bet you're thirsty."

She didn't answer right away. Just stood staring at her emotionally absent mother.

"Sure, bro. I'm whatever you say I am." She tore her gaze from her mother to smile back at Aaron and they headed back into the kitchen, leaving her mother, speechless and staring after her.

Chapter Thirty

W hat the fucking fuck are you doing?" Aaron whispered as he and Olivia stood before the fridge. He obviously was worried their parents and friends would overhear them from the other room, but she realized she honestly couldn't care less.

She laughed, glad her anger and hurt were suddenly giving way to apathy and sarcasm.

"I don't think I've ever heard you cuss quite like that, bro. You sound almost as bad as I do now."

He grabbed her shoulders. "What's come over you? Are you drunk?"

"No."

"High?"

She sighed. "No."

"Don't tell me you've just suddenly lost your mind."

"Apparently, that's exactly what's happened."

"Oh, no." He rubbed his forehead. "Not today, Olivia. Not at Molly's party. Can't you wait to have a high noon showdown with Mom another time? I promise there will be ample opportunity."

"I'm just so sick to death of her snotty self-righteousness. She was about to criticize my body in there, Aaron. After all the hard work I've put in, she was about to cut me down and tell me I'm too big and too muscular and too masculine. Just like she's always done. Do you know what constantly hearing that has done to me over the years? Do you know how much shame I've felt about my own body? How uncomfortable I've been in my own skin? All because I don't fit her definition of perfection? Well, fuck that, Aaron. Fuck it. And fuck her."

"Shh!" His eyes grew so big she thought they might literally pop out of his skull.

She swatted his hands away from her shoulders and pulled open the fridge. "And it's not even just about that. It's about everything. I can't ever seem to do anything right. But don't worry, I'm not going to say anything. Not today." Maybe not ever. Who knew? She obviously wasn't ready to even calmly confront her on her judgments about her body, much less anything else.

Would she ever be able to totally and completely put her foot down?

She cracked open a can of Diet Coke and slurped, hoping for its black tar heroin to vein effect, despite not having had one in forever, following Eve's advice. But she scowled when she found the flavor to be offensive and the carbonation way too overpowering, like it was eating away at her throat. She dumped it in the sink and searched for a glass instead. She filled it with ice and water and opened the fridge again.

"Then will you please take it down a notch?" Aaron said. "This tough girl attitude even has my butt puckering. I'm worried the ass that's going to get kicked in this whole thing will somehow end up being mine."

She cracked up.

"I'm serious, Olivia. I've even had the benefit of being around to witness this evolution of yours and I'm still scared to death of the way you looked at Mom in there. In fact, right now, I'm ready to run for the hills and leave everyone else to fend for themselves."

"Even Molly?" She closed the produce drawers and shoved containers of milk and orange juice and soda aside, growing frustrated.

"Molly? Oh, you mean my daughter? Oh, wait, you mean your little clone? She's been just like you are now even before you were! That girl can definitely hold her own. I don't have to worry about her at all in this case."

"I am kind of proud, now that you mention it. Actually, more than proud."

"You should be. She doesn't just love you. She idolizes you now. She refers to your changing as the Evolution of Olivia."

Olivia warmed. "Does she really?"

"Yes." He bumped his way in. "Now, what the hell are you looking for?"

"Lemon."

"Lemon?"

"For my water."

"You have to have lemon for your water now?"

"It would be nice."

He cussed again and dug in the back of the top shelf and handed her a green plastic bottle with a yellow lid. "As good as it gets."

"Lemon juice? How old is this?"

He shrugged and closed the door. "Beats me."

She struggled with the lid but finally got it open. After she added some to her water, she walked to the back door and slipped outside, wanting to check in on Molly and her friends. The three girls fell silent when they saw her, but Molly perked up.

"It's okay. It's just Auntie Liv. She's cool."

Olivia smiled and shook their hands. "Hi. Cool, here. Nice to meet you."

They laughed.

"This is Carla and Sam. They're in my dance class."

"Oh, of course. I thought I recognized you. When's your next recital?" She loved watching Molly dance and often wished that she, too, was just as coordinated. Molly had even tried to show her a few moves over the years, but it had always been disastrous, ending with her and Molly on the floor laughing hysterically.

"This fall," Molly said. "Only, Auntie Liv, we're taking hip-hop this time, so it's going to be awesome."

"No kidding? Think I might be able to pull off a couple of those moves?"

"Um, no." Molly laughed. "I think it's safer for everyone if you just hang up your towel with the dancing, Auntie Liv."

"Is she that bad?" one of the girls asked.

"Scary bad," Molly said.

"I'd argue, but it's true," Olivia said. "Aren't you guys hot out here?"

They shrugged.

"Come on. Come inside. You can hang in the front room. I promise I'll keep an eye out for the troglodytes."

Molly laughed. "The what?"

"Cave dwellers. Never mind. Come on, come in where it's cool. It's your damn party. You shouldn't have to hide out here in the heat like you've done something wrong."

The girls followed her inside and Molly smiled at her with obvious appreciation. Olivia winked at her and the adults were now the ones who fell silent as they entered.

"These young ladies are going to hang out in the front room where there will be gossip, girl talk, and excessive cellular phone use. That means no sticks in the mud allowed. Especially you, Mr. Dudley."

He looked offended and then embarrassed.

The girls hurried to the front room while she sipped her water in the kitchen. Aaron stood next to her, still rubbing his forehead, something they'd both always done when they were nervous, even as kids.

"You know, if you keep doing that, you're eventually going to hit your gray matter. And doing so will no doubt send you into shock and awe, seeing as how you've always been so convinced that you have no brain to begin with. Another one of Mom's finest achievements."

She had been too big and muscular, and Aaron had been too hyper and intellectually underachieving.

"Right now, I really wish I didn't have one," he said. "Because the one I do have is bombarded with worry and a growing sense of impending doom."

"You've got to stop doing that, Aaron. You aren't responsible for keeping the peace. It's not your job and it never should've been."

"If I didn't, and if I don't, well, then we just may not have a family, Olivia."

"Then we may not, Aaron. And if that were the case, it would in no way be your fault."

"You don't understand."

"I do, actually. More than you know. But I also know that this is something you're going to have to face and deal with on your own. Letting go of what's been engraved into us all our lives is far from easy. It's scary. I know you know that because you have let go of some things. And you've been all the better for it. But there's more to be done. For the both of us. I just hope we can someday find the courage to do it."

She sipped more of her water and was about to turn to join the girls in the front room when Aaron spoke.

"Wait." He leaned back against the counter. "When are you going to tell me what's really going on with you? I know something is. And it's more than just your seeing someone, or the working out and personal trainer thing."

She thought of Eve and that familiar rush of desire and giddiness ran through her. But soon came the anxiousness of her confessed love, along with the regret and disappointment from her continued inability to confront her parents. Why did everything always have to be so complicated? Why couldn't she and Eve just relish and enjoy each other on a private plane of existence somewhere? Without all the added bullshit of ever-changing emotion and other people and life in general?

"When I'm ready to share it and you're ready to hear it," she finally said.

"What makes you think I'm not ready to hear it now?"

"Because you're still worried about Mom and Dad getting upset about things. You're still trying desperately to keep the peace. So, I can't tell you yet, Aaron. Because if I do and you're still feeling like you are right now, all strung out and stressed, it would only cause you more chaos and more stress. You wouldn't know what to do because this will be something you won't be able to fix. You'll be torn. Torn between your love for me and your innate sense of responsibility to them. And I'm not doing that to you. I love you too much."

She paused for a quick breath.

"And all of that is second to that fact I'm still not ready myself. So, for now, for today, let's buck up and prepare ourselves for the arrival of more tweens. Molly's a riot so we both know more will be coming."

"This is true. I think she invited like fifteen."

"See? Now that's something we really should pray about. We're gonna need a lot of strength and patience, and obviously that's not just in dealing with the girls. We've got the party poopers to contend with as well. So, let's say a silent prayer and steel ourselves. We've got to run this shindig."

Aaron stepped up to her for a long embrace. "I love you, crazy sister of mine." He kissed her cheek.

"I love you, too." She held his face and grinned. "Bro."

CHAPTER THIRTY-ONE

I'm not sure I can do it," Olivia said as she continued to pump her legs vigorously on the stair stepper. "I know I should, just because of my belief in animal rights alone, but I haven't totally looked into the science behind it. Not yet anyway."

Eve checked the numbers on Olivia's machine. She had been performing at a pretty high level of resistance for fifteen minutes straight, and she was still able to speak, an improvement from last week alone. They'd been hitting the cardio hard the last three weeks, gradually increasing with every workout.

"Ah-ha," Eve said, stepping back to reach into her gym bag. She held up a large book. "Behold, the science."

"*The China Study*?"

"Yep. You read this, you'll never look back. Totally changed my life."

"Okay, I'll give it a shot."

Eve put the book in Olivia's bag and zipped it closed. Then she squirted two sips of water into Olivia's mouth. They'd been discussing diet a lot lately and Olivia had been very curious about her veganism. She was so full of questions and seemed to have this drive to learn about everything. Eve found it so sexy.

"But, tofu, ugh," Olivia said. "I don't even like thinking about it."

"Aw, you get used to it, and honestly, it's not so bad. Besides, I have a million recipes," Eve said. "Judging by the laws of physics alone, you're bound to like some of them."

"Are you offering to cook for me?"

Eve almost said sure but stopped short. She actually would really love to cook for her, but the thought struck that part of her that was still anxious about the whole love thing. That part of her that kept people at bay and allowed Olivia to only get so close. She was still a little surprised at just how far Olivia had gotten. It was like she was inching closer and closer with each stimulating word, sigh of pleasure, moving glance, and heartfelt laugh. Eve had been so caught up in her, in every single thing about her, that she'd missed the quiet advance toward her innermost self. But now Olivia had reached that protective part of her and she was knocking on the door and ringing the bell, forcing Eve to decide if she was going to let her in or not.

"I wouldn't go that far," Eve said, trying to sound a little playful while still rejecting the idea.

"That's too bad. I almost got excited picturing you in my kitchen, making us dinner every night."

Eve blinked. That was exactly what she'd pictured herself. Cooking for her, every night. She imagined standing at the stove with Olivia coming up and embracing her from behind. Telling her how good the food smelled while she lightly kissed her neck. Asking her what she was making while teasing her ear. That kind of familiarity and sweet affection wouldn't seem as intimate as their wild sex to most people, but to Eve it far surpassed it.

She forced herself to swallow and to again sound light-hearted.

"Your kitchen? No way. It's too small. I need room for my masterpieces."

"Well, I've only ever been to your place twice and it wasn't because I was invited. So, my kitchen was what naturally came to mind."

Oh, no.

Eve's heart began to race.

"And I don't know," Olivia continued, looking wistful. "For a moment, I kind of liked thinking of you there, in my home, in my kitchen."

Eve struggled to calm her rising panic. She thought for sure that Olivia could see it all over her face. But she didn't seem to. Instead, her soft smile faded, and she looked away as if she'd shared too much.

Like maybe she had a similar part of protection in herself, causing her to pull back.

Eve had seen her react that way before. Quite a bit lately.

Eve's heart ached, pretty sure she knew what it meant.

Olivia was struggling with her feelings too.

She recalled the last couple of weeks and realized that though they had worked out and spent time together, and the sex had still been great, things had changed between them. While they obviously both absolutely loved giving each other pleasure, the long, deep stares they used to share in doing so had been avoided, along with the soul exposing revelations that often went hand in hand with their cries of pleasure and pleas for more. Now the sex was more needy, aggressive.

They were at the point where they were both confident and they knew each other well, so they gave and took with no hesitation or inhibition. So much so, that Eve had began joking to Karen that she and Olivia were almost killing each other. And last night had been no exception.

Eve rubbed the crook of her neck and checked her reflection in the mirror behind Olivia. She'd awakened that morning to find a sizable mouth mark there along with another one on her shoulder. They went nicely with the fingernail scratches that still remained on her back from three days before. Thankfully, the T-shirt she'd had to wear was covering all of it.

"Okay, you can stop now," Eve said, stepping up to turn off Olivia's machine. But Olivia pushed her hand away.

"I can go a little longer."

Eve raised her brow. "You sure?"

"Yes. I want to." She continued, lowering the level only a little.

Eve smiled. Olivia was now a full-fledged fitness junkie. She was addicted to those endorphins.

Olivia caught her. "You're pretty proud of yourself right now, aren't you?"

Eve gave a half shrug. "Maybe a little. But mostly I'm proud of you."

"Really? Should I ask you to show me how proud you are?"

Eve grew closer and rested her forearms on the top of the machine.

Oh, God, I'm doomed.

She's just so irresistible.

Despite her awareness of what was happening between them and the uncertainty they both felt, she still couldn't help herself. She wanted her.

"I'd love to show you how proud I am. In any way you want. Just as soon as you finish your workout."

"Any way I want? Does that include anywhere as well?"

Eve smiled, though confused.

"Okay, then. I want dinner. Made by you. In your kitchen. And then, after we eat at your table, I want—" She glanced around to see if anyone was close enough to overhear. Then she continued in a whisper. "I want to come. So very hard. Just for you. And then, I want you to do the same. So very hard. Just for me. I want to do it all in your bed. Wrapped in your sheets. In your room."

Eve blinked in quiet disbelief again and felt the blood rush from her face. She glanced down and realized she'd somehow backed away without knowing it.

Olivia climbed from the machine. "What's wrong?"

"My place?" Eve gripped the back of her neck. Olivia had been to her place, yes, but she'd been right, it wasn't due to an invitation. She'd come by to drop off some of Eve's freshly laundered clothes that had been accumulating at her place and then later to pick up a kettle ball Eve had told her she could borrow. Eve had never outright kept her from her place, but she'd never exactly invited her either. She'd never really given much thought in doing so. Probably because she never had before. Keeping things casual and away from the privacy of her home had simply become her routine.

But now, with Olivia asking, wanting to be there, inside her world, her safe place…she was feeling overwhelmed, and she grappled to find the right words. She knew what it would do to her to have Olivia in her home. Just imagining it was causing her heart to swell. It would send her emotions over the threshold and her wall would break and Olivia would be able to get all the way in. But how could she tell her that? How could she tell her that the thought of her being in her home made her feel both elated and terrified?

This time Olivia seemed to be able to read the fear and discomfort on her face, because she, too, paled and appeared crestfallen.

"I shouldn't have asked." She hurried to gather her things.

"Where are you going?"

No. No. Oh, fuck, make her stop.

"I just remembered I've got other things to do tonight."

But she was upset. It was more than evident in her short, clipped movements and lowered tone.

"Olivia," Eve tried.

Say something. Anything.

"Don't go. We aren't even finished with your workout—"

"I can do it on my own. In fact, maybe that's what I should do from now on."

Eve held her arm, desperate. "Olivia, no. Don't say things like that. You don't mean it and it only causes us both pain."

She pulled away and shoved her things into her bag and then did the same with her towel.

"Actually, I do mean it. I mean, who are we kidding, here? What the hell are we doing?"

When Eve could come up with nothing to say, Olivia zipped up her bag and slung it over her shoulder. She turned to go, giving Eve a serious, scorching look, full of pain and anguish. Eve felt the slap of it and she touched her own face, convinced her skin was stinging.

Olivia, if she noticed, didn't seem to care.

"Let's face it. You're scared, I'm scared. We're both just totally chicken shit. The fucking...it's fine. Well, it's better than fine, it's beyond fucking fantastic in fact, but it's not going to protect us and it's not going to save us. Life and emotions and all the bullshit that comes with that, will eventually creep all the way in. And it's more than obvious that neither one of us is ready and or willing to deal with that."

She walked away and Eve ran after her, angry at herself for not having any words to stop her. People stared after them as they crossed the gym. Bobby glanced up from the front desk and asked what was going on, but neither of them answered. Olivia pushed out into the hot evening with Eve right behind her.

"Olivia, will you stop," Eve finally said, gripping her arm once again. But Olivia kept yanking it away, hell-bent on getting to her car.

When she did, she fussed with her keychain like she was trying to find the right button to unlock it. The setting sun was obviously hindering her as she squinted and cussed. But the light wasn't the only thing burning in her eyes, there was hellfire there, Eve could see it.

She finally hit the right button and opened her door to toss in her bag.

She faced Eve, seeming as though she had more to say.

"Every time I try to convince myself that I'm ready to handle my feelings for you and I push on this invisible, unspoken line between us, you pull away or get quiet and distant. Or like tonight, which was totally new, you nearly shit your pants with panic. That hurts me, Eve. Not just because it solidifies the fact that you don't feel as strongly as I do, but because I don't ever want you to feel scared or panicked and I don't ever want to be the cause. It just kills me to think that I am."

Eve felt her throat tighten and tears threaten, and she gulped, needing to get rid of both, their presence totally unexpected. Olivia was watching her, waiting. Eve wanted more than anything to argue, but again no words came. And suddenly she understood why. She couldn't argue with Olivia because she was right. She did pull away. She did get distant. She was scared. And tonight, she had panicked. She wished none of it were true, but sadly it was.

All of it.

"I don't know what to do with you," Eve said, saying the one and only thing that came to mind. It was the truth. The undeniable truth. She couldn't come up with anything that would keep Olivia in her life for just a little while longer, while she desperately wished for answers that never seemed to come.

She rubbed her brow as a heavy sadness settled over her.

"Oh, my God, I just really don't know." The tears threatened again, and she covered her mouth, as if she could hold them in. Somehow, though, she managed to say one final thing. The only truth that remained.

"I'm so sorry. I'm so sorry, Olivia."

Olivia stared at her as if she were searching, trying to find any tiny piece of evidence she could to prove Eve was lying. When she seemed to find nothing, her already pained face went void of any emotion at all. She frantically wiped away some falling tears.

"Okay, then." She opened her car door and gazed beyond the parking lot. "Just so you know." She took a deep breath. "When I tell someone that I love them, I really mean it. It's not something I can just turn on and off." She wiped at more tears, like she was agitated, but wouldn't look back at Eve. "I meant it when I said it to you. And I mean it now. I love you, Eve Monroe."

She climbed into her car and Eve turned away, unable to look at her anymore, for her words alone had just fully infiltrated and they carried nothing but pure, raw, unfiltered love, pain, and regret. They surged through her as if they'd been injected with a long, piercing needle straight into her vein, hitting her so hard she bent and clutched her abdomen and knew without a doubt, that these were the very feelings that she'd never wanted to experience and the reason why she kept people out.

She staggered, seeking the safe haven of her own vehicle. When she found it, she crawled inside, saw Olivia drive away, and then pounded on her steering wheel while screaming into the oncoming evening. She did so until her fists were throbbing and her voice caved.

Because the woman who had moved her like no other had just told her she loved her and then walked out of her life.

And she'd let her go.

Chapter Thirty-two

E ve, honey, stop," Karen said from behind, sounding extremely fatigued.

Eve finally slowed as they reached the top of the mountain at Thunderbird Park. They were on another early dawn run and she'd already ran the trail twice before Karen had insisted on joining her for this one.

She shook out the tightness in her legs and took in big lungfuls of air. She absolutely loved that pleasant wide-open feeling in her chest that she often got when she did hard cardio. It made her feel so fucking alive, which was a feeling she hadn't been experiencing a lot lately despite her intense workouts. She'd shut off so completely she was now numb to everything, even the little things.

"Jesus, Mary, and Joseph, you're going to kill me," Karen said as she stumbled with her hand on her hip. She crossed to the large rock and sat.

Eve turned her head, trying not to picture Olivia and the way she'd looked sitting in the same spot.

"You shouldn't sit right now," Eve said. "You know better."

"Yeah, well, fuck the rules. I'm dying."

"I told you, you didn't have to keep up," Eve said.

"What am I supposed to do, Eve? Just sit back and watch as my best friend kills herself on a fucking mountain?"

Eve gave her a look.

"I'm not killing myself. I'm just going hard." She walked around with her hands on her hips.

"I know exactly what you're doing. You're trying to cope with your pain through exercise."

"So?"

"So, you're doing too much, going too hard."

Eve laughed. She was so damned dramatic. So what if she wanted to lengthen or intensify her workouts? And who cares why she was doing it? It's not like she was doing drugs.

"And don't tell me there's no such thing as too much exercise. You're full of shit."

"I'm fine."

"You're obsessed. And fucking whacked out crazy. For Christ's sake look at yourself."

Eve looked down at her bright yellow sports bra and black runners shorts. "What?"

"You have an eight-pack, Eve."

Eve ran her fingers over her etched muscles. "So?"

"You've never had an eight-pack, no matter how hard you've worked before."

"So, why can't you just be happy for me then?"

Karen stood and threw her water bottle at her. It stung her arm and fell to the ground.

"Ow! What the hell?"

Karen stalked up to her with daggers in her eyes. "You want me to be happy for you? For what? For a stupid eight-pack? Did I mention that I can also see your ribs? Yeah, very sexy, Eve. I'm so impressed. You are at the very peak of performance. Congratulations."

"Karen, come on, calm down."

"You're starving yourself while pushing your body beyond the brink. I'm surprised you haven't passed out yet. But give it time. Give it time."

"I'm not starving. I just...I'm not as hungry anymore." Her appetite had decreased quite a bit since the last time she'd seen Olivia, but she was still eating enough, wasn't she? She thought back over the last few days, trying to remember what she'd had. She'd eaten her meals and snacks and finished most of them completely. But had she increased her food intake for her added exercise? Had she compensated? It was like she had no self-awareness anymore.

"I don't want to hear anymore bullshit. I'm so sick of it. I'm so sick of it I'm about ready to tell you to fuck off once and for all."

To Eve's horror, emotion began to tighten her throat, just as it had the last time she'd seen Olivia. She was so shocked at feeling anything at all, she almost fell backward as Karen poked her in the chest with her finger. Her eyes, just like her words, seemed to be full of venom.

"I mean it, Eve. You won't listen to anything I have to say. You just placate me or flat-out ignore me. You're so hurt and so depressed, and so damned determined to punish yourself, I'm afraid you'll soon be too far gone for me to reach."

She pushed harder with her finger.

"I can't watch you do this. I can't watch you disappear into yourself. I refuse to watch my best friend kill herself, no matter how she's going about it or how slowly she may be doing it. I can't, Eve. So, you need to do one of two things, here. You either need to pay real close attention and really listen to what I have to say, or you need to tell me good-bye."

She lowered her finger and looked away as tears filled her eyes. Eve tried to hold herself together.

She grabbed her head, totally overwhelmed, realizing what was going on.

Someone else was banging on that fucking protective door of hers, forcing her to feel, to hurt, to panic.

Only this time it was Karen. Her best friend. And she was so serious it was scary.

"Not you, Karen. Not you, too," Eve said, dropping her hands.

Karen had turned to face the rising sun. Her arms were crossed and she kicked absently at the ground. "Does that mean you're willing to talk? And more importantly, listen?"

Talking with Karen was the absolute last thing she wanted to do. No, all she wanted was to push her body, to feel that sweet burn, to feel those beautiful endorphins while all the rest just faded away. Why couldn't Karen let her do that?

"Well?" Karen was waiting for an answer.

Eve closed her eyes, truly terrified. She couldn't lose Karen, too. She'd truly be lost at sea without the ever-glowing lighthouse of her friendship. And even though Eve didn't want to feel those painful emotions or face anything that might bring them up, she honestly didn't want to die or disappear. Without Karen, she knew she might very well become so consumed with sadness, she might just fall into the looming darkness and be lost forever.

"Okay," she finally said.

Karen turned and dropped her arms to her side, but she didn't look any different.

"All right, we'll talk on the way down. But I swear to God, Eve if you take off and run from me because you don't like what you hear, then that's it. I will not try to talk to you again."

"You want to do it now? Like now, now?"

Oh, God.

I need time. Time to prepare. To ease myself into this.

"Yes, Eve. It's now or never."

Eve hesitated.

"Fuck this, I'm gone," Karen said and started to walk away.

"Wait," Eve said, pushing all thought from her mind. She was going to force herself to listen before she could put any more thought into it. It was the only way.

"Go ahead," Eve said. "I'm here."

Karen was quiet for a moment. She spoke, her voice softer. "I'm only going to do this once. So, please, just listen without saying anything. Without any interruptions and then you can say whatever it is you want. Deal?"

"Deal."

They reached the trail and slowly began the descent back down.

"The first thing I want to tell you is how I much love you. You're not only my best friend, you're like a daughter to me. I'd go to the ends of the earth for you. And I don't feel that way about many people. But you're different. You're a really, really great friend and you're so kind to people and patient and you're always willing to help someone, whomever they may be. You give a lot of love, Eve. Everyone in your life feels it. Sometimes I look at you as you interact with someone and I think, my God, she's pure love."

Eve held her chest, moved.

"But, my darling, you are a hard person to love in return."

Eve stopped, stricken.

Karen tugged on her. "Let me continue."

They started to walk again.

"What I mean is, you refuse to accept any love given to you. You do. You're kind and caring and gracious, but when someone tries to love you, you shut down. Think about how long it took you to even allow me to pay for your meal? I'm still only allowed to do so much for you and I'm the person closest to you."

She stared down at the trail.

"Which leads me to your love life. I've watched you do your thing for years now and, Eve, I've never been fond of the way you go about things. I don't like your refusal to let anyone get close. I know that you know that because I've told you. It's caused more than one argument between us, and for the most part I haven't said anything about you settling down anymore because you've insisted that the way you do things is your choice. But now, with what's going on, I can no longer keep my mouth shut, my dear friend. I'm going to give you my two cents on everything."

She glanced over at her.

"Because this insane little way of life of yours is destroying you."

Eve's breath hitched as she listened. Karen wrapped her arm in hers.

"I admit that I didn't initially like this whole Olivia thing. I thought she sounded like trouble because she was so different from you and because I was sure she would continue to toy with your emotions and eventually hurt you. I didn't think she would do it intentionally. I thought she'd do it because she was so confused and repressed. So, I didn't encourage your seeing her."

She sighed.

"But as I've watched this relationship with her develop, I've seen something in you I've never seen before. And from what you've been telling me about her, she sounds like someone I would be very fond of. And she hasn't behaved like I expected. She didn't use you as an experiment. She fell for you. She loves you. And, Eve, let me tell you, I'm over the moon about that. To know that someone sees you the way I do, someone you actually like in return, it just makes me so happy."

She gave her a gentle squeeze.

"Now, I don't know everything about this relationship, so, I can only tell you what I see and what assumptions I've made based on knowing you like I do. And even though you haven't told me what led to things ending with Olivia, which, I might add, is unlike you, I think I have a pretty good idea."

She lowered her hand to grip Eve's.

"I think she got too close. I'm not sure how she did it, considering your adamant determination to keep your affairs casual, but she did. She snuck in under the wire. My guess is that you were, like I tried to tell you, completely smitten with her. And that was so unexpected and felt so incredibly good, you ignored your long-held boundaries. You didn't pay attention and in she came, sliding right under that wire, climbing right over that wall. And when she got through and pushed a little more, tried to get a little closer, well, your internal alarms finally went off and you realized, 'Oh shit, how did she get in here?' So, you did just what I'd expect you to do. You kicked her out and you closed down. And if this had been any other woman under any other circumstance, that would be the end of the story."

They slowed as they trekked over a rocky patch in the trail.

"But this isn't like any other circumstance, is it? No. Which is why you've totally lost your shit. You're sad and depressed and hurt and confused. But more than that, Eve, you're scared. And you're so upset with yourself for allowing yourself to get to this point, you're not only punishing your body to help yourself cope, you're punishing yourself for letting her slip in. And you're punishing yourself for pushing her away. Because you know you've hurt her. And that, my friend, that is eating you alive. That is literally killing you."

Karen stopped and placed her hands on her shoulders.

"Because this is not just any other woman. This one is special." She reached up and held her face and Eve trembled, the surfacing emotion in her becoming more and more difficult to contain.

"You're in love with her."

Eve grabbed her wrists and tried to pull them from her face, but Karen held tight.

"You love her, Eve."

Eve again tried to pull away.

"I'm not letting you go until you face that. So you can struggle all you want." When Eve finally stopped, Karen pulled her closer.

"That's why her hurting is damned near killing you. That's why your own pain is fiercer than it's ever been. You love this woman. You love her like you've never ever loved anyone else."

She pulled Eve down so their foreheads were touching.

"And that's okay, sweetie. It's okay. It's okay to love her."

Eve fought the oncoming emotion with all her might, tightening every muscle and fisting her hands, but she could no longer do it. Karen was reaching inside and jump-starting her heart, and the damn broke and Eve broke down and sobbed. Karen enveloped her, and Eve fell into her as if she needed her strength to remain standing at all.

"I know, hon. I know. You cry all you want. I'm right here."

They stood there for what felt like an eternity as the sun rose and shined just as bright and hot as ever, as if the day wasn't any different from any other.

But to Eve it was.

To Eve, this day was very different.

Today was the day the breath of life reentered her body and soul.

And she knew nothing would ever be the same again.

CHAPTER THIRTY-THREE

Olivia was breathing hard, and her face was coated in sweat. She had that excited thrumming coursing through her, and considering her recent lifestyle change, being in such a state was expected and not at all unusual. But this time, her condition wasn't the result of a workout.

"You ready?" Aaron asked.

She tried to control her heart rate, but it was damn near skipping over itself. Aaron's voice was muffled, and she could hear her own breathing inside the racing helmet. She wanted to wipe her brow but couldn't with the thick gloves on her hands and the goggles on her face.

The motorcycle vibrated beneath her, and she was squeezing the brake so hard her hand tingled. She looked at Aaron who had his hand on her shoulder. He had on Wayfarer sunglasses and a Monster baseball cap. His motocross racing jersey whipped against him in the breeze.

"Olivia?"

"I'm nervous." She winced as she said it, wanting to be composed. However, she was refusing to let it stop her.

He smiled and squeezed her shoulder. "I would be worried if you weren't."

She glanced ahead at the surrounding desert full of green brush, cacti, and sparse trees. A well-worn trail awaited her, this one a basic large oval without any hills or jumps. Aaron had tried to reassure her that she'd be fine, but she was still anxious, feeling the harnessed power shaking between her legs.

"You don't have to do this," Aaron said, and not for the first time.

"No, I want to." She had to do this. She wanted to feel that rush of adrenaline just like Eve did when she pushed the envelope. Taking risks that Olivia wouldn't have dared dream. Eve had told her all about her daredevil stunts one night after sex, filling her in on skydiving and bungee jumping and riding dirt bikes as a kid. All of it had Olivia so aroused and excited, she'd began touching her as she talked about it. Soon they'd both gotten so turned on, the tales were lost in the darkness as they'd made love once again.

Now Olivia was on a dirt bike herself, hoping it would make her feel close to Eve in some way and foolish and desperate enough to try. She'd thought about calling her or seeing her, but that would be pointless given the way they'd left things. They'd just end up in bed, and while that was certainly not anything to complain about, it wasn't getting them anywhere. She had tried for more and Eve turned her down. But now, after having thought things over, she wondered what would've happened had Eve been willing to get more serious. She knew now that she wouldn't have been totally comfortable and that her own fears, which sadly she still had, would have once again stood in her way.

Pushing Eve even though she wasn't ready herself and expecting her to ignore her own trepidations and just jump right in with her, had been wrong. But coming to that realization did little to help the situation between them. She knew she owed her an apology, and she hoped some day to be able to give it to her in person. She also hoped to offer her more than an apology should that day ever come. She hoped she would be able to really, truly, seriously be able to offer her whole heart, having worked through all her issues and fears.

If Eve rejected her then, then she would let her go. But for now, even though they had no contact, she kept her close inside, held onto her tight, and prayed for the strength and insight it would take to change.

She squeezed harder on the brake. What would Eve think of her doing this?

She'd fucking love it.

Olivia gave Aaron a nod.

"Watch that throttle, now," he said. "I don't want you flying off the back of the bike or going headlong into a saguaro."

She nodded again, having listened thoroughly to his warning about a "whisky throttle" earlier. Slowly, she released the brake and gave some throttle, kicking the bike forward. The sudden jolt shocked her, and she immediately understood what he'd been trying to say. She braked and tried again, this time more prepared. The bike lurched, but she eased off the gas quickly and managed to balance for a few yards before the bike wavered. She stopped, feet on the ground, grateful for Molly's boots and that she already had such big feet. Aaron was right there next to her in no time.

"You're doing great. Just keep at it and you'll get the hang of it."

She gave him a thumbs-up and went again, doing nearly the same thing, only riding a little farther. She tried over and over, making good way along the trail. Soon, she was so focused, the world around her faded and she could only think of one thing. Impressing Eve.

She pretended she was there watching her.

If I go harder and faster, will it turn her on, just like hearing about her escapades did me?

She tensed her muscles and increased her speed as she realized and accepted what was plainly obvious. She still wanted Eve to want her.

It was crazy. But then again, this whole stunt was a bit crazy. But the dream of being close to Eve and Eve wanting her was all she had now, and ridiculous or not, it was helping her get through, one day at a time. And there was nothing wrong with that, no matter what Jake said or how often he said it.

He was a great friend and he was there for her, there was no denying that. But he had been telling her to let Eve go, that she had to, for her own benefit. That she'd done all she could by telling Eve that she loved her. But Olivia disagreed. She just couldn't let her go. Not yet. She wasn't ready and she couldn't help but think that maybe there was a reason why she couldn't. Like maybe there was some sort of fate waiting to play out. It was the kind of thing she read about in books and she knew most people didn't believe in such things. But she was a firm believer in the kind of love and romance she read in books and saw in movies. Especially in having experienced it herself.

And according to the romance writers of the world who literally bled all over the page as they poured out their hearts, that kind of love doesn't die.

She grinned as she was finally able to balance and began to gain some ground. She rounded the trail five times before she eventually pulled up next to Aaron and killed the engine.

She tore off her gloves, goggles, and helmet and climbed from the bike. Aaron parked it and she hopped with joy when he came to join her.

"That was so much fun. Why didn't you tell me sooner?" They sat on the tailgate of his Ram truck and she slid on her sunglasses. She drank from a cold bottle of water Aaron had fished out of their cooler behind them. He cracked open a Mountain Dew Kickstart and slurped.

"So, you like it, huh?"

"Like it? I didn't want to stop. I just wanted to keep going faster and faster, whether I was ready yet or not. What a head rush," she said.

They bumped shoulders and stared out at the vast desert. The sky was just a shade darker than baby blue, and the breeze continued to press against them. It was a beautiful day, and with this latest conquest, it should be one of her greatest days ever. But with the absence of Eve, it felt bittersweet.

"What's her name?" Aaron asked, leaning back on his hand.

Olivia stared at him, stunned.

"The woman you've been seeing. What's her name?"

Olivia choked on her water.

Aaron remained calm next to her as she had an internal nuclear meltdown. She wanted to run, to escape, but she was frozen. She couldn't move.

Not now.

Not now.

Not when everything is still such a mess.

"It's okay, Olivia, you don't have to be afraid."

She forced a swallow and focused so hard on a distant saguaro she worried it might burst into flames.

"How did you know?"

He shifted a little. "I've always known."

She looked at him. "You couldn't have."

"Really, Olivia?"

"What?"

"You're gonna sit there and act like the whole thing with your youth leader at church didn't happen?"

She sat very still, now confused as well as stunned.

"Remember Sarah Benson?"

She reared back as the name registered.

"Oh, my God." She hadn't thought of her in years, and flashes of the past began to come at her like quick jabs from a prize fighter. One right after the other.

Aaron leaned forward. "You didn't remember?"

"Not until just now."

"You had it so bad for her. You followed her everywhere."

Her mind spun as memories came. She struggled to make sense of them, to put them all together. She saw Sarah's face, remembered that Sarah was sixteen when Olivia was thirteen. She remembered the two of them together, talking, laughing, and the way she'd felt so excited and happy when she was with her. And then, she remembered a specific moment. She saw the angles of Sarah's face lit up in the streetlight. They were sitting just outside the church in the dark. It was late summer. Olivia could still hear the cicadas and smell the oncoming rain. Not just any rain, but that dusty, monsoon rain. She felt Sarah put her hand on hers and trace her fingers up her arm. She saw the look in her eyes, like she was in a deep dream and never wanted to wake. She saw her eyes close as she leaned in and kissed her.

Olivia touched her mouth, still recalling the warm, gentle probe of Sarah's lips. She could still feel her and feel the sizzling voltage that struck her in response. It had been so instant and so enticing, she had clung to her, never wanting the feeling to end. And then, suddenly, there was a gasp and a shriek and a flicker of distant lightning. They were torn apart and taken away. She remembered angry voices, whispers of embarrassment and shame as she was hurriedly put in the back seat of her parents' car.

"Mom and Dad, they knew," she said, looking to Aaron for confirmation.

"Yes."

"We were caught."

"Yes. But it was kept very, very quiet. The only people who knew were Mom and Dad, her folks, and the pastor. And, well, I knew you were in love with her. It was more than obvious. And I figured out pretty quickly what happened in having to be around all the hush-hush that followed."

"That's why we left that church," Olivia said softly.

"Mom and Dad pretty much flipped out. We changed churches, friends, nearly everything. You were really devastated. Really, really broken. You wouldn't talk to anyone. You just holed up in your room."

She wiped a tear, unable to remember any of that, but imagining the pain her young self must've endured. "I blocked all of that out, Aaron. I didn't even remember her at all until you said her name just now."

"You were really messed up over it," he said. "And it's not like you were given any help or comforted or shown any understanding. The whole thing was just swept under the rug, and Mom and Dad controlled and smothered you more than ever."

He reached over and touched her hand. "I'm sorry, Olivia. I'm sorry you were treated like that and I'm sorry I wasn't there for you."

She wiped more tears and leaned into him. "You were young, too. You didn't know what to do."

"I knew enough to know that Mom and Dad were wrong in how they treated you."

"Yeah, well, there's no surprise there, is there?"

He grew quiet and they both seemed to get lost in the desert before them.

"Do you want to talk about her?" he asked. "This woman you're in love with?"

"Is it that obvious? That I'm in love?"

"Yes, Olivia, it is. You haven't changed much in the way of love since you were thirteen. You still wear your heart on your sleeve and when you're in love, like back then, it shows in everything you do and say. That's how I knew you weren't in love with Kenny. I knew who you really were. And I should've said something. But you were so far gone and so controlled and so scared to rock the boat with Mom and

Dad, I knew you'd never listen to me. And I knew you'd never admit your feelings for women. Not at that time. Denial isn't just a river in Egypt, you know? It can be a very powerful thing."

He nudged her and smiled. "So, who is she, this new wonder woman of yours? She must be something wonderful, because my sister never has, with the exception of Sarah Benson, given her heart to anyone."

Olivia hugged his arm. "She is, Aaron, she's so very special."

"Then why did it end?"

"How did you know it ended?"

He raised an eyebrow. Letting her know once again how obvious her feelings were. And she had been really down. How could he not've noticed?

"Because we're both afraid."

"Of what?"

"It's difficult to put into words. I think we're both afraid of what really loving each other would mean. We would have to completely open up and let each other in. We would have to trust, and in doing those things, our lives as we've come to know them would change forever."

He sighed. "Know what I think? And this is coming from your dopey grease monkey of a brother. I think that in order to be brave, you first have to be vulnerable."

"I hate feeling vulnerable." She still couldn't believe she'd told Eve she loved her. Had she not been caught up in the afterglow of passion, she probably wouldn't have done it. She was definitely paying the price for that venture with vulnerability. Eve's silence had been a terrible rejection and it still hurt.

"I know, you moron, I'm talking about you. I know you hate it, I do too. But if you never allow yourself to be vulnerable, then how can you ever be brave? And who wants to live their life afraid? Haven't you had enough of that for a hundred lifetimes, Olivia? Aren't you tired?"

"Yes, I'm so tired."

"Then stop. Just open yourself up and go with the flow." He nudged her again. "You never know where it might lead. And the not knowing what's around the corner when you're open like that, well, that's better than any damn adrenaline rush you could ever hope to experience."

"You're smart as hell, you know that?"

"I have my moments." He grinned and wrapped an arm around her. His smile faded as he grew serious once again. "Mom and Dad, though. That's going to be rough. I think Mom suspects because every time she calls, she asks if you're dating."

"Oh, God." Her stomach plummeted. "I guess she is, considering what happened with Sarah. Everything she's said to me lately makes so much more sense now."

"I want you to know I'm here for you this time around. If and when you ever tell them, if you want me to, I'll be there."

"Thanks. I just don't know if I can do it. I have these moments of courage and determination, but then they just seem to vanish."

"It'll happen when it's supposed to." He pulled her tight. "So, what do you think? You gonna give that whole vulnerability thing a try? So you can unearth some courage and do all the things you want to do with your life? Like riding that bike today?"

"I don't know. I'll think about it."

"You can do it. Just take it slow and easy," he said.

"Are you telling me to watch that whisky throttle again?"

He laughed and tugged on his ball cap. "Yep, I sure am."

CHAPTER THIRTY-FOUR

Eve sat in her Tahoe with the music low and her windows down. It was early evening and the neighborhood was quiet, lit up here and there by streetlights flickering to life. Olivia's house was across the street with light burning at the door and glowing behind the blinds. Eve wondered if Olivia was sitting down for her evening meal or curled up with a book or maybe, just maybe, thinking about her.

It seemed all Eve could do was think about Olivia. What was she doing? Was she okay? Was she sad? Devastated? Lost? Had they done the right thing in ending it? Could they ever fix things? Did Olivia even want to?

She didn't know the answers to any of those questions, but she had still been determined to come here. Whatever Karen had done and said to her on that mountain, it had opened up the floodgates and she'd been drowning in emotion ever since. She was facing things she'd never wanted to, feeling things that stabbed her in the gut, sharing things she'd never told a soul.

There was only one person who she hadn't said anything to. The most important person of all. Would she offer a hand and pull her out of her drowning sea of emotion? Or would she leave her for the fishes? Regardless, she had to do it, she had to try. It didn't matter how scared she was, she owed it to Olivia to do this.

Eve eased up her windows, removed her key, and slid from the SUV. She locked it with the remote as she jogged across the street to Olivia's front walk. She stood there for a moment to gather herself, opening and closing her fists, trying to breathe deeply, until eventually, she hurried to the front door. She rang the bell right away, before she could turn and high tail it out of there. She tried shoving her hands in the pockets of her jeans, but it felt awkward. Instead, she fingered through her hair and pressed her lips together, hoping she still looked okay, and then feeling foolish because she was unable to come up with a reason why she wouldn't still look the same as she had half an hour ago at her own house. After all, she'd only obsessed over her appearance, changing outfits five times and retouching her makeup a few times more than that. She finally settled on a pair of designer jeans and a tan sleeveless sweater that Karen said looked nice on her.

Eve heard the door unlock, and she held her breath as it was slowly pulled open. A young girl smiled at her and spoke.

"Hi."

"Is—Olivia here?"

"Yep. Hang on a sec." She closed the door a little and called out, "Auntie Liv, someone is here to see you." Her face popped back into the doorway. "She's coming."

"Oh, okay." She noticed how much she looked like Olivia. "Are you—Molly?" Olivia had spoken of her niece often, always commenting on how well she thought the two of them would get along. But sadly, they'd never gotten to meet.

The door opened more, and Olivia gasped when she saw her. Eve backpedaled some, upset that she had caused such a strong reaction.

"I'm sorry, I didn't know you had company," she said. "I didn't mean to—I shouldn't have come." She started to walk away, but Olivia stopped her.

"Eve, wait." She stepped outside in her bare feet, flannel night pants, and a tight, threadbare tank top.

Eve had to force herself not to stare at the now well-defined muscles of her arms and shoulders, as well as the perfect swell of her breasts stretching the fabric of the tank top. She looked better than ever, putting even the photos Eve had of her on her phone to shame. No camera could truly capture Olivia.

"What is it that you needed?" Olivia asked softly, crossing her arms over her chest, as if she suddenly realized that her shirt was less than adequate.

It was a natural response for one to have when they felt exposed, especially in being outside their home, but even so, Eve felt a sting of rejection, like she no longer had the key to the most spectacular of castles. She now had to wait at the gate and there was no guarantee she'd ever get back in, much less be given a key.

"I was hoping we could talk."

Olivia searched her face with the beautiful gray eyes Eve had missed and been dreaming of. Though they weren't currently full of lust or passion or…love, Eve was so grateful just in seeing them and she found herself captivated all over again. So much so, that she almost missed the way Olivia was trying to read her. Like she didn't want Eve to notice she was doing so.

"Oh?"

And then a slight pink tinted her cheeks as that seeking gaze quickly swept her up and down and then paused to linger on her mouth before returning once again to look into her eyes. It had happened in a millisecond, but Eve had seen it all and she knew what it meant.

Oh, holy fuck.

She still feels it.

She still wants me.

Can she see how badly I still want her?

Eve took a step toward her, almost reached out to cup her jaw and take her with a long, deep kiss, but she stopped, wrestling with restraint.

"I have some things I need to say." She tried to concentrate as best she could, but her presence alone was having a significant impact on her. "Things I need to say. I was hoping you'd be willing to listen."

Olivia looked away as her face was overcome with what appeared to be heartfelt emotion.

Oh, my dear sweet Olivia.

It had always been difficult for her to hide her feelings with her, though she'd tried so hard sometimes. That part of her was still very much the same.

"I don't know," she surprised Eve in saying. "That may not be such a good thing right now."

This part, however, was new. Eve wasn't sure how to respond.

She didn't have to.

"I know how we both feel, Eve. So, unless something drastic has changed, wanting each other physically just isn't enough, no matter how intense it is."

"What if I told you something has changed?"

"I'm not sure I'd believe you."

"Why not?"

She rubbed her temple. "I'd wonder if this change came to be just so we could fall into each other's arms, only to do all of this over again and arrive at the same ending. I miss you so much it literally hurts. And I know you miss me, or you wouldn't be here. But we can't do this again. We can't. It would be like building your dream home without a foundation. It would never stand."

She was so strong now, so firm in her beliefs and opinions. She knew what she wanted, and she wasn't going to settle. It was beautiful. She was beautiful. And Eve didn't know if she wanted to smile or cry. She didn't know whether to tell her the truth or just let her go.

She only knew that she wanted for her happiness. And she'd do anything to make that happen. Even if it meant walking away.

"You're right. It wouldn't," Eve said. They were silent for a moment as Eve searched for words. But everything she came up with wasn't enough, and Olivia deserved to have it all. She was put on this earth to have it all. She was someone who was unmistakably made to love. "I don't want to cause you any more grief or any more pain. So I'm going to go. But I want you to know one last thing. I want you to know that this change that I speak of, it didn't come about because we ended things and I realized I missed our physicality. It was always there. I just refused to accept it."

She turned her head and wiped at a tear. Crying was something she did now. Not very often and never in front of anyone other than Karen. But she was doing it. She still hated the way it made her feel though. It did not ever, in any way, feel good. She saw Olivia come toward her out of the corner of her eye, and she knew she'd better go or she'd never be able to.

She just had one last thing to say and she looked directly at her, needing to do it right.

"I'm sorry I was such a coward. I'm sorry I kept pushing you away."

Olivia blinked quickly as tears formed. When she spoke, it seemed to be a struggle.

"You aren't the only one who was a coward," she said. "God, I still am. I still have things to face." She laughed. "Why you put up with me when I was too afraid to even be around you is something I've never understood." She shook her head. "I was so God damned afraid of who I might really be because of the way you made me feel. But you hung in there. And you were kind and understanding and patient. Why did you do all that when it would've been so much easier for you to just walk away?"

Eve closed her eyes, searching for strength now. The words that would answer this question, she had. Because the answer to this question hadn't been hard to find.

"I thought you were worth the risk," she said. "Even though I had no idea what would happen or where it would lead, you moved me so profoundly there was no way I could walk away."

Olivia smiled softly. "And God knows you love your risks."

"That I do." She smiled back at her. "You were the best one by far, Olivia. And so worth it. My God, you were so worth it. You still are."

The door opened and Molly hurried out to wrap her arms around Olivia. She grinned up at her.

"Popcorn's ready."

"Oh, good. I'll be right in, okay?"

"Huh-uh," Molly said. She looked at Eve. "I think your friend should come too."

"Oh, honey, I don't think—"

"You haven't even asked her. And you're already being rude by not even inviting her in." She took Eve's hand. "Come on. We're going to watch *What About Bob?* Have you seen it?"

"I have seen it," Eve said, being urged along after her. She looked to Olivia unsure what to do, but Olivia only shrugged as if she, too, were helpless.

"Isn't it hilarious? Auntie Liv has never seen it."

Eve stopped just outside the door and aimed her question at Olivia.

"Is this—okay?"

She laughed and walked up to place a gentle hand on the small of her back.

"You don't know my niece," she said. "Even if this wasn't okay, Molly would make it so that it was. She's very strong headed."

"I wonder who she gets that from?"

Olivia narrowed her eyes. "Get inside before I change my mind."

Molly tugged again and Eve stumbled along after her, once again back into Olivia's home. She'd moved the furniture around and the whole place smelled of freshly popped popcorn. Eve still felt at home there. She wished she'd made Olivia feel the same way in hers. Not doing so, she knew, would be something she'd always and forever regret.

CHAPTER THIRTY-FIVE

Eve glanced over at Olivia when she lightly tapped her shoulder. She was sitting on the opposite end of the couch, and Molly was sprawled out between them, her head resting on a throw pillow on Eve's leg. She was snoring softly, and Eve could see her eyes moving behind her closed lids.

"Is she asleep?" Olivia asked, leaning forward for a better look.

Eve nodded. "I think she's dreaming."

Olivia came to Molly's side and gently shook her awake. "Mols, come on, sweetie, let's get you to bed."

Molly stirred and sat up but slurred her words with eyelids still half closed.

"I don't wanna. Wanna stay up with you guys."

"Shh, maybe another time. Come on, now." Olivia helped her stand and then helped her walk through the living room where they disappeared into the hall. Eve scooted to the edge of the couch, not quite sure what would happen next. Should she offer to go? Or ask again to talk? But Olivia returned rather quickly, and she was playing with her hands, letting Eve know she was nervous, too.

Eve stood, knowing she should probably go. It was past ten and neither of them had intended for this to happen. It just kind of did.

"Thank you for letting me stay," Eve said. "I had a really good time." Molly was so much fun, just a kid so full of love and promise and adventure. Eve imagined she was looking at Olivia at that age, and it both warmed and broke her heart. She'd probably been a lot like Molly, yet all that wonderful hope and happiness and energy had been stifled.

"We loved having you," Olivia said.

"She reminds me of you, you know," Eve said.

Olivia laughed a little. "She's a character."

"Like I said," Eve said with a smile.

"She's crazy about you," Olivia said, absently picking at the armrest of the sofa.

"What about you, Auntie Liv? Are you?" Eve flushed both with yearning and embarrassment. The questions just came to voice, as if they hadn't been birthed in her mind, but in her mouth.

Being in that house with Olivia was doing a lot more to her than she realized. And she knew with what she'd just said, she was either going to hold Olivia tight and tell her everything she should've told her a long time ago or Olivia was going to insist that she leave. But leaving on her own, she now knew, was going to be very difficult.

Olivia looked up at her quickly and crossed her arms over her chest, just as she'd done outside.

Eve's heart pounded.

"Olivia," Eve said. "I can't seem to shut up and I can't bring myself to leave. Say something, anything. For God's sake, help me."

"You know how I feel about you, Eve. It's no big secret."

She sounded stern, like she was trying to be firm.

"You still…"

"Of course." She stared right into her, and Eve watched as the stone look to her face crumbled and raw desire crept in. And when she spoke again, she sounded raspy and strained, her voice giving way to her passion. "What, you think I can just shut that off somehow? Like I'm some kind of person who can turn love on and off like a light switch? I told you I'm not like that. I love for life, Eve. I wasn't bullshitting you when I said that. The way I feel about you, it isn't just going to go away or disappear, no matter how badly I may need it to." She began to tremble, and her voice was threatening to cave altogether.

Eve approached her, uncertain and hesitant, but wanting to hold her, to comfort her.

"Don't you get it, you crazy woman?" Olivia said, taking a step back as Eve neared. "I love you. That hasn't changed. That will never change. God, how can you be so smart and so stupid all at once?

How can you be so gentle and kind and insightful and be so clueless? How—"

Eve stepped into her and held her face with both hands. "I love you."

She felt Olivia shudder and her own eyes burned with tears.

"I love you," she said again.

Olivia was searching her for answers once again. This time frantically. "But—"

"I should've told you a long time ago. I should've said it when you first said it to me, and I definitely should've said it that night in the parking lot at the gym. But I can't go back. I wish I could, but I can't. All I can do is tell you now. That's why I came here tonight."

"But you almost left earlier without telling me."

"Because a part of me thinks you might be better off. Don't you see yourself at all, Olivia? You deserve so much more. You deserve someone who can tell you how they feel no matter how scared they might be. You deserve all the love in the world, and I—"

"You what? You can't give it to me? You don't want to give it to me?"

"I want to give it to you so badly it's quite literally killing me. But I know I'm not perfect. I've got issues with trust and with sharing my feelings. And I definitely know I'm not good at doing this. I truly have no idea what the hell I'm doing. I don't know if this is the right thing to do for you, and I don't know if I'm saying things the right way. All I know is that I'm taking another risk, and yes, I may love taking risks, but when it comes to my heart, I'm truly fucking terrified. But you, Olivia, as I said before, are worth it."

She held on to Eve's wrists. "I don't need you to be perfect. I just need you. The you who is standing in front of me now. The you who has deep feelings and emotions. Because I already know they're there. You don't have to hide them from me."

"You don't have to hide either. From anyone. Not me, not your family, not anyone. There's nothing wrong with who you are or the way you feel."

She fell into Eve's arms and they stood there just holding one another while the television flashed and Molly slept peacefully down the hall.

When they parted, Eve stroked her cheek with her thumb, smoothing away what was left of her tears.

"I should probably go," she said, even though it was the last thing she wanted to do. "Molly's here and I can tell she doesn't know. I don't want to make things uncomfortable for either of you."

But Olivia held her tight. "No, don't leave."

"I can't stay, Olivia. You know what will happen if I do."

"We can behave. We aren't totally incapable of keeping our hands to ourselves."

Eve raised an eyebrow and Olivia laughed.

"Please, stay. I want you in my bed, next to me."

Eve lightly kissed her face and shushed her. "I'm making an executive decision here. I'm going." She pressed her finger to Olivia's lips to keep her from protesting. "You don't want Molly to find out by walking in on us in bed together. It wouldn't matter if we locked the door or tried to wake extra early. If she were to wake up at all during the night, she would figure things out. She's well old enough to. And I know you don't want her to learn about you that way."

Eve kissed her face again and headed for the door. She unbolted the lock and pulled it open, intent on turning and kissing Olivia good night one last time. But she jerked with shock when she found a man standing there, looking as confused as she was.

"Who are you?" she asked.

"Who are you?" he asked in return.

Olivia rushed up next to her and opened the door all the way. She gasped just as she had when she'd first seen Eve that evening.

"Kenny. What the hell are you doing here?"

Eve was suddenly ablaze with anger. She knew who he was. Olivia had told her all about him.

"What am I doing here?" he said. "I told you yesterday I wanted to talk. And when I called today, Molly said you weren't available. I told her to tell you I was going to drop by after my shift tonight."

Eve looked from him to Olivia, still reeling with anger but also with something new. Something else was trying to take root.

Jealousy.

"You're talking to him again?" she asked, totally incredulous. She thought Olivia hated him. But then she recalled her words from just moments before. When Olivia loved, she loved for life.

"Yes, she's talking to me," he said. "Not that it's any of your business." He shifted his leer from Eve to Olivia. "Who is this and why is she in my face?"

"I'm Eve," Eve said, pushing past him to step outside. "And I'm leaving."

She was so hurt and confused and riddled with fury, she couldn't think straight. She was on autopilot and her autopilot was making her run. Far and fast.

"Eve, no." Olivia caught up to her and hurried alongside her in her bare feet. "This is not what it looks like. I had no idea he was coming."

"Maybe not, but it's obvious you two have some things to discuss. And I really wish you would've told me you were talking to him again."

They crossed the street to her Tahoe, and it lit up as she unlocked it with her remote.

"When was I supposed to do that? Within the last couple of hours of us finally speaking to each other again?"

"Yes, before I—"

Olivia grabbed her by the arm and turned her to face her.

"Before you what? Told me you loved me?" She pressed her lips together and nodded like she knew better. "So, what, you wouldn't have told me you love me if I'd told you he'd been calling me and bugging the hell out of me? Well, here's what I wish I knew before you told me you loved me. I wish I'd known just how shallow and conditional your love actually is."

She tried to stifle a cry that seemed intent on breaking through. Eve reached out to her, but Olivia pushed her hand away.

"Please, don't. Just don't. I, apparently, have enough shit to deal with. Because I now have to go deal with someone else who is insisting they love me. Only difference is, this one," she said, hitching her thumb back toward him. "This one, I don't love. I never have. So, go, Eve. Just go. I just want you both to fuck off. Because I simply can't handle anymore."

She spun on her heel and stalked back toward her house where Kenny waited by the door, watching.

"Olivia, wait!" Eve wanted to die. Olivia's pain was killing her, and she didn't know how to make it stop. She wanted to run to her, to tell her she had it all wrong and that her love for her was completely unconditional. But Eve knew she'd fucked up and almost said the exact opposite when all she'd meant was that she didn't want to get hurt if Olivia was somehow back with Kenny. That, though, was fucked up too. How could she have ever thought she was back with Kenny after all the things Olivia had said to her tonight? What the hell had she been thinking? Was she really that jumpy and panicked in response to having opened up to her?

Olivia didn't look back and Eve climbed in her SUV. She watched as Olivia squared off with Kenny and jabbed a finger at him. He shook his head and said something in return, but Olivia pushed past him and slammed her door closed behind her. Eve waited, making sure Kenny left. He eyed her the entire walk to his car, so she stayed for another half an hour to make sure he didn't come back. When he didn't, she considered going to knock on the door, to see if Olivia would talk to her, or as she'd wanted before, to just listen. She owed her a huge apology and she knew she had to do whatever it took to deliver it to her face to face.

But there was Molly to consider. She was possibly awake now, with the loud voices and the door slamming. And if she wasn't, Eve didn't want her to wake to any drama between her and Olivia.

She had to go.

She started the engine and drove away slowly, wishing once again that life had a rewind button.

CHAPTER THIRTY-SIX

"Can we take this thing off now, please?" Olivia stumbled a little as Molly led her by the elbow.

"No, you're wearing a blindfold for a reason. This is a surprise."

"I don't like surprises," Olivia said, being guided up a couple of steps. She heard people talking as they walked by them.

"It's your birthday, so get over it," Molly said.

"This is all your idea, isn't it?" Olivia asked.

"Yep."

"Should've known. Now I'm really scared." It was Saturday afternoon, her thirty-third birthday, and by all accounts, a beautiful, beautiful day. But it wasn't as beautiful as it could've been. She tried not to think about how she'd spent every waking moment the last couple of weeks clutching her phone and checking it for a text or a message or a missed call. But there had been nothing. She really hadn't thought she could ever feel any more devastated than she had the night she'd said good-bye to Eve in the parking lot at the gym. She'd been wrong. Devastation, it seemed, could be intensified, multiplied, and stacked upon. To what end? She didn't know. She was terrified that it would continue to build upon itself and last for all eternity, keeping her in a heartbroken hell she wouldn't wish on anyone, not even the devil himself.

Molly stopped them and brought her focus back to reality. "I'm gonna get the door."

Olivia heard and felt a whoosh of air as a door was opened.

She grinned right away as they stepped inside. "I know where we are."

Molly led her on. "Just keep walking."

"We're at Fajitas. I would know that smell anywhere."

"Keep walking, smarty-pants." Molly tugged her along, and Olivia knew they were now past the hostess stand and fully inside the restaurant. The air was cooler and smoky with the scent of fire grilled onions and peppers, steak, chicken, and shrimp, and freshly made tortillas. It was her favorite place to eat, and sadly, she hadn't been there in years. She was touched, though, that Molly remembered how much she loved it.

They headed up more steps and then stilled. She could feel Molly bobbing up and down next to her. "Okay, you can take off your blindfold."

Smiling, Olivia removed the blindfold, which was one of Aaron's very few dress ties, and took in first her brother, who sat at the end of the table, and then the two people sitting on the bench side facing her. She laughed, short and sharp, and then went silent in both total confusion and shock. Aaron stood and grabbed on to her as if he knew her world was tilting. Molly continued to bounce with excitement.

"Surprise!" Molly said, extending her hand outward toward their guests.

Aaron spoke into her ear. "I know you weren't expecting this, but for Molly's sake, please try to hold it together." He squeezed her arm. "You can do this."

Olivia nodded and tried her best to recover quickly with a smile, but everything around her had morphed into a blur.

"Happy birthday!" Molly said, now tugging on her arm. "Are you surprised?"

Her sweet face was so full of joy and an eagerness to make sure she was happy.

"Yeah, I'm, uh, definitely surprised."

Aaron returned to his seat, but he was watching her carefully, like he was worried she might actually fall over.

"Awesome!" Molly quickly pulled out a chair. "You sit here. Across from Eve. And I'll sit here and, Dad, you stay over there next to Jake."

Olivia eased into her seat cautiously, convinced the whole world would just disappear beneath her and she'd be falling and flailing into a never-ending abyss. She gripped the table and used it as an anchor, seeking some sort of stability. She couldn't bring herself to look at either Jake or Eve. They both had the ability to see right into her soul without her having to say a word. And she didn't want to be seen like that at that moment. She wouldn't be able to handle it.

She didn't dare sip her water for fear that everyone would see the glass tremble. As for any other thinking or reasoning or planning, she was hopeless. She had no idea what was happening, how it was happening, or what she was going to do about it. She just knew that Eve, who she had only managed a fleeting glance at, was sitting right there across from her, looking like the drop-dead gorgeous blonde that she was in a dark green halter top and deep red lipstick. She was so impossibly gorgeous and so incredibly close, Olivia wondered how she was able to even keep breathing in and out like a normal person. Or how she was even conscious at all. Maybe she wasn't. Maybe this was a dream.

Could it be?

Slowly, she moved her gaze across the tabletop and up to Eve's face. She was sitting with her elbows on the table, hands clasped under her chin. She was looking at Molly and smiling in the way that adults do when they don't want a child to know that they are really worried about other things. Olivia allowed herself the great pleasure of a long stare, tracing the contours of her face, the line of her jaw, the fullness of her lips. The sweet bliss of studying her relaxed her a little too much, though, and Eve, as if she'd felt her eyes lightly grazing her skin, shifted her gaze and caught Olivia looking. She studied Olivia in return and appeared anxious but sincerely concerned, with the polite interested look she'd given Molly, gone. The change was subtle, so subtle the others probably hadn't noticed. But Olivia had and it was more than evident that the other thing she was worried about, the one she was trying to hide from Molly, was her.

"Happy birthday," she said, the usual confidence in her words absent. "Molly invited me."

"Oh." That explained, not only her presence, but her obvious anxiousness about it as well. She had come out of obligation, probably uneasy about having to tell Molly no. Olivia glanced away from her, hurt by the realization and upset at herself for feeling that way.

"Aaron invited me," Jake said, also with a rather guarded smile. His all-knowing eyes held hers, silently letting her know he was aware of the awkward situation but that she had his support regardless. He gave her a wink and sipped his water, and she was so grateful for him at that moment, she wanted to hug him so hard his bones would break. If only she could. If only he could voice his support out loud, to reassure her, to tell her to hang on. But he couldn't. He just sat looking at her in his purple V-neck T-shirt and his perfectly styled hair. Olivia couldn't help but notice how much he and Eve looked alike with their blond locks, golden tans, and carefully chosen outfits. They were an exceedingly beautiful pair with extremely big hearts, and they both had an inner access to her that no one else ever had. By all accords, it should've been a really happy moment, with her heart full and carefree and her world dancing and bright. But it wasn't. They were obviously just as uneasy as she was. Jake because he knew all about her last encounter with Eve. And Eve because of the way that last encounter had turned out. Still, she wondered, how did things get this way? How did they end up like this? How did they end up here, staring at each other uncomfortably across a table at a birthday dinner?

"We had to get in your phone," Aaron said. "But I swear I only looked at your contacts."

"Thankfully," Molly said, crossing her arms proudly, "I remembered your password."

"When did you—oh, right." She'd given it to Molly one day when they were out shopping. She'd needed her grocery list on her phone. So, she'd given Molly her password while she kept shopping, putting items in the cart. Molly read the list aloud and then returned the phone to her purse quickly. She hadn't had time to look at anything else, and Olivia never worried that Molly might remember the password. She looked at Aaron, hoping he hadn't seen all the texts and photos she'd saved from Eve. She just hadn't been able to delete them.

Besides, she didn't think she could ever just erase Eve. Not her words or her photos. Not any part of her for that matter.

"I wanted you to have the best birthday ever," Molly said. "With the people who love you the most."

Olivia kissed her temple. "Thank you, sweetie."

"Are you happy?"

"Yes. I'm happy."

Molly furrowed her brow. "You're smiling but you look sad."

Olivia wrapped her arm around Molly and reassured her. "I'm not sad, silly. Just surprised is all. This is all very unexpected."

"But in a good way, right?"

"Right."

Molly only knew what she'd been told and what she'd seen. She knew that Eve was a very good friend and that they cared about each other very much. And she'd seen them together that night at the house, laughing and joking together as they'd watched the movie and talked and munched on microwave popcorn. Molly had seen and no doubt felt the love they had for each other, even if she didn't quite sense or understand just how deep that love went. She had obviously enjoyed being with them because she'd asked to see Eve for the following two weekends, confused as to why Olivia wouldn't even try to invite her over. Olivia had just told her that Eve was very busy with work. She hadn't known what else to do.

Their waiter arrived and Olivia hoped that Molly would move on to another topic and that she'd somehow be able to get through the afternoon. He took their order and brought their drinks, and everyone chatted except for Olivia, who sat quietly watching. Jake, it seemed, would be no problem. He talked with Aaron, and when he did look at her, it was to smile or wink. He knew she was devastated and confused about what to do with Eve. So, he'd done what he always did. He gave her the best advice he had, encouraging her to go talk to her, because he was pretty sure that Eve had just panicked in seeing Kenny. He said it would've freaked any lesbian out to suddenly be faced with a girlfriend's ex-husband or boyfriend, especially if he acted like they were somehow still connected or together. And in addition to that, Eve was the only woman Olivia had ever been with, so Eve might have always worried, subconsciously or not, that there was a chance Olivia might, at some point, want to go back to men. The whole thing, according to Jake, was like a lesbian's worst nightmare.

She stirred her iced tea with her straw, quietly observing while Eve was listening to Molly. She was paying close attention to her and seemed to be enjoying herself. Eve was very good with her, and she obviously cared about her. It almost made Olivia tear up as she watched them interact. Molly would be heartbroken if she never saw Eve again. Olivia understood that feeling all too well, and she prayed against all odds that things didn't turn out like that. She prayed that somehow, someway, Eve would be in their lives for a long time to come.

"I hope we aren't too late to join the fun," a male voice said from Aaron's end of the table.

Everyone turned and Olivia felt her chin drop. Her mother and father stood next to Aaron, holding a wrapped gift.

Chapter Thirty-seven

Oh, my fucking God.

Shock, panic, and whatever else anyone could possibly feel in a similar situation caused Olivia to stiffen in her chair. She was still and composed on the outside, which she found odd considering nothing but total chaos was taking over the inside.

Facing death, she reasoned, would be better than her current position.

And to add to the tension that was already hanging in the air, no one said anything. Not a word. Aaron looked as shocked as she did, and Molly seemed to share her preference in facing death based on the way she had her head in her hand, staring down at the table. There was no way she would've invited them. They were the fun killers, the party poopers.

Her father seemed to sense everyone's confusion.

"Molly told us all about her big plans for a surprise birthday dinner, so we decided to surprise Olivia too."

"But you live in Rocky Point," Molly said, rubbing her forehead. "You said at my birthday you wouldn't be back in the States until Christmas."

Olivia's father continued, giving Molly a pat on the shoulder.

"Well, a friend asked me to play in a golf tournament at the last minute, so we said, what the heck? Let's go play golf and wish Olivia a happy birthday, too." He kissed Olivia's cheek as he handed over the present.

"So, happy birthday," he said. "I hope we aren't imposing."

She hugged him from her seat. "It's nice of you to think of me," she said. She just wished it had been any other day but this one.

Her mother did the same as her father, kissing her cheek and wishing her a happy birthday, though she was more reserved and formal, with her rigid posture and put-upon smile. They took the two seats closest to Olivia. Her mother, across from Olivia on the bench, and her father at the end of the table to her right.

Their choice of where to sit was as perfectly innocent as their arrival, but still just as nerve-racking. Because her mother, the ever-hunting, ever-seeking aggressive bird of prey, was now sitting right next to Eve, causing Olivia to almost have a coronary.

Molly tugged on Olivia's sleeve and whispered in her ear.

"I didn't think they would come. Honest, I didn't."

"I know, hon. It's okay."

But things were far from okay. Her mother introduced both herself and Olivia's father to Jake and Eve, and Olivia could tell by the look on her mother's face, she was confused as to who they were, never having seen them before.

"You're Olivia's friends, then?" her mother asked right away.

"I go to school with her," Jake said. "And we study together."

Her mother nodded and then looked to Eve.

"And I—" Eve suddenly flushed, and Olivia did as well. Just what was it that Eve did with her? Oh, right, have wild, crazy, passionate, mind-blowing sex. Olivia stared at the table, unable to look at Eve, and massaged her temple.

"Work out with her," Eve finally finished. "We work out together." She quickly grabbed her water and drank like she was parched. Her nervousness was as unusual as it was obvious, and Olivia only grew more anxious, knowing that if Eve, who was normally walking, talking confidence, was reacting to the heavy weight of the moment, then this entire birthday celebration was seriously fucked.

Olivia looked to Aaron for some sort of help, but he had assumed Molly's earlier posture of sitting with his head in hand. He knew how fucked up the situation was, and she knew he was no doubt worried about just how much more fucked up it could get.

"Eve's a personal trainer," Molly said. "She kicks serious butt."

"Oh," Olivia's mother said. She smiled but it was hardly genuine.

"She said she can bench press Auntie Liv. She's that strong."

Oh, dear God. My mother is literally picturing Eve lifting and manhandling me at this very moment.

I'm going to die. I am. I'm going to die.

And apparently, Jake was picturing something similar.

He coughed into his hand, trying to hide his laughter, and sipped his water. He turned his head, refusing to look at her.

Aaron, who had looked up, was now as red as Eve and he, too, was avoiding her gaze.

Her mother was studying and smoothing the back of her hands, her discomfort and disapproval apparent.

Her father, however, seemed to be oblivious to what Molly's revelation inferred.

"So, are you the one who whipped Olivia into shape?" he asked Eve.

Eve glanced at her before she responded, obviously unsure what she should say. But Olivia had no answers. Eve widened her eyes at her, as if trying to get her to say something, do something, anything, but Olivia didn't. She couldn't. She was frozen with no words and no plans of how to survive.

"I—showed her a few things," Eve finally said.

Again, Jake coughed, and Olivia's mind was right there with him.

If they only knew what all she's shown me.

Eve's flush deepened, as she also seemed to realize the way her words could be construed. She cleared her throat.

"But Olivia did all the work."

"Well, she looks fantastic," her father said. "Stronger than ever. And so do you. You've got some substantial muscle yourself."

Eve smiled but her nerves were still showing. "I like feeling strong."

Olivia's mother, whose pinched face showed her displeasure with the conversation, turned to both Jake and Eve.

"So, Jake, tell me, are you married?"

It sounded like a polite inquiry and a harmless change in topic, but Olivia was aware that it was so much more than that.

Oh, shit.

This time it was Jake who cleared his throat. "No, ma'am. I'm not married. Haven't found the right one, I guess."

"Surely, you have a girlfriend."

"Uh, no." He laughed a little. "No girlfriend here."

"You're not involved?"

"No."

"What about you, Eve?" her mother asked, her focus now on what Olivia knew was her intended target.

Eve drank more water. "Same here."

"You're both single?" She was not happy with that information, and it was evident by her tone. "That's hard for me to believe. You're both so good-looking and polite. I don't understand why you aren't both married."

"Maybe we're both terrified of commitment," Jake said. "I know I am."

There was some light but forced laughter around the table. The tension still hung heavy in the air. Even Molly seemed to feel it.

"Auntie Liv, open your presents."

"Shouldn't we wait until after we eat, Mols?" Aaron asked.

Molly slumped like the wind had vanished from her sails. "I guess."

"How about I open just one?" Olivia said, giving her an encouraging nudge.

Molly perked up.

"Okay! But I get to pick."

She rounded Aaron's chair to sift through gifts that Olivia hadn't seen on the bench next to Jake. She chose a small, rectangle shaped present and bounded back up to Olivia to hand it over.

"This one's from Eve."

Olivia was so overcome with anxiousness she felt like her head was going to explode and some sort of fucked up confetti would fly everywhere.

"Maybe—" Eve started. "You should—"

Olivia questioned her with her eyes.

"I was just going to say—" She shook her head. "Never mind. Go ahead."

Olivia's skin was now aflame, and Eve's hesitation didn't help.

What had she gotten her?

It couldn't be anything that bad. The gift was too small for lingerie or anything else along those lines. And Eve would never give her something like that to open in front of anyone.

"Open it, Auntie Liv," Molly said. She clapped her hands in excitement.

With everyone's eyes on her and her heart in her throat, Olivia carefully removed the wrapping paper to find a dark blue velvet box. Time seemed to stand still, and she felt perpetually stuck in that moment, halfway between scared to death and irresistibly curious.

Eve had gotten her something personal.

Meaningful.

Olivia knew it just as sure as she knew the stars would come out at night and the sun would rise in the morning.

She slowly opened the box. A beautiful, elegant gold bracelet glistened in the overhead lights. Molly gasped and Olivia couldn't breathe. She tried so very hard to hide her feelings and reaction.

"Take it out," Molly said.

Olivia removed the bracelet from the clasps, noticing that it had a name plate, like an ID bracelet. She could see the etching on the plate, and her hand began to shake as she thought of what might be engraved on it. She was dying to know, but she wasn't about to share it with the group. The gift was beautiful and special, which meant that whatever was written was something very dear and personal. She tried to return it to the box, but Molly, who seemed to be more excited than she was, wasn't about to let her put it away.

"Here, I'll help you." She took the bracelet and helped Olivia put it on.

The bracelet glimmered and shined, and Jake and Aaron stated what a nice gift it was and how good it looked on Olivia. Her mother and father remained quiet, but her father, who sat with his chin resting on his hands, did look at her like he was pleased for her.

She took a deep breath and smiled as platonically and politely as she could at Eve. She was expecting a similar smile in return, but something had seemed to overcome Eve as well, because she was now staring intently at her, silently reiterating all the things she'd ever said to her, in the moments of heated passion and in the intense moments they'd shared staring into each other's eyes. Eve was giving all those words and emotion back to her, with the bracelet and with her heavy, heart drenched gaze.

I am so in love with this woman.

I'm about to dive into her and swim so far and so deep that the entire world and everything in it will just fall away.

But I can't.

Not here.

Not now.

Someone tear me from this trance.

Someone help me, please.

Jake, the great savior that he was, stood and excused himself, claiming he needed the restroom. He touched Olivia on the shoulder as he walked past her and then widened his eyes at her when he was behind her parents, silently telling her to wake the fuck up and get a grip.

"Wait, Auntie Liv, I think it says something," Molly said, angling her head as she repositioned Olivia's arm to look at the bracelet.

Olivia held her breath.

CHAPTER THIRTY-EIGHT

"Mols," Aaron said. "Mols, you shouldn't—"

"It says," Molly said, ignoring him, "For Olivia. Walk in courage. Live in love."

The table was once again silent and Olivia couldn't bear to look at anyone other than Molly, who was just as happy as ever.

"That's really nice," Molly said, sitting down in her chair. She wadded up the wrapping paper and handed it to Aaron, along with the box. "That's a really pretty bracelet, Eve," Molly continued. "Too bad you weren't at my birthday party."

Eve, who was still staring at Olivia, tore her eyes away and looked at Molly. She laughed. Molly laughed along with her. "I'm not saying my presents were bad or anything, I'm just saying I wish you had been there to give me one from you. Because, I mean, wow. You're coming for Christmas, right?"

Olivia's father laughed a bit as well, but Olivia sat wound tighter than a top, listening so hard for Eve's reply she knew she could've heard a pin drop.

Please say yes.

For Molly.

For me.

Jake returned from the restroom and looked to Olivia.

"What did I miss?"

"Here we are, folks," their waiter said, coming up from behind. He, along with another waiter, set out all their food, and though it looked absolutely delicious as it still sizzled in the pans, Olivia didn't feel like eating.

Everyone else apparently did, however, because they all began digging in, passing around the tortilla bowls and the refried beans and pico de gallo. Olivia made herself a shrimp fajita for show and took a few bites. Eve did the same, only without any meat. She was chatting politely with Olivia's parents, mostly with her father, about golf of all things. She knew Eve played, but she didn't know how much she really liked it, and Olivia wondered what else she didn't know about her. And more importantly, if she'd ever get the chance to find out.

Eve continued talking to them, very gracious and genuine despite knowing how they felt about homosexuality. But that was Eve. She was kind. To everyone. And when she glanced at Olivia from time to time, Olivia could still feel the heat from that powerful stare. The bracelet had obviously come from her heart and soul, and Olivia could sense that Eve wanted to say so much more. They both yearned to talk, but they were currently trapped and muted by an unspoken boundary that, Olivia realized, had kept her from happiness her entire life.

Yet there she sat. Motionless. Voiceless. Unable to fucking rise up and do anything about it. Just like she'd been that very first day at the mountain when she'd been unable to climb from her car.

This is no mountain.

This is my life.

What she said and did in the next few moments could cause her to lose her parents or Eve. For life.

She was more torn and terrified than ever.

"What's wrong? Aren't you hungry?" Molly asked, looking at Olivia's half eaten fajita.

"Oh, I just had a lot to eat before you came to get me. I didn't know we were going out to eat, because someone surprised me, remember?"

Molly seemed satisfied with her answer and everyone finished eating, seemingly unaware of her inner turmoil. Molly was still determined to play hostess, and after the waiter took their plates, she brought Olivia her remaining gifts and cards. She paused with one card in her hand.

"This one is from Eve. It was probably supposed to go with the bracelet. You should probably read it first."

"Molly," Aaron said, this time in a firmer tone. "Let Auntie Liv decide what she wants to open and when, okay?"

"But you always tell me to read the cards that come with my gifts first. That they are the most important thing because they mean more than the present." She searched Olivia's face for clarification. "Right, Auntie Liv?"

"Yes."

Olivia took the card, which was in a light blue envelope, and opened it. She quickly read the endearing well wishes for a happy birthday and then focused on a folded piece of paper that appeared to have a longer and handwritten message. Her mouth went dry, and she knew she should put it away and thank her and read it later, in private. But Molly was standing there expectantly, and as she opened it and skimmed the first few words, she couldn't help but want to read the rest. She simply couldn't stop herself and she read on. In front of her parents, her friend, her brother, and her niece.

In front of Eve.

She read with her chest wide open and her heart exposed and beating for all to see.

Dearest Olivia,

On this very special day, everyone is coming together to celebrate you, to show you how much you mean to them. I've been lucky enough to be invited to this remarkable occasion, and I will forever be grateful, because I get to see you again. I know you aren't expecting me to be here, and I don't even know if I'll be here with you when you read this. Because there is a possibility that my presence may upset you and that I may have to leave and possibly never see you again. The mere thought of that kills me, but I would understand, because I've hurt you.

I've hurt you terribly, not once, but twice. I can tell you I'm sorry, I can apologize from now until the end of time, but I know it would never be close to enough. So, I will just say this.

I love you, Olivia.

Truly, madly, deeply, and all the adverbs anyone has ever used to describe the magnitude of their love.

I love you wholeheartedly, with all of my being, and without condition.

I love you now, at this very moment, tomorrow, and all the days to come.

And I loved you all those days ago, when I first saw you and every day that has followed.

I love you whether you tell me to go or ask me to stay.

Whether I get to see you every day or never see you again.

I love you, Olivia.

May you have the happiest of birthdays. Today, next year, and all the years to come.

And I, too, will continue to celebrate this day. Today, next year, and all the years to come.

Because this is your day.

Olivia's day.

The day the woman I love like no one else came to be.

And that's a day I will always thank the stars above for.

I love you.

Now and always,

Eve.

The paper shook in her hands and tears blurred her vision as she battled to control her emotions. Molly touched her shoulder, and the cries broke through.

"Auntie Liv,' she said softly. "Are you okay?"

Olivia forced herself to nod and swallow, doing her best to settle down. She wiped her eyes. "Yes, angel. I'm okay." She folded the note and placed it back inside the card and slid the card back into the envelope.

"Well, I think I've had about all that I can stand for one evening," Olivia's mother said, tossing down her napkin.

Her outburst was so sudden, and her unhappiness so blatantly and freely expressed, Olivia could tell everyone was truly startled.

"You're free to go, Mom," Aaron said, which also seemed to surprise everyone. "You aren't being held hostage."

"And why should I leave? I'm not the one doing anything wrong."

"Oh, but you are," Aaron said. "You're being rude and you're ruining Olivia's birthday celebration."

"I'm not the one who's ruining everything. I'm just speaking the truth. This—" She waved her hands like she was lost for words. "Whatever it is, is getting out of hand."

"What is it exactly that's getting out of hand, Mom?" Aaron asked. "Olivia getting a gift that means something to her? Or getting the gift from someone who also means something to her? Which is it? Or could it be both? Just exactly what is the problem?"

"You know darn well what the problem is," her mother said, slamming her hand on the table. "It isn't me and I'm not going anywhere."

Eve stood and reached for her purse. "I'll go," she said, her voice tight.

"There," Olivia's mother said. "The problem is leaving."

Eve gaped at her. She gave a little laugh. She then looked at Olivia for permission to lash back, or for support, or reassurance, but Olivia was consumed by the raging turmoil rising inside her. She wanted to stand up, to scream, to yell, to say everything she'd ever wanted to say to her mother. But Molly was right next to her. She was watching. She was listening. And Olivia wasn't about to do wrong by her and lose her cool and verbally attack her mother just because the release would make her feel good. If she was going to do this, she had to do it right. She wasn't yet sure what that was, but she knew if she opened her mouth to say anything at that moment, she'd lose herself to anger and resentment, because it was now boiling inside her.

Eve took her silence as cowardice, and her face fell. She slung her purse over her shoulder.

"You're right, Mrs. Savage, I seem to be the problem. And the problem is now leaving."

She scooted out and around Olivia's father.

"After all, I'm not in the business of ruining birthdays and put-on puritan family get-togethers."

She walked behind Olivia and stopped as Molly stood.

"Eve, why are you leaving?"

Eve knelt and gently held her shoulders. She was so close Olivia could smell her perfume causing the reality of the situation to smack her upside the head.

Eve was leaving.

Her mother had insulted her.

God, no.

Olivia grabbed Eve's forearm, trying to ensure that she remain. But Eve ignored her and spoke directly to Molly.

"Because sometimes adults are really stupid. We say and do stupid things and we're sometimes too stubborn to admit when we're wrong. And when that happens, like right now, it's best if one adult leaves rather than stay and argue. Especially when that adult has no support and her arguing would only cause more chaos and pain."

"But I don't want you to go," Molly said.

"I have to, sweetie. It's what I have to do. For myself. Maybe someday you'll understand."

She kissed her forehead and tore her arm from Olivia's hand to walk away.

No.

No.

Oh, God, no.

Olivia stood, completely panicked, and called after her. Eve kept walking without looking back. Olivia started to give chase, calling out again, desperate to reach her and grab hold and never let her go again. But Aaron cut her off and held her in his arms.

"It's best if she goes," he whispered. "For right now."

Molly ran up and hugged her hard from behind. Olivia turned and held her tight and continued to cry. Aaron led them both back to their seats, holding on to Olivia's shoulder and brushing her hair away from her face. He knelt beside her.

"Can you do this?" he asked softly.

She nodded.

"I'm right here," he said. "I've got your back."

She wiped her face and nodded again. He returned to his seat, and Olivia did her best to regain her composure. Molly was looking at her with her wide, curious eyes. She was concerned and confused, and Olivia knew that Aaron was right. It was now time to speak her truth.

Not just for herself, but for Molly.

"Please, tell me what's wrong, Auntie Liv. Why did you cry when you read the card? Why are you crying now?"

Olivia touched her face and closed her eyes. So many things went through her mind and so many feelings rushed through her body. But only one word stuck and remained, flashing on and off like a neon sign, demanding to be seen and heard. It was the word that encased and explained it all.

"Love," she said, holding Molly's face.

"Love?"

"Yes, my sweet girl. Love."

"But the card was from Eve."

"Yes, it was."

Molly continued to search her face with eyes that were wild and seeking. Olivia could almost see her mind at work as it came upon new things. Things she might have known about but had never stopped to fully examine until now.

"You—love Eve?"

Olivia covered her mouth as more emotion rocked through her.

"Yes, I do. I love her very much."

Olivia heard her mother say something under her breath, but Molly never broke eye contact with Olivia.

"And Eve—loves you?"

"Yes."

"You love her more than Kenny?"

Olivia laughed through her tears. "Oh, God yes. I love her more than Kenny. I love her more than anyone else in the world." She lightly poked her with her finger. "Except maybe for you."

Again, her mother started, but this time her father shushed her. Olivia's sole focus remained on Molly.

Molly held her hand. "This is why you suddenly got so happy, isn't it? It was Eve."

"Yes."

Her face clouded. "Is it why you've been so sad, too?"

Olivia took a deep breath. "Yes."

"But why?"

"Because it's ridiculous, that's why," Olivia's mother said. "Two women loving each other. It's absurd and it's wrong, and Molly should not be exposed to this." She looked to Olivia's father. "Why aren't you saying anything? Why aren't you doing something?"

"What is it you want me to do, dear?" he asked.

"Tell her no! Tell her she can't do this!"

"She's an adult," he said. "What we say, what we think, it no longer matters."

"And as for *my* daughter," Aaron said. "I would appreciate it if you would shut up and let Olivia speak. I want Molly to hear this. I want Molly to know what love *really* is."

Olivia's mother reared back as if she'd been slapped, and Olivia looked back at Molly.

"I've been sad because love isn't always easy. There are sometimes things that get in the way and try and stop it."

"Like Grandma?"

Olivia heard Jake laugh.

"Well, yes. Sometimes it's other people, sometimes it's just life and the circumstances you find yourself in."

Molly was quiet for a moment with her mind obviously back at work. She spoke with a strong voice, louder than before, and she stood tall and proud.

"Then don't let anything stop you, Auntie Liv." She gave Olivia's mother a stern look. "Not Grandma and Grandpa, not life or any silly little circumstance." She looked back into Olivia's eyes. "Just love."

Olivia smiled and pulled her in for a long, firm, hug. She cried again, and when Molly finally pulled away, she too, had tears in her eyes.

"Go do it, Auntie Liv," she said softly. "Go love."

"I second that," Jake said, rising.

"So do I," Aaron said, also coming to a stand.

"Me, too."

Olivia turned to see her father standing. Her mother was beside herself and insisting that he sit down.

"This isn't about us," he said to her. "It's about our daughter. And despite what we think or believe, I want her to be happy. I want her to be happy above all else because I love her." He smiled at Olivia through tears of his own. "Go, hon. Go be happy," he said.

"All right, Grandpa!" Molly said as she encouraged Olivia to stand.

Olivia looked at them all with every last ounce of love she had. Even her mother, who refused to look at her.

"Thank you," she managed to say.

Then she took her purse from Molly and left them standing at the table.

It was time to go be happy.

It was time to just love.

CHAPTER THIRTY-NINE

Eve couldn't settle down. She'd driven home like a maniac, yelling and cussing, lost and aimless, not having the slightest clue what to do. The pain she felt rivaled what she could only imagine being stabbed repeatedly by a knife would feel like. It was relentless, eviscerating her over and over. Having an awareness as to why it hurt so bad didn't stop it. It didn't help at all. Nothing could tame this kind of pain. Pain that rooted in rejection.

How could Olivia do that? How could she sit there and not stand up for them, for the way they felt about each other? How could she sit in silence and let someone, anyone, insult the person she supposedly loved without even trying to stop them?

Olivia had always been scared to confront her parents, but Eve never thought she'd just bow out and sit in silence when it came down to either her parents or her. Especially not after all they'd shared and confessed recently. The Olivia she knew now was stronger than that. Wasn't she?

She cussed again, ran her hand through her hair, and paced.

She'd never been so angry. So fucking hurt. So…just completely dumbfounded.

She stilled at the sound of her doorbell. She knew who it was, and she stalked to the door, yanked it open, and jabbed a finger at Olivia, ready to let her have it with both barrels.

"How could you—"

But Olivia came right at her, causing her to stumble in reverse, her face just inches from Eve's, her eyes boring into her. She slammed the door behind her, and when Eve tried to speak again, she backed her to the wall and pressed a finger to her lips, silencing her.

"It's time," she said, her voice strained. "No more fear. No more running. No more hiding. I love you. You love me. Everyone knows. I told them and I'm ready to tell the entire world. I'm sorry I didn't have the courage to do it sooner. I'm sorry I let my mother speak to you that way. That will never, ever happen again. Because you are all that matters. You are all I care about." She lowered her finger and spoke softer. "You are the one I'm madly in love with."

"You told them?" Eve asked. She was stunned from her close proximity and the way she'd come in and took total control. Not to mention what she'd just said.

"I did."

"Molly?"

Olivia smiled. "She told me not to let anything stand in my way. She told me to just love."

"Just love."

"Yes."

"Is that why you're here?" Eve asked, her own voice husky.

"Yes. It's time to just love."

She looked intense and serious, like she'd just walked a tightrope a hundred stories high and she couldn't wait to tell her about it, having conquered the greatest risk of her life. She was still wearing the navy pin-striped vest and rolled denim capris, and Eve was sure she'd come straight from the restaurant. She'd probably sped just as Eve had. She was a woman on a mission, a woman who had finally found herself and was willing to do anything to live that truth.

Eve reached up to touch her face, moved to tenderness, wanting to ease her intensity. They had both been through a gamut of emotions in the last couple of hours. Olivia more so than her, and she wanted to comfort her, to let her know she was safe now and loved beyond measure.

But Olivia grabbed her hands.

"No," she said. "I've waited my whole life for this moment. Waited my whole life for a love like this. Waited with more restraint and self-control than you'll ever know, to completely take you, to truly have you, and to…" She leaned in and spoke in her ear. "Fucking taste you."

Eve shuddered.

"And I can't wait any longer."

She pinned her hands above her head and lightly pushed her body against Eve's while teasing her lips with her own.

"Don't even think about moving," she said. "Because I'm not letting you go for at least the next few hours. And if I could somehow hold you this close to me for longer, I would." She teased her again with her lips. "I don't ever want to let you go again."

She kissed her, deep and slow, claiming her completely with her ambitious and patient tongue. She kissed her like she wanted to see, feel, and experience every last inch of her and then burn those things into her memory.

Eve felt herself falling into her, the strings of her intimate and most sensitive places being played again and again with the slick, purposeful probe of her tongue. Until eventually, she fell limp against the strength of her body, knowing that she was gone now, done for, helpless. Another person had total control. Had her by her very soul. And it felt fucking wonderful.

She moaned into her mouth and Olivia groaned in response and then tore away to attack her neck, causing her to sigh with pleasure. She loved the feel of Olivia's hot mouth sucking and nibbling at her delicate skin. And she did so thoroughly, devouring first one side and then the other, taking time to tease her ear, knowing exactly what that did to her.

"Am I getting to you, Eve Monroe?" She lightly sucked her ear lobe. "Am I turning you on?"

"Yes," Eve breathed. "And you know it."

"Maybe. But I'll always want to hear you say it."

"You are," Eve said, jolting at the feel of her tongue in her ear. Every single inch of her skin tightened and came to life. "You're— turning me on. So very much."

Olivia groaned again.

"The way you look, the way you smell, the way you feel, I can't fucking take it," Olivia said. "I want to make you come, Eve. Right now. Right fucking now."

She held Eve's hands together and then traced her free hand down to the waistband of her jeans. She hurriedly unfastened her thick belt and her pants and eased herself down into her panties.

Eve made a noise and startled again as Olivia found her flesh.

"Jesus Christ, you're wet." She slid her fingers up and down, stroking the length of her. Eve clenched her eyes and continued to make involuntary noises as her hips began to move, her body trying desperately to fuck Olivia's hand on its own accord.

"You're throbbing," Olivia said with a raspy voice, sounding like she was in disbelief. "Oh, my dear God, I can feel how badly you want it."

She worked her flesh carefully, prolonging her touch, extracting more and more pleasure, her own excitement evident in her breathing and in her voice.

"You're about to come in my hand," she said.

"Olivia," Eve said, eyes now open and trained on hers.

"Tell me," Olivia said. "Tell me you want me to make you come."

"Oh, God, Olivia. I want—"

"Yes, baby."

"Make me come."

Olivia stopped and released her hands. She dropped and tugged off her jeans and panties, tossing them both aside, like they were a frustrating barrier to what she wanted most. Then she rested on her knees and looked up at Eve. She eased her legs apart.

She slightly touched Eve's aching flesh with her lips, teasing, testing. Eve tangled her hands in her hair and shook and sighed, her kisses getting longer, heavier, eventually finding her most sacred place.

"Olivia," Eve said, the eventual press and movement of her tongue so fucking good her legs trembled. "You feel so good on me. Ah, God have mercy."

Olivia moaned and licked the head of her clit dead on, full and heavy and then all around.

Eve threw her head back and called out, completely lost and overtaken with the onslaught of pleasure. She couldn't ever remember it being this good. This fucking mind-blowing and intense. It was like she was being made love to for the very first time, and it was far surpassing any memory she still had of anything previous. Because this time she was being taken by someone she was crazy in love with, madly in love with. Someone she wanted desperately. Someone who wanted her just as desperately in return. Someone who was showing her just how much she wanted her with her mouth and heavy tongue. And she wasn't afraid, and she wasn't holding anything back. She was taking her. Giving to her. Hell-bent and determined to give her everything she had. And holy fucking Christ, was it good.

"You taste like heaven," she said, taking tiny pauses to speak. "I'm never ever going to want to stop doing this."

"I don't want you to," Eve breathed as she returned to her and began the slow assault with her tongue once again. "Oh, fuck, Olivia. Yes, love. I will always want you to do this." She looked down at her and watched as she devoured her. "I will always want your mouth on me. Ah, fuck, yes."

"Then why did you make me wait so long?" Olivia said, looking up at her with a grin.

"I have no idea."

Olivia snuck out her tongue and teased her.

"None. Oh, Jesus. No, fucking clue. I think I was—wanting to make sure you were ready."

"Oh, I've been ready, baby. Can't you tell? Can't you feel how badly I've wanted this? How badly I've wanted to make love to you with my mouth? To feel you against my tongue and taste your very essence and savor it as I give you all the pleasure I possibly can?"

She licked her, flicking her clit.

"Yes—I can feel it."

"Can you?"

"Yes."

"Feel it some more."

She attacked her again, pressing her mouth fully against her, where she French kissed her cleft, swirling and swirling, until Eve was completely engorged and struggling to stand. Olivia somehow knew exactly what to do, where to touch and for how long, as if she'd studied her for years, and was the utmost expert in her sex and desire. She gave and gave to her, bathing her with her tongue, bringing her to the brink of ecstasy and then slowing and removing the weight of her, careful not to send her over too soon.

Eve knotted her fingers in her hair, holding her head fast to her, loving the loss of control, loving that she was at her complete mercy, loving that it was Olivia who was taking her. Eve was in her world and Olivia was leading her by the hand, showing her all the pleasure it had to offer. It was beautiful and magical and the most erotic place she'd ever been.

"Olivia. Olivia." She kept sighing her name, and eventually the sighs gave way to cries and her cries became louder and louder. Her eyes were closed and her head back; she was totally caught up in the movement of Olivia's head and the manipulation of her tongue. She could feel nothing else. Register nothing else.

There literally *was* nothing else.

Her body was wide open, taking in pleasure, consuming it quicker and fiercer. She clenched handfuls of Olivia's hair and moved against her. Olivia, with her aggressive hunger and audible noises, continued to tell Eve without speaking just how much she was enjoying herself and just how well she knew her, able to sense that her orgasm was right there, ready to crash down upon her.

"Yes, baby," was all she said, and Eve shook as the sensation of her hot mouth seared into her once again.

Eve clenched her eyes and clenched Olivia's head.

It was there. It was right there. She could feel it and it was fucking monumental.

"Olivia, I love you," she said. "I love you. I love you I love you I love you."

Olivia took her in her mouth and sucked her off, hard and unrelenting, giving her the gift of the most earth-shattering climax she'd ever had. It hit her so forcefully it almost knocked her off her feet and she had to hold on to Olivia so tightly she worried she was hurting her.

But Olivia only groaned and sucked her more vehemently, ensuring she would feel everything the orgasm brought for her.

"Fuck, yes," she cried out. "Fucking suck me, baby. Don't stop." She tensed and arched as all the pleasure Olivia had stirred to life within her, gathered, and rained down upon her, covering her solely and completely, drenching her from head to toe.

"I—love—you." The cry was so loud and guttural it felt foreign to her, as if it were coming from somewhere other than her. It poured up and out of her while the orgasm poured down on her. Both tearing her to sweet, sweet pieces, until she was left absolutely vanquished, whispering the words while close to collapse.

Olivia gently removed herself from her and stood to embrace her, holding her tight.

Eve closed her eyes and even though cries and pleasure had just exploded out of her, she felt full and warm, with every dark corner inside lit up and glowing. She clung to Olivia with weak arms and inhaled the skin of her neck while the powerful strength of her body held her upright. She was so strong. So heartfelt. So passionate. She was like the perfect puzzle piece that slid right into place inside her, fitting into all the gaps, a truly snug fit.

That was them. Two strong individual puzzle pieces, coming together for a perfect fit. Creating the beautiful scene of what would be their life.

Eve held her closer and cried then.

And for the first time in her life, crying felt good.

Chapter Forty

Olivia sat on the large rock taking in another spectacular sunrise. She was mesmerized by its brilliance and enjoyed basking in the new light after having just finished her run up the mountain trail. She could feel her body recovering, but her raised pulse and strong breathing were of little concern and she paid little attention. She was growing more and more used to vigorous exercise, and her body had adapted. She didn't struggle like she used to when she ran, and when she did push herself, she was able to recuperate quickly. But the best part was that she craved her workouts now just like Eve said she would. When she didn't work out, she felt unfocused and frustrated and cranky. And she wasn't the only one who noticed. Her loved ones were quick to tell her when she was being a bear, many times even suggesting that she go for a long run or spend an hour lifting weights.

A breeze stirred, and she absently rubbed the chill that tickled her moist skin. The mornings were cooler now, and soon she'd have to cover up instead of wearing just an athletic bra and runner's shorts. That didn't bother her. She loved this time of year and thought back to how far she'd come since spring. She couldn't believe all that she had accomplished. It was almost surreal. She now had the two things that had seemed damned near impossible to get.

She was fit, able to run and lift like a well-trained athlete. She was tight and hard as a rock with defined muscle, and for the first time in her life, she was proud of her body. She was healthy and strong, and she loved the way she looked and the way she felt. She couldn't imagine ever going back to the way she was before. She'd been awakened and shown a new, better way to live, and oh, what a life it was turning out to be.

"Hi."

Olivia turned and found Eve standing on the trail with her hands on her hips. Similar to Olivia, she had on nothing but a purple sports bra and a pair of black leggings. Her hair was in a ponytail, and she pushed her sunglasses up to rest on her head, just like she'd done all those weeks ago when they'd first met.

"Hi."

"You look like you might need some help."

Olivia saw the corner of her mouth lift.

"Oh, yeah?"

"Uh-huh."

"And let me guess, you're the one who's going to help me."

"I am."

"What makes you so sure I'll let you?"

"Because I'm the woman for the job."

"You are, are you?"

"Yes. And I think you're well aware of that."

"I see."

"You don't see anyone else up here do you?" she asked, glancing around. She walked slowly toward her. "Nobody else is coming to your rescue. Just me."

"You're right." Olivia's voice weakened as she watched her move. "There's only you."

Eve came to a stand before her. Her eyes were alive, and she looked driven and a bit…ravenous.

"You will always be the only one," Olivia said.

"Are you admitting that you need some help, then?"

Olivia reached out and tried to touch her, but Eve swatted her hand away.

"Well?" She was fiery and feisty, and the way her eyes flashed, Olivia knew she was wanting to dominate.

Olivia swallowed. "God, yes, I need help."

"You better get up then, so I can take a look at you."

Olivia stood and Eve swept her up and down with her hungry gaze. Then she took a step closer, so that they were inches apart.

"You look really good to me," she said.

"Do I?"

"Yes. Incredibly good. But…" She ran her finger down the center of Olivia's body until she came to the top of her shorts. "I think you need some help here."

"Where?"

"In here." She slid her hand into her shorts and panties and halted as she reached her center. She grazed her with her fingertips, and Olivia gripped her wrist and clenched her jaw. She rose to her tiptoes and made a small noise.

"Yes," Eve said. "I think you need some help right here. I'm concerned that you can't feel as well as you should. I think maybe I should touch you to be sure. What do you think?"

"Mm. Yes. Please."

Eve sank her fingers into her folds and glided up and down.

Olivia jerked and her whole body tightened. She tried to form words, pleas of approval and pleas for more, but Eve was rubbing her so intently, she couldn't focus on anything other than the pleasure shooting out from her clit.

"Can you feel me?" Eve asked.

"Ye—es."

"Are you sure?"

Olivia clung to her shoulder. "Yes. Fuck yes."

"I'm not totally convinced." She increased her speed and intensity. "I think I better make completely sure. You know, touch you until you scream and crumble and come all over my hand." She leaned in and nibbled her neck and worked her way up to her jaw and then to her lips where she grinned and licked her with flicks of her tongue.

"What do you think? You want to come all over my hand?"

"Yes."

"Then do it. Look into my eyes and fucking do it. Look into my eyes and see how much I love you. How much I want you."

Olivia stared into her and saw her beautiful soul where love and desire and everything that made Eve Eve, existed. She saw all of it. Felt all of it.

And Eve could tell.

"Now come, Olivia. Come for me at this very moment at this very spot. Right here. Where I first laid eyes on you. Where I fell for you."

Olivia felt herself going over. She held her tighter.

"Yes, love. Come."

She broke completely open then and cried into the rising sun as the orgasm pulsed through her, saturating every single nerve ending she had with raw, delicious pleasure, over and over. The power of it just kept multiplying, and it felt so good she stared into Eve with disbelief, wondering if it would ever end and hoping like hell that it wouldn't.

Eve only grinned at her as she continued to give, her own desire more than apparent in her naughty look of lust. She was more than enjoying herself, and Olivia knew that from then on, anytime Eve grinned at her like that, no matter where they were, she'd get wet. She'd get wet and crave the all-knowing touch of her fingers.

Olivia clenched her eyes as one final surge tore through her, leaving her delirious and exhausted. She laughed softly and looked at Eve with heavy lidded eyes.

"I was such an idiot back then," she said, and Eve looked at her in confusion. "When I refused your help. What the hell was I thinking?"

Eve laughed and eased her hand from her shorts and held her hips.

"You're stubborn."

"And prideful."

"Yes."

"Thank God, you insisted. Thank God."

"I'm stubborn, too."

"Yes. You are."

"We probably shouldn't argue very often then."

"Probably not."

"You should just agree with me all the time."

Olivia laughed. "I don't think so."

"No? Well, at least agree with me on the next few things I have to tell you." She reached up and touched her face.

"Okay. I'm listening."

"I would like for you to meet my mother."

Olivia could see that she was serious and even a little emotional.

"You know I check in on her a lot. So, next time I go, I want you to come with me."

"I would love to."

Eve smiled and ran her thumb over her bottom lip.

"Really?"

"Of course. I know how much you love her. And I want to know every single part of you and your life."

"There's something else," she said.

"Okay."

"I want to take you somewhere next week. It's Thanksgiving and you won't have class."

"Oh? And where, dare I ask, do you want to take me?"

"Mexico."

Olivia grinned so big it hurt her face. "Are you kidding me?"

"Aaron told me you already have your passport."

"I actually do, yes. We all got one when my parents first moved down there, so we could visit. I just—never wanted to."

"Well, what about now? Do you want to go? With me? I've got the reservations all set up at hotel Karen. They're guaranteed."

"Hotel Karen?"

"Her beach house."

Olivia looked at her in disbelief. "Get out of here."

"I'm serious."

"A beach house? A house. On the beach. Like for real, on the beach?"

Eve laughed. "You step off the back patio into sand. The ocean is right there in front of you."

"Oh, my God."

"Is that a yes? Do you want to go?"

"Do you even have to ask? Yes, I want to go. Abso-fucking-lutely."

"It was the beach house that cinched it, wasn't it? Not me."

Olivia pulled her closer. "Oh, no, it was you. I'd go anywhere in the world with you. The beach house was just an added bonus."

"Ah, okay."

"Will I get to meet Karen?"

"You will, yes. She'll be there for the first two days and she's so excited she won't leave me alone. She keeps texting me asking me all kinds of questions about you. Does she like this or that, or what about this."

"I can't wait to meet her."

"You two are going to hit it off, I have no doubt. And you'll probably gang up on me. That wouldn't surprise me at all."

Olivia fell silent and Eve continued to look into her eyes.

"Spill it." It was what she said now when she could tell that something was bothering her. "You're thinking about your parents, aren't you?"

"Yeah."

"You still haven't heard from your mother?"

"No. Just my father. He calls, but she refuses to speak to me. He always has an excuse for her."

"Give her time, love. She might come around."

"I don't know." Her mother icing her out still hurt, no matter how much she talked about it and tried to accept it.

"We can always stop by and see them," Eve said. "Give them a little surprise like they did you on your birthday." She grinned. "Eh? Wouldn't that be fun?"

Olivia laughed softly. "That would be one heck of a surprise, that's for sure."

"I know you're hurting and I'm so sorry." She brought her hand to her mouth and kissed it. "I'll just have to do my best to try to distract you."

"Now, thinking about that makes me feel much better."

"I thought it might."

"Oh, it does."

Olivia smiled at her and felt tears well. One slipped down her face and Eve smoothed it away.

"Something else?" she asked, her voice high with concern. "What is it? What's wrong?"

"Nothing," Olivia said. "Everything is…right. Everything is so right it's overwhelming. Just before you got here, I was thinking about how I have the two things I thought I'd never have."

"Yeah?"

"I'm fit and healthy, that's one."

"And what's the other?"

"Love. Honest to God, real, true, make your heart pound and your head spin, wildly passionate, comes from the depths of your soul, sacrifice anything for it, love. I have it. I have you. And I can't believe it."

"Sometimes I can't either."

"You have changed my whole life, Eve. I keep comparing it to being awakened. Like I've been asleep for my entire life and suddenly this beautiful and alluring woman walks into my room and wakes me, causing me to stir to life and feel and experience and really, genuinely live. I don't know how I can ever thank you for that."

"You just did."

"I don't think what I just said is near enough."

"Your continued happiness is. That alone is more than enough, and, Olivia, it's all that I want." Her gaze drifted down to Olivia's mouth and her eyebrow lifted. "Well, maybe not *all* that I want."

Olivia groaned as she saw the hunger return to Eve's eyes. "Jesus, God, I love the way you want me."

"I love the way I want you, too."

"Let's get out of here so I can take my turn and have my way with you."

Eve laughed and Olivia shushed her with a finger pressed to her lips.

"But first, a kiss."

They drew closer, so close Olivia could feel her breath as it collided with her own.

"You got it," Eve whispered.

Olivia kissed her then right there at the very spot where they'd first met.

Right there against the backdrop of another rising sun.

The End

About the Author

Ronica Black lives in the desert Southwest with her menagerie of animals and her menagerie of art. When she's not writing, she's still creating, whether drawing, painting, or woodworking. She loves long walks into the sunset, rescuing animals, anything pertaining to art, and spending time with those she loves. When she can, she enjoys returning to her roots in North Carolina where she can sit back on the porch with family and friends, catch up on all the gossip, and relish an ice cold Cheerwine.

Ronica is a two-time Golden Crown Literary Society Goldie Award winner and a three-time finalist for the Lambda Literary Awards.

Books Available from Bold Strokes Books

Everyday People by Louis Barr. When Film star Diana Danning hires private eye Clint Steele to find her son, Clint turns to his former West Point barracks mate, and ex-buddy with benefits, Mars Hauser to lend his cyber espionage and digital black ops skills to the case. (978-1-63555-698-8)

Forging a Desire Line by Mary P. Burns. When Charley's ex-wife, Tricia, is diagnosed with inoperable cancer, the private duty nurse Tricia hires turns out to be the handsome and aloof Joanna, who ignites something inside Charley she isn't ready to face. (978-1-63555-665-0)

Love on the Night Shift by Radclyffe. Between ruling the night shift in the ER at the Rivers and raising her teenage daughter, Blaise Richilieu has all the drama she needs in her life, until a dashing young attending appears on the scene and relentlessly pursues her. (978-1-63555-668-1)

Olivia's Awakening by Ronica Black. When the daring and dangerously gorgeous Eve Monroe is hired to get Olivia Savage into shape, a fierce passion ignites, causing both to question everything they've ever known about love. (978-1-63555-613-1)

The Duchess and the Dreamer by Jenny Frame. Clementine Fitzroy has lost her faith and love of life. Can dreamer Evan Fox make her believe in life and dream again? (978-1-63555-601-8)

The Road Home by Erin Zak. Hollywood actress Gwendolyn Carter is about to discover that losing someone you love sometimes means gaining someone to fall for. (978-1-63555-633-9)

Waiting for You by Elle Spencer. When passionate past-life lovers meet again in the present day, one remembers it vividly and the other isn't so sure. (978-1-63555-635-3)

While My Heart Beats by Erin McKenzie. Can a love born amidst the horrors of the Great War survive? (978-1-63555-589-9)

Face the Music by Ali Vali. Sweet music is the last thing that happens when Nashville music producer Mason Liner and daughter of country royalty Victoria Roddy are thrown together in an effort to save country star Sophie Roddy's career. (978-1-63555-532-5)

Flavor of the Month by Georgia Beers. What happens when baker Charlie and chef Emma realize their differing paths have led them right back to each other? (978-1-63555-616-2)

Mending Fences by Angie Williams. Rancher Bobbie Del Rey and veterinarian Grace Hammond are about to discover if heartbreaks of the past can ever truly be mended. (978-1-63555-708-4)

Silk and Leather: Lesbian Erotica with an Edge edited by Victoria Villasenor. This collection of stories by award winning authors offers fantasies as soft as silk and tough as leather. The only question is: How far will you go to make your deepest desires come true? (978-1-63555-587-5)

The Last Place You Look by Aurora Rey. Dumped by her wife and looking for anything but love, Julia Pierce retreats to her hometown, only to rediscover high school friend Taylor Winslow, who's secretly crushed on her for years. (978-1-63555-574-5)

The Mortician's Daughter by Nan Higgins. A singer on the verge of stardom discovers she must give up her dreams to live a life in service to ghosts. (978-1-63555-594-3)

The Real Thing by Laney Webber. When passion flares between actress Virginia Green and masseuse Allison McDonald, can they be sure it's the real thing? (978-1-63555-478-6)

What the Heart Remembers Most by M. Ullrich. For college sweethearts Jax Levine and Gretchen Mills, could an accident be the second chance neither knew they wanted? (978-1-63555-401-4)

White Horse Point by Andrews & Austin. Mystery writer Taylor James finds herself falling for the mysterious woman on White Horse Point who lives alone, protecting a secret she can't share about a murderer who walks among them. (978-1-63555-695-7)

Femme Tales by Anne Shade. Six women find themselves in their own real-life fairy tales when true love finds them in the most unexpected ways. (978-1-63555-657-5)

Jellicle Girl by Stevie Mikayne. One dark summer night, Beth and Jackie go out to the canoe dock. Two years later, Beth is still carrying the weight of what happened to Jackie. (978-1-63555-691-9)

Le Berceau by Julius Eks. If only Ben could tear his heart in two, then he wouldn't have to choose between the love of his life and the most beautiful boy he has ever seen. (978-1-63555-688-9)

My Date with a Wendigo by Genevieve McCluer. Elizabeth Rosseau finds her long lost love and the secret community of fiends she's now a part of. (978-1-63555-679-7)

On the Run by Charlotte Greene. Even when they're cute blondes, it's stupid to pick up hitchhikers, especially when they've just broken out of prison, but doing so is about to change Gwen's life forever. (978-1-63555-682-7)

Perfect Timing by Dena Blake. The choice between love and family has never been so difficult, and Lynn's and Maggie's different visions of the future may end their romance before it's begun. (978-1-63555-466-3)

The Mail Order Bride by R Kent. When a mail order bride is thrust on Austin, he must choose between the bride he never wanted or the dream he lives for. (978-1-63555-678-0)

Through Love's Eyes by C.A. Popovich. When fate reunites Brittany Yardin and Amy Jansons, can they move beyond the pain of their past to find love? (978-1-63555-629-2)

To the Moon and Back by Melissa Brayden. Film actress Carly Daniel thinks that stage work is boring and unexciting, but when she accepts a lead role in a new play, stage manager Lauren Prescott tests both her heart and her ability to share the limelight. (978-1-63555-618-6)

Tokyo Love by Diana Jean. When Kathleen Schmitt is given the opportunity to be on the cutting edge of AI technology, she never thought a failed robotic love companion would bring her closer to her neighbor, Yuriko Velucci, and finding love in unexpected places. (978-1-63555-681-0)

Brooklyn Summer by Maggie Cummings. When opposites attract, can a summer of passion and adventure lead to a lifetime of love? (978-1-63555-578-3)

City Kitty and Country Mouse by Alyssa Linn Palmer. Pulled in two different directions, can a city kitty and country mouse fall in love and make it work? (978-1-63555-553-0)

Elimination by Jackie D. When a dangerous homegrown terrorist seeks refuge with the Russian mafia, the team will be put to the ultimate test. (978-1-63555-570-7)

In the Shadow of Darkness by Nicole Stiling. Angeline Vallencourt is a reluctant vampire who must decide what she wants more—obscurity, revenge, or the woman who makes her feel alive. (978-1-63555-624-7)

On Second Thought by C. Spencer. Madisen is falling hard for Rae. Even single life and co-parenting are beginning to click. At least, that is, until her ex-wife begins to have second thoughts. (978-1-63555-415-1)

Out of Practice by Carsen Taite. When attorney Abby Keane discovers the wedding blogger tormenting her client is the woman she had a passionate, anonymous vacation fling with, sparks and subpoenas fly. Legal Affairs: one law firm, three best friends, three chances to fall in love. (978-1-63555-359-8)

Providence by Leigh Hays. With every click of the shutter, photographer Rebekiah Kearns finds it harder and harder to keep Lindsey Blackwell in focus without getting too close. (978-1-63555-620-9)

Taking a Shot at Love by KC Richardson. When academic and athletic worlds collide, will English professor Celeste Bouchard and basketball coach Lisa Tobias ignore their attraction to achieve their professional goals? (978-1-63555-549-3)

Flight to the Horizon by Julie Tizard. Airline captain Kerri Sullivan and flight attendant Janine Case struggle to survive an emergency water landing and overcome dark secrets to give love a chance to fly. (978-1-63555-331-4)

In Helen's Hands by Nanisi Barrett D'Arnuk. As her mistress, Helen pushes Mickey to her sensual limits, delivering the pleasure only a BDSM lifestyle can provide her. (978-1-63555-639-1)

Jamis Bachman, Ghost Hunter by Jen Jensen. In Sage Creek, Utah, a poltergeist stirs to life and past secrets emerge.(978-1-63555-605-6)

Moon Shadow by Suzie Clarke. Add betrayal, season with survival, then serve revenge smokin' hot with a sharp knife.(978-1-63555-584-4)

Spellbound by Jean Copeland and Jackie D. When the supernatural worlds of good and evil face off, love might be what saves them all. (978-1-63555-564-6)

Temptation by Kris Bryant. Can experienced nanny Cassie Miller deny her growing attraction and keep her relationship with her boss professional? Or will they sidestep propriety and give in to temptation? (978-1-63555-508-0)

The Inheritance by Ali Vali. Family ties bring Tucker Delacroix and Willow Vernon together, but they could also tear them, and any chance they have at love, apart. (978-1-63555-303-1)

Thief of the Heart by MJ Williamz. Kit Hanson makes a living seducing rich women in casinos and relieving them of the expensive jewelry most won't even miss. But her streak ends when she meets beautiful FBI agent Savannah Brown. (978-1-63555-572-1)